Three Songs for Courage

MAXINE TROTTIER

TUNDRA BOOKS

Published in Canada by Tundra Books,
75 Sherbourne Street, Toronto, Ontario M5A 2P9

Published in the United States by Tundra Books of Northern New York,
P.O. Box 1030, Plattsburgh, New York 12901

Library of Congress Control Number: 2005927011

Library and Archives Canada Cataloguing in Publication

Trottier, Maxine

Three songs for courage / Maxine Trottier.

ISBN 978-0-88776-745-6 (bound).–ISBN 978-0-88776-831-6 (pbk.)

I. Title.

PS8589.R685T47 2006   JC813'.54   C2005-902891-2

We acknowledge the financial support of the Government of Canada
through the Book Publishing Industry Development Program (BPIDP)
and that of the Government of Ontario through the Ontario Media
Development Corporation's Ontario Book Initiative. We further
acknowledge the support of the Canada Council for the Arts and the
Ontario Arts Council for our publishing program.

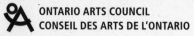 ONTARIO ARTS COUNCIL
CONSEIL DES ARTS DE L'ONTARIO

Typeset in Bembo

Printed in Canada

1   2   3   4   5   6   13   12   11   10   09   08

For those who fought.
We owe you greatly.

prologue

Erie View, a small town nestled on the shoreline of its namesake, has changed a good deal over the years. It's a trendy place now, where couples come to weekend at the inns or bed-and-breakfasts that line Laurel Creek. There are new restaurants – you can get Italian, Greek, or French cuisine and even gourmet pizza – rather a step up from the french fries and hot dogs that were once a staple here. It certainly is cleaner now that the smelt no longer run (Lake Erie pollution took care of them), and the fish flies are only a minor irritation. (Oh dear! Lake Erie strikes again.)

Yet, there are those who think that Erie View has lost something in her transition from small town Ontario to stylish beachfront resort. They miss the old times, the old places.

The Sand Club burned down in 1978. What a place that was in its time. Guy Lombardo, Lionel Hampton, Louis Armstrong – all the big names played there, and summer wasn't complete until you danced just once with your sweetheart while the revolving globe spattered you with light. On the morning after the fire, the parking lot looked like a senior citizens' caucus, with elderly people having come miles for one last look at a landmark that was now no more than a smoldering reminiscence.

Fishing tugs like the old *Better B Good* ply the lake's waters elsewhere, the Palace Theater has become a venue for artsy, indecipherable stage plays, and Hawk Point, that quintessential make-out spot is now, ironically, a wildlife refuge where parking in a car after dark will likely result in a ticket rather than a kiss.

Denison's Fries, Franks, and Foam closed years ago. Denison's couldn't compete with fast food and playrooms where children capered until they were close to puking up their cardboard burgers. Besides, Denison's had been a drive-in, a relic, a restaurantorial dinosaur. No one wants a drive-in these days.

The Yorktown to Erie View Railway? It doesn't run anymore. The engines are silent; the Victorian interiors of the finely appointed cars are now just so much rotten wood and moth-pocked fabric.

The circus no longer comes to town. No more big top, no more kids trying to get work helping set up in the hope of free tickets. No daredevils have been fired from cannons in Erie View, no sinuously exotic woman has walked a tightrope, not one terrier has worn a starched ruff and walked on its spindly hind legs to a calliope's wheezing rendition of "Barnum & Bailey's Favorite" in . . . well . . . a dog's age. And that is a long, long time.

Besides, where would they pitch their tents? Victoria Park and the baseball diamond are now covered with condominiums, blocky and graceless, an angular contrast to the big old cottages and houses that once bespoke a different way of life. A time when you mowed your own lawn and then sat out back to drink iced tea – real iced tea with rectangular ice cubes and crescents of lemon floating in it – on a porch that could have used painting.

Not the same place anymore, really.

But, if you stand on the beach late at night when a dark wind is blowing off the water and waves march in from the lake, a white and undisciplined battalion, sometimes you can almost hear something. Especially if your youth is woven into the fabric of the place, green and changeless.

As is Gordon Westley's.

It isn't the ghost of carousel music. Nor is it the heady, gut-thumping beat of rock and roll, of maybe, say . . . Bill Haley's "Rock Around the Clock." No, it is a bittersweet song, which even after all these years takes Gordon a good deal of courage to face without weeping.

On the evening before July 1st of 1956, though, Gordon is as yet unacquainted with that particular sheet music. He is sixteen years old, he has money in his pocket, and he is ready for what will surely be the most carefree and wonderful summer of his life.

Funny how you can be so very wrong about things, isn't it?

chapter 1

"Live well. It is the greatest revenge."
- Amos Littlebird, Odawa Sachem

It all began with Lancer Caldwell's butt, a butt of the cigarette variety. Lancer, slim and darkly handsome, was a two-pack-a-day man, having gradually worked his way up the smoking ladder since the age of eleven. The relentless seed that had rooted itself in the lower lobe of his right lung just last month, the one that had begun his road trip down the Highway of Cancer would never kill him, though. Lancer was destined to meet his Maker in a rather different fashion.

Although he had enjoyed his cigarette, on this sweltering Saturday evening the Players weren't doing all that much for him, and so he stopped his immaculate pre-war Dodge coupe, took careful aim and flicked it out the car's open window. Then Lancer opened a beer and drove on.

If Lancer had been anywhere but on Walnut Street, the butt's destination could have been one of a dozen places. It might have fallen to the sidewalk to be retrieved by some little kid who would later light up and pass it around the circle of his admiring friends. It might have rolled under a bush to smolder a while and then go out. It could have scored a direct hit on the Westleys' fat lump of a cat that was dozing in the shade, crouched beneath the mailbox. It could have landed straight up on a fresh coil of dog crap, instantly creating an obscene birthday cupcake.

But instead, it landed a direct bull's eye on the hood of Gordon Westley's freshly waxed, '50 Pontiac.

■■■

Gordon's bedroom was an oddity in Erie View, as were all the bedrooms in his home. That was because he had the use of his own private en suite bathroom. The Westleys' Walnut Street house, a fifteen-room clapboard colonial cottage, had been in the family since its construction in 1894. His paternal grandfather, long since dead, had owned a lucrative plumbing business and the place was lousy with bathrooms, water closets, showers, and sinks. Like many of the houses on the beach, the Westleys' had a name. *Brierly*. Although Grandpa sometimes called it *Shithouse on the Midden* or *Poopoire Manor*. When out of his daughter's and son-in-law's hearing, of course.

The Westleys were old money. On the rare occasion that he was dragged to the Red Cedar Country Club by his parents, Gordon had heard the term whispered about them more than once. A lot of people spoke thoughtlessly when a kid was around. Kids' hearing really didn't develop until they were about twenty, after all. Kids didn't speak *adult* and so you could say just about anything in front of one and it wouldn't really register: *Gordon Westley and his family are a bunch of stuck-up assholes, Louise Westley walks around like she has a broom up her ass, Ben Westley is a lush, the little brother Stan stinks; he should be put away somewhere so he isn't around normal children, but they are ooold money.* It gave Gordon the creeps. Old money sounded like something out of a Dracula movie. Old money was what Bela Lugosi carried in his cape pocket. It was what Frankenstein used to buy new bolts for his neck. It was what the witch in *Hansel and Gretel* used to purchase baking supplies. It definitely gave Gordon the heebie-jeebies.

Old money aside, Gordon loved the big place, something he had been careful never to admit to his friends. You could definitely love a car or maybe even a girl, but never a house. His bathroom and his bedroom were refuges, mostly because his mother flatly refused to enter either of them. This phenomenon had concurred at roughly the same time as the abrupt onset of Gordon's puberty three years ago, with the overnight sprouting of his body hair, the changing of his voice, and growth spurts of almost frightening proportions. His little brother, Stan's, rooms were still within his mother's domain, but his? She treated them like she did his father's den: male territory that she would no more trespass upon than she would have stepped into Kitchie's Pool Hall.

Although this had its disadvantages and Gordon had to maintain his suite himself, it was a situation that did not cost him much sleep. There was a point where the piles of clothing and damp towels *did* have to be taken down to the laundry, but that point was usually a distant speck on the horizon, something Gordon could stare at for days and never see coming closer. Sort of like walking to the Rocky Mountains.

As for personal bodily cleanliness, that was an entirely different matter. Gordon was a fanatic. He usually took several showers a day; the house had two enormous water heaters courtesy of dearly departed Grandfather Westley, plumber unparalleled. This was Gordon's second Saturday shower, the most important one of the week, a shower that he treated with more reverence than the waxing of his car, The Chief.

He turned on the bathtub taps, letting the water run over his fingers until it was the right temperature (hot enough to parboil lobsters), then he pulled the shower curtain shut and flipped on the shower. Running shoes, socks, jeans, T-shirt, and underpants fell to the floor. Gordon stepped into the tub and let the hot water cascade over him. He soaped himself thoroughly with Lifebuoy, leaving his hair for last. No Lifebuoy for the old Westley locks, for that he used Prell shampoo. Then a long, long rinse, breathing in the steam, eyes closed, head back. Water off. Done.

He drew back the shower curtain, stepped out, grabbed a clean towel that was hanging on the rack, and padded, naked, into his bedroom. After the jungle-like atmosphere of the bathroom, the bedroom was quite refreshing. Gooseflesh pimpled his body as he toweled himself dry. It was a fleeting thing though; by the time he was scrubbing at his hair, his body was lightly sheened with the fresh, clean sweat of male youth.

Gordon dropped the towel and stared at himself in the dresser mirror. He thought he looked pretty good. He had been working on his tan since the long weekend in May, and his skin was a pleasing shade of golden brown. Except for what his swim trunks covered, naturally; his buttocks and lower belly were pale. The Westley bayonet was looking fine, cringing a little it must be admitted, in its nest of blond pubic hair, but that was only the cool air. It fit well with the rest of his body, Gordon thought, not small and skinny like Henry Morton's – they all saw each other naked when changing for gym – or huge and meaty like Marty Fallbrother's. That thing was not only fearful, it had a wart.

No indeedy, thought Gordon, as he selected clothing for the evening; nothing wrong at all with the old Westley bayonet. He dressed himself in a clean version of what he privately called HIS UNIFORM. Skid mark free underwear, (his skids marks were small and discrete, while his brother Stan's clung to *his* underpants with the tenacity of limpets, impervious to bleach and repeated washings; Stan's underpants usually looked like the entire 7th Armored Division had skidded through) white socks, line-dried jeans still redolent of beach air, a white T-shirt, and black high-top running shoes.

Now for his crowning glory. He uncapped a tube of Brylcreem and squeezed out a liberal application, rubbed it onto his palms, and fingered it through his hair. He began an endless series of re-combs as he strove for that elusive goal; the faultless duck's ass. It was a modified duck's ass, unfortunately, a modest pompadour with the sides swept back. His father, who had served as an officer in the Canadian Army during WWII, and his mother, who had served alone as an army wife those six long years, wouldn't let him grow his hair any longer than it was at the moment. Therefore, achieving the ideal duck's ass was something of a challenge.

Gordon combed and patted and smoothed, then combed more and tucked and patted, and then for good measure combed some more. He did this with the same concentration he would affect when playing pool at Kitchie's after going to the movies this evening. The blood began to drain out of his upraised arms, but Gordon didn't stop. Maybe someday they would find him dead in his bedroom, all the blood having settled in his lower legs and feet, but his duck's ass would look great. When it was exactly right, when duck-ass excellence had been achieved, Gordon wiped the comb with a handkerchief and pocketed both. Wallet, car keys, matches (his pack of Black Cat cigarettes with only two smokes missing was in his car's glove box), and he was ready.

Gordon exited his room and descended the stairs soundlessly, hoping to avoid his mother, who had the hearing of an Egyptian fruit bat, and who would question him more thoroughly than Dick Tracy grilled thugs in the funny papers. He stepped over his grandfather's obese and lazy cat. Old Butcher Dougie (named for Sir Douglas Haig, the British officer responsible for half a million *British* casualties in a single 1917 campaign), was stretched out in the most inconvenient place possible, this time at the base of the stairs. Success. Front door closed behind him with nary a snick, he paused for a moment and breathed deeply, inhaling the all-pervasive smell of an Erie View summer, a mixture of lake weed, dead fish, grilling meat, and just a suggestion of car exhaust. There were his wheels. The Chief, parked with its rear end to the house under a big maple tree, looked ready and oh so fine.

At dawn that day, before it got too hot and before working around the house for his mom, Gordon had spiffed up The Chief. Radio playing softly (rock and roll sounded stupid when it was played softly, but if he woke his parents at that hour it would have meant an instant grounding), he had quickly lost himself in soapy water creaming down the car's green sides, the suds sheeting off when he turned the hose upon them. Then came the patient drying with a chamois cloth, the application of the wax in slow sensual strokes and once dry, its brisk removal. The Chief. The Pontiac's hood ornament had given him the idea for the name. It suited the car exactly.

Gordon vaulted off of the porch and cut across the lawn. He would pick up Frank, Tony, and David, in that order he decided, not because it would save time, which it wouldn't. It actually would take longer, since he would be backtracking up and down Main Street four times, but that was the key point. Main Street. See and be seen in his beloved Chief.

Gordon set his hand on the door handle. Later he would not be able to clearly recall the next few seconds when the blood began to roar in his ears with a thunder that drowned out all other sounds. He let his hand fall to his side unable to take his eyes from the cigarette butt, the very dead cigarette butt that had burned itself out on The Chief's hood.

chapter 2

"Friendship makes prosperity more shining and lessens adversity by dividing and sharing it."

                - Amos Littlebird, Odawa Sachem

"Sonofabitch. Sonofabitch! You sonofabitch! YOU SON-OFABITCH!" Each sonofabitch grew louder and more elongated until Gordon was howling.

"Gordon!" shouted his father through the open window of his den.

"SONOFABITCH!"

"What the hell's going on now?" muttered his father. He threw down his paper and walked through the house, the sonofabitches becoming fainter as he did so. Fainter but still there, until he flung open the front door.

"SON! OF! A! BITCH!"

His father crossed the lawn in a few quick strides. Ben Westley was a big man, an older and much weathered version of Gordon, with the same straight nose, striking blue eyes, and blond hair. Gordon had been five years old the first time Ben had seen his son, Louise having been newly pregnant in 1939 when he left for England. He had felt nothing for the boy in the beginning, but then his love began to grow slowly like a locomotive laboring on a steep grade, then picking up speed until it was a runaway. And Ben Westley, frightened by the intensity of that love, did the only thing he could do. He hid it.

"You don't stand out here on this front lawn swearing at the top of your lungs," he said, his voice measured and slow. "As long as you're under my roof you will be civil. You know how your mother feels about that sort of language. I am very disappointed in you, Gordon. Look at me when I speak to you!"

Gordon turned and faced his father, his eyes glassy with unshed tears, and whatever displeasure Ben felt evaporated. He hadn't seen his son cry in years, not since their old cocker spaniel, Rusty, had died in its sleep. Stan cried all the time; he had made an art form of it with every part of his body involved. You could hear him for blocks. But not Gordon. Gordon's tears came unwillingly, as though something were being torn from his very soul.

"Sorry." Gordon struggled to control his voice. It wasn't manly to cry. Men — *real* men like his father and grandfather, war heroes — didn't cry. "It's just . . ." He pressed his lips together to keep his chin from quivering. "My car. The Chief. The hood."

His father moved past Gordon and looked down at the cigarette butt.

"Sonofabitch," he whispered.

"No kidding," said Gordon, wiping furiously at his eyes. He picked up the butt and hurled it onto the grass. "Look at that, will you! It'll never come out! It'll take me a year to save enough to have it repainted." Somebody had done it on purpose, he thought grimly, already beginning to dream of revenge.

"Not so fast." His father pulled out his handkerchief, spat on it and rubbed at the mark, leaning over the car's hood until the residue of ash was gone. He straightened. "It'll compound out."

"But what about tonight? It's Saturday. I can't drive The Chief on a Saturday night when it's looking like that!"

His father's brows lifted. "Then, I guess you stay home."

"But I'm supposed to pick up the guys! We're going to the Palace to see *Rebel Without a Cause*."

"Again?"

"Well, yeah."

"Then I guess you drive your car the way it is," said his father. "Your choice, Gordon. You want to cut off your nose to spite your face, it's your choice."

"I'll go," said Gordon softly. "I can't let The Lakers down."

The Lakers. It was what his son and his friends called themselves. "No, you can't let your friends down."

"Dad?"

"Yes, son?"

"How do I look? I mean, do I look like I've been . . . you know."

"You look like a guy going out on the town to me. Nothing more; nothing less."

"Don't tell Mom." Gordon knew his father. He told Mom *everything*.

"Sworn to secrecy. Now get the heck into that car. You don't want to miss the Rocketman serial, which is your all-time favorite, as I recall."

Gordon made a gagging noise as he opened The Chief's door, slid in, and started the engine. He turned on the headlights and the radio.

"Gordon?" His father took out his wallet and tossed a five-dollar bill onto his son's lap. "This one is on me. Be careful and be home by eleven." He didn't bother to mention Kitchie's, knowing Gordon would go anyway.

"I will. Thanks. Thanks, Dad."

Ben Westley watched his son pull out. The taillights flashed; Gordon signaled a right turn and drove onto Walnut Street. Ben shook his head. It had seemed like a good, no, a *grand* idea at the time, an idea reluctantly agreed to by Louise. Gordon's sixteenth birthday and all,

but he knew now that he should never have given him
that car.

■■■

When he was driving, Gordon Westley ceased to exist.
Instead, behind The Chief's wheel was Wesser, the leader
of The Lakers, the greatest bunch of guys in Erie View.
Wesser did not emerge if Gordon had to drive his mother
somewhere. When driving his mom, Gordon sat straight
and kept his hands in the eleven and two o'clock positions. He braked gently at stop signs and checked left and
right with exaggerated care. That was not the automotive
modus operandi of Wesser. Oh, no, no, no.

Wesser drove with style.

He cranked up the radio, leaned over the steering
wheel and sort of wrapped his left arm around the entire
thing, and cocked his head a little. Wesser tried a slight
sneer, but he could never hold on to one. It gave him a
cramp in his cheek. So he settled for what he was certain
was a very nonchalant expression. That he resembled
nothing more than a demented Quasimodo never crossed
his mind.

Down Walnut, hang a right at Blane Avenue (Wesser
didn't *turn* the wheel, he palmed it), accelerate (Wesser
believed in jackrabbit starts and high speed, even though it

meant that The Chief burned more fuel than the Queen
Mary), come to a screeching stop at the red light (Wesser
believed in running red lights, but not when there was this
much traffic. Wesser was suave, but not stupid), and then a
left turn onto Main, where Wesser slowed to approxi-
mately the speed of a pope's funeral cortege so that he
could check out the action (which really meant checking
out the girls).

Checking out the action was something you had to
appear *not* to be doing. This was most effectively achieved
by squinting. That way Wesser could see who was on the
street and who was doing what without actually seeming
to care. So, Wesser squinted and hunched, a mutant James
Dean with pinkeye.

There wasn't much action yet because it was only –
Wesser had to stop squinting so he could see his wristwatch – 6:10. The real action would begin after the show,
but you never knew. Carol Reynolds *might* be coming out
of Floyd's Market after running an errand for her mother.
Patty White *could* emerge from the library; it had been
known to happen. And Mary Davidson, the gorgeous
Mary Davidson, the girl for whom Wesser (and Gordon)
longed above all other girls, might suddenly appear.

None of this happened, unfortunately, so The Chief
rolled down the five blocks of Main Street that mattered –
the Main Drag – as The Lakers so cleverly put it, and then
hung a right on Willow.

Gordon slowly pulled to a stop in front of Frank Thibodaux's house. He didn't dare squeal the tires. The only time he had done that, Frank's mother had come racing out with a wooden spoon. Frank's mother was from Montreal. She weighed in at about 250 pounds and looked like she could beat the snot out of John Wayne.

"You make dat tire noise again, eh, and you gonn' be sorry. Dat noise, it get Gran'père's parrot goin', dat noise. Dat parrot get goin' and den he start sayin' bad swears, him." She had crossed herself. *"Den Gran'mère, her, she get goin' and wanna start anudder goddamn' novena, eh? Den Frank's père, him, he wanna strangle da goddam' parrot and den I get in on it, me. You got it? Eh?"*

Gordon had gotten it.

He simply pulled to a stop and waited for Frank, who had been watching for him and was already out the door. Gordon now got on perfectly well with Mrs. Thibodaux, but preferred to avoid the parrot, a malodorous, evil-eyed creature named Barbette that was continually in molt and could projectile shit with the accuracy of an army sniper.

"Wesser, my good man! How they hangin'?" Frank pulled open the car's door and got into the front seat.

"Just fine, Beery. Just fine."

Frank was known as "Beery" because he was the most reliable source of that divine brew for The Lakers. Frank knew more older guys who were occasionally willing to buy small amounts of beer for them than the rest of The

Lakers put together. He had beer source radar. And he spoke French. So, it was the migrant workers from Quebec, men who worked on his Uncle Seraphim's tobacco farm that he would hit up with remarkable success, which was a good thing, since like the rest of The Lakers, Frank wasn't old enough to buy beer himself. Even if he had had a fake card, he would never have passed scrutiny. Although he had the same fair skin and thick black hair as his family, he was small and fine-boned, the exact opposite of all the other Thibodauxs, who ranged from large to huge to gargantuan. Gordon had once considered the possibility that Mrs. Thibodaux had perhaps slept with Mr. Silvers, the milkman. He had quickly discarded the idea, since Mrs. Thibodaux was *Frank's mother*. Your friend's mother wouldn't do that. Besides, Mr. Silvers would have been crushed flat.

"Onward, Wesser," said Frank grandly, as Gordon pulled away from the curb and headed back to Main Street. He smoothed a hand over his dark pompadour, pulled a pack of Players out of the rolled sleeve of his T-shirt, and lit up. Frank, whose idol was Elvis, wouldn't have been out of place sitting on Edgar Bergen's lap singing "Love Me Tender."

Unlike Gordon, who was once more draped over the steering wheel, Frank was slouching, as was his style when riding with The Lakers. He slid down until only his eyes and his pompadour showed. His right arm hung out the window, cigarette loosely held between his fingers. Frank burned more cigarettes than he actually smoked.

He jerked up and cried, "Look, look, look! Instant boner! Pull over!" Not that he actually had a boner; it was just something he said when he saw certain girls. "Pure boner material," Frank whispered.

Gordon pulled over. The provider of the imaginary boner was Charlene Cheyenne, a mildly pretty brunette who affected a Marilyn Monroe style of walking when she was out of her parents' line of sight. Charlene's little sister Marlene — one of Stan's friends — was with her. There was another Cheyenne sister at home, a baby named Arlene. Gordon sometimes wondered what the Cheyennes would call their next kid. Sardine, maybe? Canteen? Vaseline? Ovaltine?

Marlene was feeding her Betsy Wetsy doll a plastic baby bottle of what looked like green Kool-Aid; the stuff had run out the hole in the doll's rear end. Its underpants were stained and Kool-Aid was running down its legs. Gordon thought that Betsy looked like she had the clap.

"Hi there, Charlene," drawled Frank.

"Hi yourself, Frank." She let one knee bend so that she was standing hip shot in her tight, pink pedal pushers and short-sleeved sweater.

"Going to the Palace tonight?"

"Uh-huh. With Carol and Patty. Soon's I take Marlene to my grandmother's place. She's sleeping over."

"See you around, then."

"Not if I see you first, Frank." Charlene turned and began a slow, slinky walk down Main. Marlene, rolling her eyes, trailed behind her sister, carrying the Betsy Wetsy by one foot, revealing its green-stained underpants to the world.

Gordon pulled out onto the street once more. David Molonovitch and Tony De Salva lived three houses apart on Chestnut Avenue, which ran off Main just four blocks ahead, but Gordon was picking them up at the corner, away from their parents' scrutiny. There they were, hands in their pockets, both the picture of coolness. A slight tap on the horn and each turned as indifferently as possible. Once The Chief had rolled to a stop, David entered the Pontiac on the sidewalk side, as Tony sauntered around the car's rear end to get in on the street side.

David "Ace" Molonovitch was Gordon's best friend. Gordon liked all the guys, but he had known David the longest, having gone all through elementary school with him. Their true bond was deeper. Like Gordon, David hadn't met his father until after the war, when Peter Molonovitch had returned home minus an arm. David's father might have slid into alcoholism – plenty did – but instead he had turned to hard work, and he now owned Molonovitch Appliances, the first store in Erie View to carry television sets. You couldn't buy a used television there though, in spite of the fact that people turned them in regularly when they were upgrading to TVs with larger screens. That was because all of Mr. Molonovitch's salesmen were veterans who were bored out of their minds with civilian life. There was an actual bar in the basement of the store, one that would have shamed any of Erie View's men's beverage rooms, and when business was slow, he and the salesmen would sit down there and drink. While laughing like maniacs, they would enthusiastically shoot the screens out of the old televisions with a variety of pistols they had acquired as war souvenirs. Gordon thought it was pretty weird, but he had to admit the noise exploding televisions made was kind of cool. Since Mr. Molonovitch and company sold far more televisions than they blew up, David, SON OF THE RCA ASSASSIN, was the offspring of a reasonably wealthy man. Not old Dracula money, obviously; it was new money, but as far as Gordon was concerned, it would still pay for a beer.

Tony "Breezy" De Salva was a big, chunky boy who lived with his father and his four uncles, his mother having died giving birth to her first and only child. Tony's place was the epitome of a male household. All the De Salvas hunted and fished. They swore and spat, scratched their crotches, and farted. Tony's nickname came from the fact that he could fart on command, even if he hadn't been eating beans. His specialty was farting in cramped places, and although Breezy restrained himself in The Chief, anywhere else was fair game. This was something for which Gordon silently thanked God as he made a U-turn and headed back up the street toward the Palace Theater.

"Wesser, good buddy!" crooned David. He leaned over until he could see himself in the rearview mirror and smoothed his almost white flattop. David had a long and narrow face to go with his long and narrow body. Everything about David – his feet, his fingers, his arms and legs – was long and narrow. He had briefly considered "Snakeman" as a nickname for himself until he realized it would make him sound like a walking penis. Besides, Ace had more style. "How goes it?"

"Absolutely cool, Ace. Couldn't be cooler. Breezy? Cuttin' any good ones lately?"

Tony's farts could corrode stainless steel; they could eat through upholstery. They could probably melt lead. Gordon was reasonably sure that someday Tony would be able to make a living welding with his ass. And the farts *lingered*. They hung around for days, foully aromatic ghosts made worse if it was damp, which of course it always was in Erie View during the summer months.

"Good barely describes them these days, Wesser, but never fear." Leaning out the open window until he could see himself in the side-view mirror, he smoothed back the slick sides of his duck's ass and checked his dark pompadour. "Breezy will never befoul The Chief."

So there they were, four sixteen-year-old boys in a '50 Pontiac rolling slowly down Main Street to the Palace Theater. Bill Haley's "Rock Around the Clock" was blaring away on the radio, Gordon was surrounded by his buddies and with his father's five bucks in his pocket, he was flush.

Let the night begin! he thought.

chapter 3

"All the world's a stage and all
the men and women merely players."

— Amos Littlebird, Odawa Sachem

The Palace Theater was only a second-run movie house; months after films had been shown in the Bijoux or the Roxy, they would emerge yet again at the Palace. The oldest theater in town, it had none of the Roxy's glitter or the Bijoux's cavernous dignity. The Palace was more like a once beautiful woman garishly done up to hide her lines and pouches and sags. It stood next to the Bayside Hotel, a pox of a building that made the Palace *look* like a palace, and which was sometimes referred to as the Main Street Riding Academy. Rumor was that you could get a woman there if you knew how to put it to the manager. Which The Lakers did not. Tony had a theory that the secret password was a knock-knock joke, as in, *Knock-knock. Whores there?* Gordon didn't think it was much of a joke, especially since Tony had never managed to come up with a punch line. Besides, Gordon had been warned so many times by his father about the dangers of "going with" a certain sort of woman (a whore, a Jezebel, a harlot), that he sometimes dreamed that his penis had fallen off. He did not want the clap. He did not want his underpants to look like Betsy Wetsy's, but wondering about it was harmless. He hoped.

There was a single parking space left on the Palace's block and Gordon scooped it up. Leaving The Chief's windows open just a crack, the Lakers walked back to the theater where they got in line for their tickets. They were early and the lights wouldn't dim until 7:00, but they wanted good seats in the section of the theater they considered their own; the balcony. It also left time for checking out the action.

Marla Jerkins was inside the ticket booth. Gordon, David, and Tony bought their tickets with no fuss. *Twenty-five cents. Thank you ma'am.* But Frank sorted his change and dropped pennies and miscounted while Marla snapped her gum and examined her blood-red fingernails. Frank did this every time Marla worked the ticket booth because he liked to look at her tits. If it was Betty Williams in the booth, he had the transaction completed in a flash, because Betty had ordinary *breasts*. Marla's *tits* were encased in two rigid cones the size and shape of clown hats. Gordon thought that the cones made Marla look like an alien, or possibly like something you might see in a circus sideshow. She could have been the star of a movie called *Invasion of the Double-Breasted Matinee Woman*. But there was no point in saying anything to Frank; he was devoted to Marla's tits.

Tickets purchased, they walked the length of the stained red carpet and delivered them into the hands of Mr. Ligonier, the Palace's manager, who took very seriously the fact that this establishment was *his* employer's theater and therefore *his* responsibility. A tall, mournful man, he would have been more in place at a funeral home than a movie house. He carried himself with the great dignity due his elevated position, keeping his eyes just above your head when he took your ticket and ripped it in half. Mr. Ligonier took your ticket with the same distaste with which he would have taken a dog turd from you. Gordon thought it might be interesting to actually substitute a dog turd sometime, but he didn't want to be BANNED. Mr. Ligonier would BAN you for breathing the wrong way if he caught you at it.

Then to the concession for popcorn and pop. The Lakers always ordered the same thing: large popcorns with extra butter and large Cokes, (fifteen cents for the popcorn and a dime for the Coke) all in cardboard containers. The concession was run by Naomi Innagadda, a tiny woman whose breasts (yes, indeed; it was all about breasts) were so pendulous that they appeared to be growing out of her waist. Naomi had a small moustache and eyebrows that resembled wooly bear caterpillars; about four feet tall, she had the temperament of a rabid wolverine. No one but Ray Charles would have lingered at the concession.

Armed with the food, The Lakers proceeded into the murky depths of the theater, where the seating arrangements were structured around a strict hierarchy. The twelve- to fifteen-year-old crowd, those too young to *legally* drive, sat in the lower part of the Palace. Guys who had wheels and the girls who knew them were in the balcony. Gordon and the other Lakers always sat in one of the front rows, preferably the very front row where they could extend their legs and relax with their feet resting on the brass railing. Anywhere else up there was okay too, in a press. Anywhere but the back row, that is.

That row was the exclusive territory of The Sultans.

Comfortably seated, Gordon watched the ushers escorting kids down the aisles. He saw one usher lean down and tell a kid to put out his cigarette. The drill was familiar. *Please put out your cigarette. This isn't the smoking section; the smoking section is over there.* SCREW OFF. *I said the smoking section is over there. Now, either put out your cigarette or move. On the other hand, I could get the manager.* SCREW YOU. The kid would then put out his cigarette, wait until the usher was out of sight, and light up again. The fact was, the entire theater was nothing more than a chandelier-lit ashtray.

Charlene Cheyenne and her friends Carol Reynolds and Patty White seated themselves behind The Lakers, or rather behind David, Frank, and Tony. Gordon was suddenly awash in spearmint gum and the scent of Evening in Paris perfume that made up part of the girls' beauty regimen. They also had their own sort of uniform: ponytails tied up with handkerchiefs, snug sweater sets, poodle skirts, bobby socks, and saddleshoes. Frank and the others turned around in their seats. Their whispers and giggles floated past Gordon, but his mind was on other things, or rather, on another person.

There she was. Mary Davidson. It was easy to find her if she was in the theater; she hated the balcony and would only sit on the main floor. Mary had class. It dripped from her, oozed from her pores, and flowed around her in a cloud that, if it could be seen, would be made of pearlized titanium atoms. It was good breeding, good manners, and good looks all seamlessly blended with a dash of *haute société*. The real thing. And she had what his mother called strawberry blonde hair, although what strawberries had to do with it, Gordon would never know. A muted shade of red, a pale coppery gold, it hung perfectly straight to her shoulders when loose. Mary almost always wore some shade of blue; when her hair was in a sleek ponytail, she would tie a blue silk scarf around it. Blue and red-gold like the lake at sunset. Now *there* was a thought he would never be able to share with anyone.

Mary and Gordon had resumed a halting friendship only a year ago. She hadn't spoken to him since the seventh grade when he had made a joke about playing connect the dots with the freckles on her nose. This had been intensely amusing to Gordon, who had not even once considered apologizing, but as the years passed, he sometimes felt as though he had let something slip through his fingers. He would see her with her girlfriends; each season she would grow more and more lovely, her figure losing its coltish lines, the hint of baby fat disappearing from her cheeks. Then one day, she was the most beautiful girl in Erie View.

It wasn't until he literally ran into her in the library where she had a part-time job last summer, knocking the dust cloth out of her hands, sending them both sliding across the newly waxed floor and under a reading room table, that something had happened. Mary might have bitten off his nose as they lay there beneath the table. She certainly looked angry enough to bite. But then old Miss Baker, calmly reading *Pride and Prejudice* at that same table, had said, "Strange way to collect dust bunnies, Mary Davidson. Might have to try it myself."

It had been a close call that day. Both of them had managed to crawl out from under the table and leave the reading room, snorting with laughter, before the head librarian had come in. Mary might have lost her job. Instead, she gained a friend. As did Gordon, although these days, "friend" didn't really describe how Gordon thought about Mary. He sure didn't have those sorts of thoughts about any of his other friends.

Gordon stared at the back of Mary's head, willing her to turn around and give him one of those smiles that made his knees weak. She didn't. She was with Laura Crane, and Laura – a striking blonde with hazel eyes – had her full attention. Mary always made you feel as though you were the most important person in the world. It didn't matter if you were some little kid she was baby-sitting, or if you were the mailman or someone she had to talk to at one of her mother's garden parties. The effect was the same. You were special. Gordon lived for those moments. But she wasn't turning around and the lights were dimming. The curtains slowly opened, the Looney Tunes music began to play, and about ten thousand popcorn boxes (carefully folded flat to gain maximum velocity) were hurled at the screen.

Mr. Ligonier came running across the stage, waving his arms over his head. He stopped at midpoint and screamed, "Cease this! Stop it right now. I will call the police! The police will be called and they'll arrest you for rioting!" Five thousand more popcorn boxes with Mr. Ligonier's name theoretically written on them cartwheeled out of the darkness. "I. WILL. CANCEL. THE. SHOW!"

Total silence except for the cartoon dialogue and background music. Mr. Ligonier wheeled on the heel of one patent leather shoe and marched back out across the stage, prudently ignoring the dozen or so boxes that accompanied him. Lit cigarettes floated and bobbed in the darkness. There was still a good deal of low, discrete chatter, since only the really young kids who came to the Saturday matinees – Stan being one of them – actually paid any attention to the cartoon.

Everybody watched the Rocketman serial though, mesmerized by its strangeness. Rocketman sucked the hairy root, but tonight he sucked it more than usual; Gordon thought it was possibly the stupidest thing he had ever seen. Rocketman, dressed in his jet packs, was hurtling though the air. Actually, Rocketman was just sort of hanging from his entirely visible wires, wobbling, grimacing against incredible g-forces, while little wisps of smoke drifted straight up from his rocket jets. It was awful.

Gordon forced himself to watch it though, so that his thoughts would not be drawn back to The Chief and the burn that still scarred its hood, so that the sick memory would not ruin his favorite night out. He nearly managed it by staring down at where he knew Mary was sitting and by thanking God that there was only one Rocketman ordeal to endure.

But when *Rebel Without a Cause* began, Mary and The Chief temporarily drifted to the sidelines of Gordon's attention. Now this was stuff worthy of his concentration. James Dean, his silver screen mentor. For the first part of the film, Gordon studied Dean, unconsciously shifting his body to mimic Dean's poses, rearranging his own features to more closely resemble Dean's expressions, mouthing the lines he knew by heart.

"Are you having a conniption or something?" Tony whispered. "I can call the usher if you're having a conniption."

"Conniption my ass," Gordon breathed. "Next time *Rock Around the Clock* is playing here and you want to study your idol's moves, I'll show you a conniption."

He didn't mean it of course. The Lakers, being the sort of guys they were, supported each other totally in perfecting their personas. Gordon's was James Dean, Frank's was Elvis, and Tony's was a bizarre combination of Bill Haley and Edward G. Robinson, whom Tony considered to be the penultimate film gangster. Gordon knew that Tony was slowly memorizing Haley's every move, the rock and roller providing what Tony referred to as the "artistic" side of his persona. *You got your artistic side and you got your hard case side. Keeps the girls off balance; don't know if they're coming or going.* In Tony's case, Gordon suspected, it would be mostly going.

David, strangely, had no persona, no idol. He was just . . . David, something over which Gordon sometimes puzzled but did not question. Yet, why would you want to be yourself when, with a little practice, you could be like James Dean? And in Gordon's case, *Rebel Without a Cause* was the textbook of choice when it came to his persona.

On the Palace's dented screen, Natalie Wood was just raising her arms to signal the beginning of the race, the car engines were revving, and even though he had seen the movie three times before, Gordon felt excitement knotting his stomach. Chicken. A deadly race of chicken where they would speed toward a cliff in stolen cars. Last one to jump from his car was the winner.

Only now, it isn't Natalie Wood who is on the screen. It's Mary, and Wesser is behind the wheel of James Dean's car. Mary's arms come down, the cars scream into action and the race is on. Wesser drives with the practiced ease of a professional (arm wrapped around the steering wheel), nerves of steel, cool as a cucumber, a motorized cliché, but a debonair one. He knows he will win this race because the guy in the other car – Lancer Caldwell of The Sultans (loser, loser) – is no match for him. But then the cliff is coming too close too fast (Wesser's reflexes spring into action), and although his honor is at stake (Wesser's no stupe), his passion for Mary is greater (pant, pant), so he flings open the car's door, hurls himself out, and rolls gracefully away. Cut to the interior of Lancer's car where he is caught (heh, heh) on the gearshift, unable to get out (heh, heh, heh!), eyes wide with terror, screaming, drooling, weeping, begging for mercy (heh, heh, HEH, heh, heh!!), begging for his life, and then (oops!), over the cliff go both cars. Bye-bye, widdle Wancer!

Of course, all of this wasn't exactly happening in the film; Gordon's imagination was simply embellishing the movie and making it much, much better. Now Mary runs into his arms and he gazes into her adoring eyes. Romantic music begins to play, he pulls her closer feeling her body (her breasts) against his body (no boner, since Wesser is too much the in-control gentleman), they kiss (no tongue, just lips . . . well, maybe a little tongue), and then she says . . .

"SHIT!"

The Sultan equivalent of Tony De Salva was Dutch Batting. Dutch didn't fart, though, he horked. Dutch was able to draw deeply from within the slimy and turgid recesses of his lungs and hawk up gobs of mythical proportion. Like Lancer, he was a two-pack-a-day guy. The gobs — something Dutch called gobberoonies — were slate-gray in color and smelled like three-day-old corpses that had been poorly preserved in nicotine. Like the Thibodaux's parrot, Dutch was a sharpshooter. He could direct one of his gobberoonies and take out a squirrel; an entire park would empty of wildlife when Dutch approached. This time though, his aim had been a bit off. Ordered to score a hit on Gordy-Wordy by Lancer and urged on by Eddie Morton, the third Sultan, Dutch, had been distracted by Natalie Wood's tits. The gob had hit David smack in the neck.

"SHIT! AW, GOD!" David wiped his hand across the back of his neck, took one look at what was there and vomited into his popcorn box, which wasn't designed to hold that much puke. It splashed out onto the floor. Tony began to gag and then gasp, "Man, oh, man, oh, man," over and over again, as though he were reciting some charm against hurling. Frank did a sympathy vomit. What looked like two gallons of semi-digested, liquefied popcorn and Coke went sailing over the balcony rail, a yellow, steaming Niagara Falls. There was horrified shrieking from below. Charlene and her girlfriends, screaming like banshees, were all but climbing over the seats and the people behind them to get away from the stench. The ushers' flashlights began to sweep upward and sideways in an attempt to pin down what was happening.

"Come on," hissed Gordon. He grabbed David's arm and pulled him to his feet. "Come on, I said! This way. Tony, get Frank." The entire first three rows of the balcony were clearing. Gordon knew – it was closer to hoped – that they wouldn't be noticed in the crowd.

Near the curtained exit at the top of the balcony, Gordon paused. There sat the three Sultans, Lancer Caldwell holding court in the middle, their feet on the empty seats in front of them, cigarettes glowing. No one, believe you me, NO ONE in his right mind sat in front of a Sultan at the Palace. Not if that individual didn't want boot imprints on the back of his head. Lancer drew hard on his cigarette and leaned back. Then because he couldn't resist the temptation to let that little ass–wipe Westley know that he had called the shot, so to speak, he saluted.

Which in the end, would prove to be a very bad call for Lancer Caldwell. Because it was at that moment that a suspicion of just *who* had thrown the butt on The Chief's hood began to form in Gordon's mind.

"A bully is always a coward."

— Amos Littlebird, Odawa Sachem

The lobby was a mob scene. Girls screeched and laughed, clutching at each other. Guys exclaimed how that had been the best, the *very* best. Mr. Ligonier was frantically questioning one of the ushers, his eyes skittering over the crowd. He went absolutely white, inhaled like a drowning man and bellowed, "STOP THE FILM! THE POLICE WILL BE CALLED. CHARGES WILL BE LAID!"

Out in the blessed sweet air, The Lakers made their way down the street away from the theater as casually as they could. David muttered, "They won't get away with this. We'll get them. It might take time, but we'll get them."

In a hundred years, maybe, thought Gordon. The three Sultans were older guys — Lancer was nineteen, anyway — who sported convoluted pompadours and full duck's asses like their leader. They drove pre-war coupes of different makes, all painted two-tone dark and light blue. The Sultans were docile enough in a low-level threatening sort of way, unless you challenged their unpredictable code of ethics and then, Lordy, Lordy, they were as mean as cat crap in a phone booth on a hot August afternoon. Especially Lancer, who had possessed since childhood a mean streak that would have made Public Enemy Number One step aside and move to the back of the line. The Sultans. Uh-huh; right. In about a hundred years.

"CHARGES WILL BE LAID!" yelled Gordon, hoping to distract David from his thoughts of suicidal retaliation. Then in a lower tone, "Puking in a public place."

"Spewing without a license," said Tony.

"Regurgitation with intent to maim," Frank offered weakly.

"It's not funny," said David, who was scrubbing at the back of his neck with his handkerchief. "I'm going home."

"Aw, come on, David," coaxed Tony. "The night is young. You can wash up at Kitchie's."

"I said I'm going home. It wasn't you he spit on, was it? It was that asshole Lancer that got him to do it. He spit on me, man! Right on my neck and on my clean T-shirt and I smell like puke . . . I'm going home."

"There's nothing on your T-shirt," said Gordon. "You got it all." His stomach was doing a long, slow roll at the thought of what David had wiped away with his bare hand. "Puke? That's nothing. You can rinse your mouth out with a Coke at Kitchie's."

"Yeah!" said Frank brightly. "Coca-Cola. The pause that refreshes *and* gets rid of the taste of vomit."

To the tune of "Jimmy Crack Corn," Tony began to sing, "*David blows lunch and we don't care. David blows lunch and we don't care. David blows lunch and we don't caaaaaaaare!*" He dropped to one knee on the sidewalk, flung out his arms and finished, "*The Sultans stink today . . . and every-day . . . and twice on Suuuuunday!*"

There was dead silence. Gordon started to say something about how brainless Tony was, when David began to laugh. It was shaky at first, but then it reached his belly. Suddenly they were all clutching at their middles, Frank was down on the sidewalk, Gordon had tears streaming from his eyes, and passersby were giving them a wide berth.

"I think I pissed myself," said Tony faintly, and of course, that started them up again. By the time they were at the door of Kitchie's Pool Hall and Fedora Emporium, their good humor had been restored and phase two of the night awaited them.

■■■

Kitchie's was one of the oldest buildings in Erie View, being part of the block up from the Palace where everything

was at least a hundred years old. Upon entering the pool
hall, Gordon's senses were assailed by *Eau de Kitchie's*, an
odor he would for his entire life associate with his teens:
cigar smoke, sweat, shoe polish, pickled eggs, and un-
emptied spittoons. The smell turned his thoughts back to
Dutch's gob, and did he ever need to push *that* baby away.
Dark oak paneled the wainscoting of the long, narrow
room; an ornate tin ceiling presided over the six pool
tables, and along the walls were ice-cream parlor chairs for
the spectators and a counter where Mr. Kitchie timed the
games and collected your money. Near the entrance was
the Fedora Emporium part of Kitchie's: the work area
where Injun Joely cleaned and blocked hats, shined shoes,
and sold cigars.

Gordon liked Injun Joely, who was a quiet, soft-
spoken Odawa man. Getting any more from him on the
subject of his Indian background or anything else personal, unless he chose to drop the occasional vague clue,
was like picking Grandpa's brain about the war. Fruitless.
Injun Joely had worked for Mr. Kitchie for as long as
Gordon could remember. He had always been at the
pool hall, sweeping up after the place closed, sleeping
there – he kept his cot under the end pool table – taking
his meals at Gertson's Coffee Shop next door. Injun
Joely bought his clothing at the church rummage sales.
He kept an old, cut-down Ross rifle in an umbrella stand
that held broken pool cues. Just in case; Kitchie's *was* a

pool hall, after all and things could sometimes get a little rough. A strong-looking, dusky-skinned man, Joely combed his gray-streaked hair straight back in a style that Gordon's dad called *wino hair* — a wino with a bad hangover and shaking hands being unable to part his own hair. But Joely didn't drink. He didn't smoke, chaw, or swear, either; at least Gordon had never caught him at it. Most of the men who frequented Kitchie's didn't really see Joely; he was just there like the brass spittoons or the pool cues. Once, years ago, wondering if Injun Joely had some sort of mysterious past, Gordon had asked his father about him.

"Joely Waters?" Gordon's father had laughed a little, but not unkindly. "Spent some time in a veterans hospital after the first war. Came from up north, if I recall correctly. They released him the year you were born." He had smiled a thoughtful smile. "I only remember that because your mom wrote me that your grandfather was well enough to attend your baptism, and for some reason, Waters was standing outside the church. Your grandfather and he had some sort of conversation, I guess . . ." Gordon always remembered how his father's voice had fallen away.

"Were they in the war together, Dad? Is that it?"

"Yes, son. I believe so. Men like them don't necessarily like to talk too much about it, though."

And so, Injun Joely had remained a mystery, an enigma — at least to Gordon who mostly didn't think about it these days. Now Injun Joely was a friend. Sort of. If a grown-up could be a friend.

David hurried through the pool hall to the rest room at the back. The hall itself might be a tad in need of a good fire hosing by Gordon's mother's standards, but the rest room was spotless. When David emerged ten minutes later, he smelled of the harsh soap which Joely kept at the sink, and the back of his neck had been scrubbed nearly raw.

"Drinks on me," said Gordon, feeling particularly generous.

Cokes in hand, The Lakers decided on a game of snooker. David told Mr. Kitchie they would play table three, which was empty. Mr. Kitchie put down his newspaper, wrote their names on his pad, and noted the time, since at Kitchie's you paid an hourly rate or minutes thereof.

For about a quarter hour, the only sound from them was the *click* of pool balls and mild swearing when a shot was missed. Gordon tried to focus, but all he could see was Lancer's sick smile, the same smile he would have had glued to his face when he defiled The Chief. With a resounding *clunk* his seven ball hit the corner pocket. The game was over. Gordon passed his cue to a guy he recognized from school, then he wandered over to where Injun Joely was re-tipping cues.

"Evening, Gordon," said Injun Joely. He glued a

leather tip onto the end of a cue. "Played a good game there. A very good game."

Gordon flushed with pleasure. "I didn't win though."

"My granddad, Amos Littlebird, used to say that winning isn't everything. In the end –"

"It's how you play the game that counts?"

Injun Joely cocked his head to one side. "No. My granddad said that winning isn't everything, that there isn't necessarily glory involved. But it's a heck of a lot more fun than losing. Ask Custer." Gordon, a bit confused, was watching him expectantly, so Joely added, "A joke, Gordon. Custer's Last Stand? The Indians won? Not Indian wisdom. Just a joke."

Gordon relaxed. He enjoyed talking with Injun Joely, but the Indian wisdom thing was a little hard to follow at times. "Oh. Right. A joke. Cool." He paused. "No glory in losing either, though, at least not in pool."

Injun Joely began to sand the bare wood tip of another cue. "On the other hand, my grandfather, who as you know was a great Sachem among my people, used to say, 'What is glory but the blaze of flame.'"

"Oh, yeah?" Gordon repeated the phrase in his head. "Keen."

"Keen? Kimosabi speak in strange tongue."

This time Gordon *knew* that Joely was kidding. Joely was a great fan of *The Lone Ranger* radio program. Injun

Joely thought that the Lone Ranger, also known as Kimosabi, and his Indian sidekick, Tonto, were hilarious.

"Yeah, Tonto? Well, this Lone Ranger's gonna chalk up a cue and hightail it over to a pool table."

Which was just when The Sultans entered Kitchie's.

"Outa my way, Prairie Nigger," said Lancer in a soft voice, soft enough that Mr. Kitchie couldn't hear him. Mr. Kitchie, who had seen a good deal of bloody combat during the last war, took crap from no one. Gordon's head snapped around. Brushing past Joely, Lancer took a cue from the rack as the other Sultans snickered. He sauntered up to Gordon, let his eyes slide over to Joely's expression-less face, and whispered, "That wagon-burner your friend, Gordie? You and Blanket Ass over there best buddies? Figures." Turning his back on Gordon, Lancer pointed at David. "You're at my table, gob neck. Oh. Pardon me. You are at my *tables*. We may want to play all these tables tonight, right boys?"

"You can't do that," said Frank above the sound of Dutch and Eddie's snorts of laughter. "This isn't your place."

Lancer's eyebrows lifted in amusement. "Not my place? Of course it is. You have to be eighteen to play pool in here. How old are you babies? Fifteen? Sixteen? Go home to your mamas, babies." He gave Frank the lightest of pushes with his fingertips.

"Leave him alone, Lancer," said Gordon, slowly walking over. He kept his voice pitched low and his back to Mr. Kitchie. "We've got every right to play here."

"Because your dad does Kitchie's books, Rich Kid? Because your old man owns a used car lot Gordy-Wordy?" His eyes flicked to David. "Another rich kid. Because your old man gave Kitchie a TV?"

"No," said Gordon. "Because the four of us put together are less of an asshole than you are. You've got no business talking to Joely that way, either. These are my friends, you perv, and so is he." He took a deep breath. "FRANCIS."

"Francis?" Dutch's laughter brayed out. "He called you, Fran —" Lancer backhanded Dutch across the mouth in a blur of motion.

"Aw, Lancer, you didn't have to go and —" Another lightning quick backhand. Mr. Kitchie looked up from his newspaper and frowned.

"Yeah. Fran-cis. Francis. It's his real name. Didn't you ever tell them that, *Francis*? Lancer is your mom's maiden name, isn't it, *Francis*?" Gordon was dimly aware that he was writing his own obituary here, but he was on a roll. "Or is that *François*?" There was a strangled laugh from Tony, cut short when Frank's elbow jabbed into his ribs.

How Constable Danny O'Driscoll had managed to enter the pool hall and make his way across the room would forever remain a wonder to Gordon. The man had cleats on his high-topped boots, for the love of God. Cleats! And he was big and heavy with a layer of fat over solid muscle. Not exactly the prima ballerina of the Erie View Police Department. And he wheezed. All the kids called him "The Walking Accordion" behind his back, since none of them were insane enough to do it to his face.

The Accordion crossed his arms over his considerable belly and asked, "Trouble? Surely, there's no trouble brewing on a fine evening such as this. Is there trouble brewing, do you think, Kitchie, my friend?"

"Aw, no, Danny. Not a tap of trouble, for if there were to be even a tap of trouble, the troublemaker would be banned from this pool hall."

"Good enough," wheezed The Accordion. "And I do believe it's damned close to your curfews, my boys, eleven being the standard hereabouts. Best be getting into that car of yours, young Westley." He hitched up his belt. "Got a mark on the hood, I noticed as I was walking my beat."

Gordon glanced at Lancer's livid face and saw a slow smile lift the corners of his thin lips. "Nothing really. It'll compound out easily." The smile disappeared, and Gordon thought, *it* was *him*!

"Well, I wouldn't want to be hearing about anything happening to that car or those who ride in it this fine evening. Having such a nose for crime as I do." O'Driscoll let his placid gaze drift over Lancer and the other Sultans.

"You're in a pool hall, my boys. Best play pool." Lancer began to step around him, but O'Driscoll lifted a hand and said, "The acoustics in my station house are better than those of this pool hall, if you didn't hear me. Best play pool and pay Mr. Kitchie for the space you've taken up these last minutes."

The Lakers wasted no time. They walked out of the pool hall, but they ran down Main Street in a blur. Once they were in The Chief, Gordon squealed out into the traffic. To hell with checking out the action or anything else.

"We are so dead! Oh, God! We are so dead!" screamed Tony, pulling down on his face so that his features were all distorted. "Dead! I want roses at my funeral!"

"Me. Not you. Me," said Gordon resignedly. "But it was worth it."

"Francis? How the hell did you know his name was Francis?" asked Frank. He had a new level of admiration for old Wesser tonight. Anybody who would take on The Sultans, anyone who would take on Lancer Caldwell, the Supreme Sultan was either very brave, or maybe screwed in the head. Frank preferred brave.

"How'd you know, Gord?" asked David.

David never addressed Gordon by his real name when they were in The Chief, while they were Lakers. He just didn't, and Gordon knew it was a measure of his awe.

"My dad told me. He ran into Lancer's father in England at the beginning of the war. Lancer's old man never shut up about his son, Francis."

Frank shuddered. "To think we practically share a name. I might have ended up a Sultan instead of a Laker."

They turned that over in their minds for a moment. The Chief rolled along Erie View's streets, the sound of the Lakers' helpless laughter streaming from its open windows as Gordon drove his friends home. With relief, he ended phase two of that Saturday night and entered phase three. Bed, sleep, and for the time being, oblivion.

chapter 5

"The pleasure of love is in loving."

— Amos Littlebird, Odawa Sachem

The next morning, Gordon was locked in mortal combat with the spiders on the lake side of the house. That's what his little brother, Stan, called it. *Locked in mortal combat*. Actually, Gordon was simply doing his only Sunday chore: sweeping spiders and their webs from the window frames and various nooks of the house.

Erie View had more spiders than anywhere else in the universe, Gordon was convinced, possibly even more than the Amazon. Maybe it was because the temperatures of Erie View summers were roughly equivalent to the climate of Venus. Maybe it was because of the plagues of gnats, fish flies, and cicadas that descended when you least expected them. Gordon wasn't sure. He only knew that every week he had to get out what Stan called the Spider

Field Sweeper – Stan watched A LOT of war movies – and get every last spider off the house.

It was a job filled with its usual joys. Using the very long-handled broom that his father had made, he worked slowly around the house, sweeping away spider webs all tangled with the shriveled corpses of insects. Stan clumped along in his braces calling out a running commentary.

"Big one there, Gordo. Huge one! A regular Goliath Bird-Eating Spider like in the 'cyclopedia! Good thing spiders are afraid of heights, eh, Gordo? Good thing they're mostly down here so's you can get 'em with the Spider Field Sweeper. Else you'd have to go all the way to the top. I wouldn't mind going all the way to the top, would you Gordo? How come there's no spiders up at the top? I seen Old Dougie eat a spider the other day, you know. Old Dougie'll eat anything, won't he? 'Cept prunes. How come he won't eat prunes, Gordo?"

Unlike Gordon, Stan had only one household responsibility, and that job was emptying and airing Old Dougie's litter box, which Dougie managed to befoul unspeakably on a daily basis. It was something Gordon would rather face death in battle than do. Dougie's box was always in the same condition it would have been, had it been used by a flock of laxative-dosed condors. There was sufficient guano in it to corner the market on the nitrate trade. It defied simile and metaphor. *Airing* the box held about as much meaning as Noah airing the Ark's bilges, in

Gordon's opinion, but Stan did it willingly, since he loved Old Dougie.

And since Stan had already fumigated the litter box, he was free to "assist" Gordon, as he called it. This involved Stan following Gordon around the house, screaming as if he were being murdered when the spiders plopped down around him. Then he would stagger madly in circles, his braces rattling, clutching at his throat, finally falling down dead. It didn't matter what Gordon said to him. Stan would repeat the performance until all the spiders – some crushed by the broom, some having sullenly crawled away to rebuild life in a more stable environment – were down.

Gordon, his task completed, gave the last spider a flick, shook off the web and then hung the broom from its brackets on the side of the garage.

"Coke, Gordo?" asked Stan.

"Just for me. You're too young for Coke."

"I'm eight. Eight isn't too young. Eight is just right."

"You'll turn into a Coke addict, your teeth will rot out, you'll start drooling. You'll get so constipated they'll need dynamite to blast your poop free, and all your hair will fall out."

"Neat," said Stan. He clumped up onto the porch, passed Grandpa who was seated in his rocking chair with Old Dougie purring away on his lap, and yanked open the screen door. Gordon heard his mother's warning about not letting it slam and then her mild admonition when it did.

Grandpa, who didn't much like loud, sharp noises, just sat there, thank God. He hadn't reacted to this one, but there was no predicting when he would. Grandpa was hard to read. Gordon had no idea what demons prowled the shadows of the old man's memory, but he knew they must be relentless and horrible. Thirty-seven years in a veterans hospital, interspersed by weekends with his family, *if* he was calm enough to be released, had done little to blunt their sharp teeth. Lately there had been an improvement, and so Grandpa had been living with them for the last month. Gordon hoped his grandfather would *stay* okay; his mental fingers were crossed that Grandpa wouldn't revisit a past so painful that it would consume his life again. Because, in spite of the old man's deeply engrained crotchetiness, Gordon liked having his grandfather living with them.

When Stan pushed the door wide with his body, an open bottle of Coca-Cola in each hand, Gordon grabbed the door's handle and eased it shut. Stan finished his Coke off with a series of gulps, burping elaborately after each one. Then he put the empty bottle on the steps and lurched out onto the beach to play.

Gordon sat on the steps next to his grandfather's chair and absently scratched behind Old Dougie's ears while Dougie slitted his eyes looking like a matted, furry Buddha. Gordon sipped the icy Coke from its green bottle and relished the time before he would go in and have a quick shower. The lake was utterly calm this morning, a huge green-gray slick. It was one of those moments when the horizon seems to have disappeared, when the smudge of the sky blends into the water. A lopsided moon was just setting, its reflection a long, straight ribbon of dull silver. There was the uneven puttering of an outboard engine as someone in a small boat emerged from the creek and rounded the breakwall with its lighthouse. *That baby needs a tune-up*, Gordon thought absently as the boat cut across the moon's reflection, setting it in motion.

"Looks like a hoopla dancer," cried Stan. He dropped onto his back in the sand and started singing "Row, Row, Row Your Boat." He was making sand angels; the beach was pocked with them. There were also several very strange sand structures, lumpy mounds that bristled with sticks. Sand porcupines, Stan called them.

Gordon sighed. "*Hoola* dancer, you twerp." His brother was very weird. He even looked weird. It had nothing to do with the braces; one of Stan's eyes was just a little higher than the other and when he smiled, one side of his mouth tilted up just a little higher than the other side. His blond hair – all the Westleys were blond – was fine and dry. And, just to complete the charming picture, he wore glasses and was a bed wetter.

Last weekend the Westleys (all except Grandpa, who felt the same way about circuses as he felt about proctologists – they're a real pain in the ass!), had gone to see the small circus that had rolled into town and set up on the baseball diamond. It had been a pretty good circus, one that boasted a pack of cigar-smoking clowns who looked at least as tough as The Sultans. They represented THE PURPLE GANG OF CLOWNDOM in Gordon's estimation. Stan had enjoyed the clowns, he had loved Madame Zaza, the tightrope walker, he had raved over the performing dogs (mongrels who probably had higher IQs than The Sultans), but he had *adored* the sideshow.

"I could work in a sideshow, doncha think, Dad?" he had asked their father. "I could play my armpit." Stan had given a demonstration, one that gained him a round of applause from both the bearded lady, Miss Divine (it was a beard so fake that it looked like a dead raccoon was hanging from her face), and The Great Lombardo, the human pretzel (whose contortions *really* would have creeped out Grandpa). This encouraged Stan to announce that when he grew up he was definitely going to run away and join a sideshow since he would fit right in. Which Gordon thought might actually be true.

But Gordon loved him anyway. It was not anything he would ever put into words; only a total stupe would go around saying he loved his brother. And Stan, odd-guy-out Stan, loved him back.

"Sometimes I wonder about that boy," muttered Grandpa. He rocked forward a little, squishing Dougie who meowed soundlessly. Then Grandpa scanned the sky, grunted and leaned back. "Strange."

"I don't know. I think it's that he's just sort of unusual," Gordon said carefully. If someone stirred the slowly bubbling pot of Grandpa's temper just a little too briskly, Grandpa had been known to show that individual *what's o'clock*, which was a smack upside the head, and which got Grandpa changed from the veterans hospital's blue denim uniform into the dreaded GRAY pants and jackets. And which also placed him in the locked ward. Gordon hadn't ever been shown *what's o'clock* and neither had Stan, but it was better not to take chances.

"Oh, he's different, all right," observed Grandpa with a certain humor. "Look at him out there. Sand in his shoes, tracking up the house, making work for your mother. And he could get piles. Sitting in the sand will give you piles. Piles on a man my age is the natural order of things. You wait, Gordon. Come the day you'll have piles so bad you want to stick a bottle brush up your ass and itch for Canada."

Gordon was unsuccessfully trying to stop *that* delight-ful scene from taking root in his ever-fertile imagination, when Grandpa rose to his slippered feet, Old Dougie sliding unceremoniously off his lap and onto the sand. Dougie responded by thrusting a hind leg up over his head and casually licking his nether region, something that always filled Gordon with a mixture of wonder and disgust, but that Stan thought was really nifty. Grandpa cupped his hands around his mouth and shouted, "Stanley Livingston Westley! Rally! Rally!"

But Stan was not moving. No way. Uh-uh. He was in no mood to play what he secretly called *The Army Retard Game*.

"Fine," fumed his grandfather. "Have it your way, soldier. Stay out there and get piles. But don't come crying to me when you do. Ha, ha! No, don't bother, because if you do, I may have to show you what's o'clock!" And with a sharp nod to Gordon, he scooped up Old Dougie, turned and went into the house.

"I hate it when he does that," said Stan in a low voice. He joined Gordon, who was still seated on the steps. "It's starting to get creepy."

"Starting?" laughed Gordon. It wasn't a very happy laugh. "Look. Just try to play along and be nice to him. That's not so hard, is it Stan? It's just a game. Sort of."

"Why does he do it? Cripes, it makes me nuts."

"I think it's because he was a soldier for so long," Gordon answered cautiously.

"Not the war? Robbie says he heard that the hospital is full of guys who were shocked by the war. Maybe hit by lightning."

Now Gordon's laughter was real. "Make that shell shocked. Some guys just couldn't handle it."

Stan fingered the medal he wore around his neck. It was one of his grandfather's WWI service medals, a treasure he had received from Grandpa's own hand when they put the braces on Stan's legs two years ago, after he had suffered through a mild case of polio. "For bravery in action" his grandpa had said. That there were hundreds of such medals forgotten in the corners of dresser drawers, and two or three were usually in the display case of Garside's Pawn Shop was meaningless to Stan. He wore the medal proudly on a steel bead chain tucked inside his T-shirt, and on the rare occasion he took it off, kept it in a cigar box on his nightstand. The medal was kind of a mess, since as he had done years ago with all his medals, Grandpa had filed his name from the back and given the front a few whacks for good measure. It might have been badly scratched, but Stan treasured it.

"Does it mean they're crazy? Robbie says it does." Stan's voice was small now, small and tinged with worry. The braces would fix his legs; they were coming off for good in just a few weeks, hopefully, but could you fix crazy?

"Robbie Colons is more of a feeb than you are, Stan, and that's saying a lot. What the hell does Robbie know? He hasn't got a grandfather who was in the hospital. He's never even been in the hospital, I bet. You have. Do those guys seem crazy to you? It's more like tired, Stan. I think Grandpa is just tired."

"Well he doesn't seem tired when he's playing the game. And he's still watching for zeppelins, isn't he? I could see him doing it."

"He was just looking at the sky, Stan. Just the way you look at the sky or I look at the sky." Now Gordon had moved into a gray area. He was not above lying; lies were often a simple matter of self-preservation. *Spitball? What spitball, Miss Walker? Oh. That one. Innocent, Miss Walker and may I say that color of orange truly suits you? I may not? Yes. Of course. I will shut up while I am ahead, Miss Walker.*

He didn't like to lie to Stan, though, but it wasn't a real lie. It couldn't be much of a lie if he told it to keep Stan from getting hurt. But the fact was, their grandpa *was* watching for zeppelins. And for fighter planes of all sorts: Fokkers, Sopwith Camels, Spads – sometimes cursing their names under his breath as he did so. Gordon couldn't ask his grandfather about the reasons for this; John Stanford flatly refused to discuss the war. *You don't want to know about them years, boy.*

"I think he is just remembering. Maybe when he looks at the sky, he's just remembering. Maybe he can't help it."

"Maybe . . . . Gordo?"

"What?"

"What're piles?"

"Oh, man! Ask Dad, okay?"

"Are piles a sex thing?"

"God; I hope not! Ask Dad; I gotta get cleaned up. Go get Robbie and meet me back here."

"'Kay," Stan answered. He heaved himself up and clumped across the porch humming "How Much Is That Doggy in the Window?" The screen door slammed, Gordon heard, "Arf! Arf!" and then he was alone.

He stood listening to his mother scolding Stan for making so much noise and laying down the law about his brother's braces being off for only a few hours so that he could play at the water's edge. There was the sound of Stan's zombie-like progress through the house, a cry of "Dad, what's piles?" his father's deep laughter and his murmured reply, an *oogy*, from Stan. (That's what he said when he found something REALLY revolting.) More clomping and the sound of the front door opening. It blessedly had no screen. Taking a deep breath, Gordon prepared himself to run the maternal gauntlet.

She was seated at the kitchen table peeling boiled eggs with a teaspoon for their "healthy" picnic lunch. Old Dougie was crouched near her feet eating an egg shell. Dougie, as Stan had earlier observed, ate just about anything.

Everyone said his parents, especially his mother, looked like movie stars. It was true; Louise Westley could have been Grace Kelly's older sister. Her pale blonde hair was worn in the same style, her voice was soft — unless she was screaming at Stan — and her smile dazzling. Gordon wasn't exactly conscious of this, in spite of what people said; she was his mom. He only knew that her housedresses were always wrinkle free, the seams of her stockings perfectly straight, that she smelled of Muguet des Bois, and that right now she was about to question him.

Without raising her eyes, as though peeling eggs was her life's vocation, his mother asked lightly, "Picking up Mary Davidson?"

Gordon wasn't fooled by her laissez-faire tone. "Yes." She knew he was picking up Mary, that her parents couldn't drive her to the beach because they were going to the Club.

She placed the peeled egg on a plate with one other. They looked like eyeballs. Eyeball picnic. Yum-o. "You'll be a gentleman, dear?" Although the words were phrased into a question, Gordon understood the implicit statement in them.

"Of course."

"Mary is a good girl." She tapped an egg against the gray Formica tabletop, slid the bowl of the spoon into the crack, and began gently lifting away the shell. Gordon peeled eggs with his fingers; Stan ripped them apart so that most of the white remained glued to the shell. His mother did it with a delicacy that was making Gordon's head swim. "She has a spotless reputation."

"I know that. So do I," he said, the highly embroidered fact rolling off his tongue more smoothly than a snooker ball on felt.

Gordon's mother set down her spoon. She lifted her eyes and met his head on, and for Gordon it was like being knocked back ten years in time. It was the you-can't-fool-me look. The you-can't-fool-me-because-I-am-your-mother-and-I-know-more-things-about-you-than-God-does look. Her spoon and her attention went back to the eggs. "Of course, dear. Otherwise Myra Davidson and I would never let Mary get into that car of yours." Gordon's mother said the word *car* the way someone else might have said *week-old moldy jock strap*.

"You can count on me, Mom. I'll be more of a gentleman than the Duke of Windsor, Cary Grant, and Fred Astaire combined. I will reek of gentlemanliness, but gotta run and have a quick shower first. Get off the old spideroo webs."

"Speak English. And don't run. Stan just made enough noise to wake the dead. Piles, for goodness sake! Your grandfather is having a lie-down and your father is reading his Sunday newspaper and wouldn't care to be disturbed by another stampede."

"Gotcha."

"And remember. Stan's braces can come off for a few hours, but not all day. That's important, dear."

It was. Stan was gradually working himself up, hour by hour, to the point where he wouldn't have to wear the braces at all. An amazing recovery, the doctors said, and Gordon wasn't going to be the one to screw *that* up. "I promise, Mom. Don't worry."

Louise Westley listened to the sound of her elder son's feet thumping down the hall and up the staircase. She shook her head. Sometimes she wondered, who was this stranger sitting across from her at dinner, eating enormous quantities of food, drinking herds of cows dry? Where was her sweet Gordy, her cuddlesome toddler; where was the six year old who had held her hand and needed to be tucked in and kissed good night? She supposed he was still inside this newest metamorphosis of her son. Rock and roll, cars, The Lakers, and yes – she knew it very well – Kitchie's Pool Hall. How long would it take all of these things to pass into history? Louise sighed again. Best not to say too much, Ben insisted. Let him stretch his wings. He's nearly a man, Louise. She sniffed.

At least he was still a clean boy.

chapter 6

"No one ever suddenly became depraved."

— Amos Littlebird, Odawa Sachem

The Chief, its practically virginal compounded hood gleaming in the sunshine, took on its exotic load in front of Gordon's house. Stan and Robbie, wearing swim trunks and T-shirts as Gordon was, were armed to the teeth with enough pails, shovels, towels, and beach toys to entirely clear the Sahara of sand in ten minutes. There was "the healthy lunch" of boiled eggs, celery and carrot sticks, pickles, ham sandwiches with the crusts cut off, and milk in a Thermos packed by Gordon's mother. Most of which would end up being buried in the sand by the little kids if they weren't closely watched. But they would be closely watched, because (thank you, God!) Mary was baby-sitting the pair of them for the day.

This was the only reason Mary would be allowed inside Gordon's car. She had seen Gordon's car, she had laid her hand upon it and stroked the paint, she had admired The Chief, oohing and aahing over its size and length (those words had nearly caused him to fall down foaming at the mouth), but she would actually *sit* in The Chief for the first time this morning. Goose bumps covered Gordon's entire body at the thought.

First, he swung around and picked up David. Tony and Frank, being Catholic, were unable to escape their religious obligations. Both their families attended 12:00 Mass and neither boy could avoid that under pain of eternal damnation. They would turn up later, maybe around 2:00, overly sanctified and raring to shake off some of that holy water.

With David sitting next to him in the front seat, Gordon drove sedately to Mary's place. When he reached Silver Birch Road — her street — he crept along at the speed of a glacier melting.

"I could crawl faster," complained Stan. "I could drag myself by my tongue faster."

But Gordon was not risking any chance of spooking the Davidsons. They were very spookable, especially Mary's mother, who apparently intended that Mary remain "sweet sixteen and never been kissed" until she was forty. Ignoring Stan's whining, he rolled up to Mary's house and parked, lining The Chief up precisely with the curb.

The Davidson abode, a mid-sized but very elegant Victorian, could have been the prototype for the words *neat as a pin*. The small back and front yards were beautifully landscaped, the interior was clean and tidy; wonderful smells always wafted about the kitchen. Mrs. Davidson was such a good baker that she always won at least one prize at the Erie View Fall Fair. Last year Gordon had heard Mrs. Colons say to Gordon's mother that in another incarnation, perhaps Mrs. Davidson had owned an 18th century *patisserie*, patronized by the lower nobility, all slavering over her tarts. Which Gordon thought sounded like Mrs. Davidson would have been running The Betty Crocker House of Bondage, Drool, and Baked Goods.

With the Davidsons watching from the doorway of their house, he loaded Mary's blanket, cooler, beach bag, and towels into the trunk, cramming them in with the other stuff, while David smiled like a cretin. Gordon handed Mary (sleeveless blouse of palest blue, hair loose on her shoulders, white tennis shorts that were just tight enough, and God in heaven, she smelled good) into the backseat where she sat between Robbie and Stan, who were both half in love with her. Her beach umbrella, he stuck crossways through the open back door windows. Gordon got into The Chief and was just turning around to say something to Mary, when Mrs. Davidson came click-clicking in her high heels, down the fieldstone sidewalk to the car, her pageboy bouncing, her crinolines swishing around her legs.

"Mary."

"Yes, Mother."

"Home by six for dinner. And you are watching the fireworks at Laura Crane's house as you promised her."

"Yes, Mother. I know all that."

Her attention floated over Gordon and found him lacking, but Gordon took no offence. All guys were lacking when it came to Mary in Mrs. Davidson's opinion. "Six o'clock, Gordon Westley, and not one minute later, mind you. I have absolute trust in your judgment as well as your ability to tell time. (Right.) As I was telling your mother last week at bridge, you have the makings of a true gentleman. (That's me. Little Lord Westley.) If you would only come to the Club with your parents you could learn to golf. Wouldn't that be nice, darling, if Gordon took up golf? Or badminton? (Dear Lord, please let a Lancaster fall out of the sky and squash her. Not kill her, just squash her a little bit so she shuts up.) You would look so dashing in plus fours, Gordon."

"Yes, ma'am." He glanced in the rearview mirror to see that Stan and Robbie each had fingers jammed up their noses as far as they could get them in, which was practically up to their elbows. "I'll certainly think about it, ma'am."

"Mother, we have to go or else we won't get a good

spot. I have to have deep sand or Gordon can't set up the umbrella properly. If it isn't set up properly, I could get a burn, and you know what would happen if I got a burn. I would peel. It would look disgusting, and people at the Club would stare, and it would be just so embarrassing I would die!"

Mrs. Davidson's hands fluttered and then settled over her bosom like two wounded pigeons. She looked like she was going to have a heart attack or something. "Oh, no, no! Gordon, you will find *deep* sand. If Mary is burned and peels I will hold you personally responsible."

Gordon started the engine and pulled away from the curb. "Don't worry, Mrs. Davidson. Deep sand it is." As he drove away, he heard *personally responsible* reverberating down the street.

"She's wearing her heavy girdle," said Mary. "Use your handkerchiefs," she tossed out absently to the boys. "Don't be repulsive." Then, "I have no idea how she can get enough air into her lungs to yell like that."

"My mom could run a hundred-yard dash in hers if it involved a department store sale," said Gordon over his shoulder. "What about your mother, Ace?"

But David was in a little bunch all wadded up against the passenger door. He was crying. "Plus fours. You in plus fours," he gasped. "And a plaid vest and a little flat hat to go with it. I can't stand it!"

"Neat," said Stan.

"You in your plus fours playing badminton in deep sand while Mary sheds skin like an anaconda," gasped David. "What does she think is under the surface of the beach? Bedrock? The Canadian Shield?"

"Probably," said Mary with patience. "My mother has never been to the beach, as you very well know, David Molonovitch. She sits by the pool at the Red Cedar Club, but she won't go to the beach. Sand fleas. You can be eaten alive she says, if there are sand fleas. And seagulls might make doo-doo on you."

"Doo-doo!" mouthed David. He could no longer speak.

"Goliath bird-eating sand fleas," said Stan. "We've seen 'em, eh, Robbie?"

"Yup. Millions of 'em," said Robbie, words that made Gordon bite down hard on his lower lip until his eyes watered. He caught Mary's disapproving frown in the rearview mirror, but it didn't help much. Once he heard Robbie say a few more sentences he would be fine, but the first sound of Robbie Colons' voice always undid him.

Robbie Colons sounded just like Donald Duck. He wasn't doing an imitation; he sounded like Donald Duck. Robbie would pass through his childhood and teenage years sounding like Donald Duck, he would enter manhood sounding like Donald Duck, he would propose to his sweetheart in the dulcet tones of Mr. D. Duck, and on his wedding night, he would cry out his pleasure – or rather quack it out – with all the passion of a pintail in rut.

Stan and Robbie carried on a disjointed and weird conversation about what would happen if somebody made a monster movie about giant sand fleas, and so by the time they arrived at Willnote Beach, the shock value of Robbie's voice had worn off for Gordon. Erie View had many private beaches, but there was nothing quite like the big public beach. Gordon saw things on Willnote that he hardly ever saw on their beach at home, and it was only about a quarter mile away. When he parked The Chief in the sandy lot on the other side of the road from Willnote, Gordon was pleased to note that the festivities were in full swing. The July long weekend on Willnote Beach hit them all with the suddenness of a summer storm when they got out of the car.

Hundreds of people had come down from Yorktown, a small city north of Erie View. Some would have driven, but many would have taken the Yorktown to Erie View Railway, with its stylishly appointed cars. Blankets and towels were spread out everywhere. A man was grilling smelt and the smell was unbelievably delectable. Little kids were making sand castles, people were swimming, and car radios were competing for airspace. Women who would never have been seen without nylon stockings on, were wearing bathing suits they probably should have burned. Potbellies that had hibernated all winter were now exposed to the daylight as men walked across the sand or lay on their backs, offering their guts to the sun. Three little kids with sand pails on their heads were having an argument about who was more powerful, Superman, God, or Santa Claus. Couples of all ages strolled by hand in hand. Just up the way, Denison's was doing a booming business. Gordon knew that in spite of the "healthy lunch," they would all be stuffing their faces there before the day was over.

They unloaded the car while David staked out a patch of sand. Blankets spread, umbrella sunk into *deep* sand, they all sat down in relief. Gordon released his brother from the hated braces and the two boys — Stan walking strangely without the weight on his legs — went to the water's edge to see what sort of booty they could find.

David stretched out in the sun, a towel thrown over his back and legs, while Mary charged Gordon with watching the boys so she could put on her suit. This he did with no difficulty, but once he caught sight of Mary recrossing that sand, her shorts and blouse tucked away in her beach bag, Stan and Robbie could have been consumed by sharks or carried off by an army of sand fleas and Gordon wouldn't have noticed.

In Gordon's besotted and hormonally driven view, she was something. Mary's deep turquoise suit was modest, even by the standards of the day, but it allowed him to see enough of her to know that beneath it she was absolutely gorgeous; long, slender legs lightly muscled from tennis, a narrow waist, and above that, the swell of her breasts. She was perfect. He couldn't let himself think about what her suit hid, though. Not that he wanted to see what was underneath it. Well, he did, but he was a gentleman and so he couldn't think like that because this was Mary. But he *was* thinking like that, and Lord in heaven, it was wonderful. Even the appearance of Lancer Caldwell and The Sultans who stood lounging against the grills of their cars in the parking lot (Way too cool to take off your leather jacket, eh, *Francis*? Well, cook away, you idiot!), couldn't spoil his mood. Although Gordon would have preferred to sit in the sun (in swim trunks, Lancer, you shithead), displaying the fine Westley musculature, Mary's invitation to share the umbrella's shade was like offering water to someone who has crawled across the wastes of the Kalahari.

"Sit in the sun if you want, though," she said. God! He was so handsome. Thick hair and straight, white teeth, and a great body. He had natural-looking muscles, unlike that imbecile Butsy Lane who was a lifeguard here at the beach. And Gordon was smart, really smart. He almost always got the best grades in everything, but he never bragged about it or showed off. He was absolutely gorgeous.

Unlike that creep, Lancer Caldwell. Mary had been conscious of various male stares following her as she walked across the beach – Gordon's in particular; she had focused on him alone – but it had been impossible for her to help glancing in the direction of the parking lot. Lancer had blown her a kiss, which she had ignored, just the way she ignored everything else he did. She had better ignore it, because otherwise she was reminded of that awful night, and she didn't want to think about it. She wouldn't think about that.

"Mary!" Cripes. What crazy dreamland had she been in for a second there? "I said, I'm fine. I want to sit in the shade." No way he was getting off this blanket.

Mary gave herself a hard mental jerk. "Are you hungry? I have Mother's watercress sandwiches in my cooler. Want some?"

"No thanks, I'm good."

"Are you going in?"

"No, I'm really good."

She stared at him. "That's good. I'm going in."

"I will too, then. So you won't drown or anything."

Mary laughed. It was a nice laugh, not a laughing-at-you laugh, but a laugh-with-me sort of laugh. Then she got to her feet and called to Stan and Robbie. Gordon, who was now walking behind her, tripped over a dog, two old men, and somebody buried in the sand, all because he couldn't take his eyes off of Mary's shapely derrière.

"Got it bad, man," said David softly. He had sat up and was watching the progress of the Lust Parade of One. He snorted when Gordon disappeared into a pit that two small girls had dug, in an attempt to reach Mongolia. Indignant cries of, "Get outa our hole, you poopee-caca-head," came faintly from their direction.

He watched Mary and Gordon standing knee-deep in the water while Stan and Robbie sat in the sand letting waves curl up over their laps in sheets of warm foam. David felt a rush of happiness for Gordon, the dink. Stretching out on his back, David hoped that Gord wouldn't fall into the pit and humiliate himself again. He was just beginning to doze, when a voice rang out.

"Hey there, guys and dolls. Make that doll. The party can at last begin because. We. Have. Arrived." It was Tony with Frank at his side.

"Whatcha got, guys?" asked David. "Gord! They're here!" he shouted though his cupped hands.

"A six-pack of Crystal Lager coming later, courtesy of Marc Ducharme," said Frank, as Mary and Gordon walked up from the water's edge. "He'll drop them off when he comes down for the fireworks. Free delivery." It was a small lie; more of a bragging lie. They might drink beers on the beach in the dark, but never during the day, and so Marc would only bring the beer after sunset. Word of public drinking could get home too easily, and they all wanted to live to be seventeen.

For a while they all just sat there, listening to Buddy Holly sing about Peggy Sue, half hearing the mewling of seagulls and the low wash of wavelets, smelling the french fries and malt vinegar.

Then Gordon leaned forward, elbows on his knees.

There were two swim platforms off the beach; one —
for people who could actually swim — was about fifty
yards out. The lifeguard only permitted its use when the
lake was reasonably calm. If the wind was high and big
waves were rolling in, a red flag would go up on the lifeguard tower. To swim at all then would be dangerous,
since a riptide would be running along the breakwall.
On *really* calm days like this one, there was also a little-
kid platform that was dragged out and anchored maybe
twenty-five feet from the waterline in two or three feet
of water. Stan and Robbie were standing alongside the
platform now, heads together. Gordon watched Robbie
climb up the platform's short ladder as Stan waded back
to shore.

Gordon glanced down at his wristwatch and began to
time what was happening. "He's actually doing it," he said
a few minutes later.

"What?" asked Mary, starting to get up. "What's
Robbie doing? Oh for Pete's sake. Not *that*!"

"What's up?" asked Frank eagerly.

"Robbie Colons? Stan's friend; the kid who lives a few
houses up the beach from us?" Gordon said.

"The neck kid?" asked Frank.

"The one and only," said Gordon. "Just watch."

"Man, Butsy Lane's gonna crap himself blind," said
David. "He will besmirch his old lifeguard pantaloons.
Serve him right. The only things he's been guarding all

day are Kathleen O'Neil's jugs. Uh, pardon me, Mary. Her figure."

"They're jugs," said Mary. "Believe me, they're jugs."

"He's been under seven minutes," said David. He had begun watching his own wristwatch when Gordon had. Not even Kathleen O'Neil's jugs, those melon-like objects of Butsy's desire and the nightly fantasy of many an Erie View lad, could distract him.

"This is going to be a good one," said Gordon. "Seven and a half minutes and counting."

Robbie Colons was a kid renowned for the amount of snot he produced. He had been subject to pulmonary difficulties all his life. A mouth breather, you could hear him coming two streets away. This winter past, he had been stricken with a terrible case of whooping cough. In a last ditch attempt to save his life – Robbie had been drowning in a sea of his own phlegm – Doctor Henderson had performed an emergency tracheotomy. Robbie's life saved, the good doctor had taken it a step further by inserting a little tin pipe into the incision so that the trache remained open. Which was why he sounded like Donald Duck. No mouth breathing for Robbie these days. It was pretty sick to look at, but Stan didn't seem to mind, and besides, Robbie had found a really cool use for it.

There he was, head entirely underwater, arms dangling in the lake, body as still as death. He was of course, breathing quite nicely through his tin pipe, which remained unseen above the water.

"A dead body! A drownded dead body on the raft!" It was Stan screaming his little guts out. Stan, the nerd, was in on it, naturally.

"Oh my God!" Butsy Lane, so called because of his habit of flexing his butt cheeks as he strode up and down the beach, half fell off the lifeguard platform and raced toward the water, spraying sand all over Kathleen O'Neil's baby oil and iodine coated bosoms. For which she did not thank him. In fact, she revealed herself to be the propri-etress of a rather interesting vocabulary.

"I christen thee Kathleen Trench Mouth O'Neil," Tony called out, tracing a cross in the air. Nice to finally put all that religious training to use.

But Gordon wasn't listening. No indeed. He was watching in rapt and mute fascination as Butsy flailed through the water and heaved himself onto the raft. He dragged Robbie out, flipped him over and leaned over him.

Now, Butsy had never actually saved anyone before, much less resuscitated a drowned kid. He crouched there, staring at strings of snot dripping down the kid's face, too disgusted to really notice the tin pipe.

"Do something!" shrieked Stan from the safety of the crowd that had gathered at the waterline. "Give him artificial perspiration!"

Knowing Kathleen would be watching, Butsy steeled

himself against the snot – God! It was the green kind! – and lowered his face to Robbie's to see if he was still breathing.

When they were only inches apart, Robbie's eyes popped open and he quacked, "I think I'm in love."

Butsy's anger was not immediate. Given a personality that was ruled by his gluteus maximi, he was limited to a few emotions at a time, and so rage could not cohabit with surprise *and* disgust within the precincts of his mind. He was stalled out at disgust. Disgust was overruling everything, it was numbah one, it was El Supremo, it was the Imperial Wizard of emotions at the moment, enabling Robbie to slip out of Butsy's arms, roll off the swim platform, and escape to shore. The sight of one snot-covered kid laughing his head off with a little four-eyed creep was enough to jolt Butsy into level two of his emotional repertoire: piss-offedness.

"Get off the beach!" he yelled, attempting to plow through the water in a manly lifeguard fashion for Kathleen's benefit. "Get off the beach!"

Gordon sighed. There was no way he was letting Butsy Lane kick Stan and Robbie off the beach. He might end up being kicked off the beach himself, but the younger kids would stay. He climbed to his feet, hoping things wouldn't degenerate into a shoving match or worse, a fistfight, when Mary held up a cautionary finger.

"I'll take care of this," she said firmly.

Mary stepped out into the sun; Stan and Robbie scuttled behind her. The image of a lioness he had once seen on some TV show flashed through Gordon's mind. Tawny and docile in repose, she had been stretched out with her eyes closed in the shade, her two cubs playing with the black tip of her tail. Then her eyes had popped open and met the camera. They were eyes of hot topaz filled with murder. Mary wouldn't be murdering Butsy, but Gordon was certain he wouldn't get off without at least a nip. Not if he pushed her too far, or made a move to touch the boys.

Butsy, his attention riveted on Mary, was about to say something, when Kathleen O'Neil cleared her throat. There was no mistaking the timbre of that sound; it rang with warning. *Ahem. Ahem! If you want even a prayer of getting your hands on my tits, Butsy, you will remove your eyes from that bitch's carcass. Now.*

Butsy swallowed, nodded, swallowed again, and tearing his gaze away from Mary – Gordon thought that Butsy's eyeballs might actually hemorrhage – followed Kathleen back to the lifeguard post.

"How does she do that?" whispered Tony. "Does she give off some baby-sitter ax murderer aura or something?"

"How do you do it, Mary?" asked Frank. "How do you bring grown lifeguards to their knees?"

"The same way I do it to the snotty little boys who are ruining my day," Mary said severely. "Come here you two. That was not the least bit funny, Robbie, and you're just as bad, Stan. Butsy *is* the lifeguard here; he has a job to do, and he doesn't need you making that job difficult." Her hands on her hips, she added, "I am definitely going to have to punish you." Stan and Robbie drooped lower and lower, looking like convicted felons awaiting their sentences. "You," said Mary, "and you," she paused, "are going to have to eat the healthy lunch!"

Robbie and Stan fell to the sand and grabbed Mary's ankles, begging and screaming, while Gordon unpacked the HL. Frank and Tony had brought food as well, so they set everything on the blanket in the shade of Mary's umbrella. The HL quickly deteriorated into a gastronomical nightmare. To Louise Westley's and Myra Davidson's tasteful picnic lunches were added a chunk of ring bologna, some pickled sturgeon's gizzards, a lump of Stilton cheese that smelled and looked like a wedge of congealed toe jam, some smoked catfish, and a huge bag of potato chips.

"Neat!" said Stan.

Emily Post would have been carried away on a stretcher had she had the bad luck to view the debacle. Frank and Tony subscribed to The Cro-Magnon School of Etiquette. They savaged their portions and didn't actually appear to chew anything. Gordon and David were a step up the evolutionary mastication chain, since at least they chewed. Robbie and Stan, who were always hungry (they ate non-stop and had the metabolisms of a pair of pigmy shrews), wore their meals. They had deviled egg in their hair, pork rinds on their shoulders, and mustard from the ham sandwiches on their cheeks. Mary? She nibbled. How you nibbled ring bologna was beyond Gordon, but she was doing it.

Half an hour later, the destruction was complete and everyone was stuffed. Mary declared a quiet hour of digestion before the boys could return to the water, although they could play at the edge in the wet sand. David put a towel over his head and fell asleep on his stomach, Frank and Tony went to look for girls, and that left Gordon and Mary – thank you, God! – alone. At least, as alone as you could be on a crowded beach.

A lifetime later, Gordon would be subject to the same illusion regarding the passage of time that affects older people. His days would fly by, which was a crying shame when you were near the end of your life and wanted to savor every precious second. Oddly enough, he was caught within the same chimera today. No matter how he willed it to drag on, the afternoon danced away with relentless abandon. Never had the sun crossed the sky more quickly; never had the hands of his wristwatch spun so frantically.

Walking down the beach with her didn't help. Joking around with the other Lakers didn't help. Not even a definitely unhealthy snack of hot dogs, fries, and Denison's famous lemonade made a difference. Before Gordon knew it, six o'clock was staring him in the face and his day with Mary was over.

chapter 7

"The heart has its reasons which
reason knows nothing of."

— Amos Littlebird, Odawa Sachem

Sometimes miracles do occur. Days ago the Davidsons
had been invited to watch the fireworks from the comfort
of Brierly's lakeside, spider-free porch. This would allow
them to drink martinis with the Westleys and listen to
what Stan called *old people music*. Benny Goodman, Ella
Fitzgerald, Duke Ellington. Old people music. Grandpa
didn't drink martinis; beer was his drink of choice, if he
drank at all. He'd as likely suck horse piss through a straw
as drink a martini, he'd said often enough. Nor did he
watch the fireworks. Gave him the creeps.

But none of that was the miracle; the miracle involved
Mary. Stan had accepted a last minute invitation to watch
the fireworks at Robbie Colons's house, thereby relieving
Gordon of the possibility of having to take his brother to

the festivities. Then Mary — in snug baby blue pedal pushers and a matching long sleeved sweater set — had unexpectedly accompanied her parents tonight, Laura Crane being mortally stricken with some female ailment. Gordon heard the dreaded *C* word whispered. *Cramps.* That would have been good enough, but the real honest to God miracle was that Mr. Davidson was sitting on their porch suggesting that Gordon might walk Mary over to the public beach to view the fireworks.

"You two youngsters just go on ahead and enjoy yourselves. Great idea, don't you think, Myra, the young- sters enjoying themselves?"

"Well, I don't know, Edgar," his wife said doubtfully. "It's dark after all."

"Happens every night about the same time." Mary's father guffawed. He might have sat there guffawing his lungs out all night had the sky not suddenly been lit by an exploding rocket. The women exclaimed, the men raised their glasses in a toast, and Mary mouthed *let's go* to Gordon.

He shrugged into his jacket and snatched up the same blanket he had used at the beach today. "We won't be late!" Gordon shouted, sort of shepherding Mary ahead of him, since he didn't dare touch her within sight of her mother. Not if he wanted his jugular to remain intact.

"Eleven o'clock," shrieked Mrs. Davidson.

"Eleven o'clock," Mary called back over her shoulder.

They walked hand in hand along the beach, just above the waterline where the sand was hard packed and smooth, past the last of the houses, to where a low wooden guardrail marked the public beach. It was lined with parked cars. The fireworks were coming with regularity now; maybe five seconds would pass and then another brilliant shower of silver or pink or gold would spray out across the sky. Clods of flaming shit could have been falling over Erie View for all Gordon was noticing. All he could focus on was Mary.

"How far do you want to go?" he asked carefully.

"What?" Mary laughed.

"I mean, do you want to walk all the way to the Sand Club? That's what I meant. Where most of the people are, or do you want to stay here where it's more private and there aren't so many people." *Jesus. I sound like an idiot.*

"I'll go as far as you want."

Dear God. She didn't mean what he hoped she was meaning. She couldn't be meaning that. "Here would be good, then," Gordon said, trying for a casual manner and failing utterly. He spread the blanket on the sand and watched as Mary sat cross-legged exactly in the middle. Then he plopped down next to her, suddenly at a complete loss. What if he put his arm around her and she pulled away? What if he kissed her and she pulled away? What if she had a fit? What if she passed out?

Mary put her hand over Gordon's. He nearly passed out. "This is really nice," she whispered. "No little kids;

I mean, I really like Stan and Robbie, but this is just, well, nicer."

This was his moment. Gordon leaned toward Mary, who shut her eyes in anticipation of the kiss and it was a good thing she did, because just before lip contact, the headlights of one of the parked cars came on, nearly blinding Gordon. But he wasn't so blinded that he didn't recognize the vehicle. It was Lancer Caldwell's coupe. Mary and Gordon scrambled to their feet to the sound of raucous laughter. Lancer doused the lights and then he and the two other Sultans climbed out of the car.

"If you don't like an audience, Westley, the beach ain't the place to be fucking," called Lancer. He lit up a cigarette. "Nice, fresh piece of tail like that deserves better than a blanket on the sand anyway. Hey, Mary!" He drew hard on his smoke. "You ain't actually gonna let little Westley pop your cherry, are you? You want a real man for that. Somebody who knows how to make it good for you."

"I don't see any real men out there," Mary said as coolly as she could. "Just a jerk." She caught hold of the sleeve of Gordon's jacket and said, "Come on. We don't need this."

Gordon felt hot rage building inside him. "Shut up, Caldwell! Keep your mouth shut about her. And stay away from my car. I know damned well it was you who threw that cigarette butt on the hood!"

Lancer threw up his hands. "Whoa! I've been told. Look at me; I'm shakin' here, just shakin'."

"Get the blanket and let's go," said Mary in much the same tone she used with Stan and Robbie.

"Listen to your baby-sitter, Westley," taunted Lancer, "or she might have to spank you. Pull down your pants and —"

Gordon moved forward, his fists balled, but Mary pulled him back and called, "Drop dead, Caldwell." Then she stuck out her tongue at Lancer, picked up the blanket herself, and dragged Gordon down the beach toward the Sand Club.

"I love a girl who knows how to use her tongue!" shouted Lancer to their backs. "Gets me all hot."

Mary and Gordon didn't say a word to each other as they plodded bleakly along. She had released his arm and was hugging the blanket to herself. It wasn't until they reached the crowded picnic tables at the back of the Sand Club that Gordon realized she was crying.

"God, Mary. Look. I'm sorry," he said helplessly. "I should have defended you better. He can't talk to you like that."

"Yeah? Really? Well, he just did." She sniffled hard. "And how could you have *defended* me?"

Gordon stiffened, horribly stung by the sarcasm in her voice. "You think I'm a coward? You think I'm afraid of him? Thanks a lot."

"No. I think you were smart to walk away with me. It's what I wanted. I mean, he carries a switchblade. They all do. I've even heard they carry guns. I know for a fact that Lancer keeps a shotgun in that place he rents from Mr. Richardson; the one the creep used to live in with his mother before she died. Mrs. Richardson told my mom so. Do you carry a switchblade? Or a gun?" She sniffled again and wiped at her nose with the back of her hand. "And you're not a coward. I know that!" She couldn't stop crying and people who were gathered near the Club to watch the fireworks were staring and whispering.

Gordon put an arm around her and led her around the side of the Club to where an enormous weeping willow stood. There was no one beneath it since the fireworks couldn't be seen through its heavy foliage. He took the blanket from Mary – she was clinging to it the way Stan still clung to his sucky Teddy bear – the gray, moth-eaten relic of his babyhood – and spread it on the bench of a picnic table, then pulled her down into his arms where she openly sobbed.

"I don't know why I'm crying. He's a puke and it shouldn't bother me. It's just that it was going to be so nice to sit there and enjoy the fireworks and everything and he made it seem . . . dirty. We weren't doing anything! He made me feel dirty."

"You're not," Gordon whispered into her hair, feeling anger build in his chest once again. She pushed away from him, but it was only so that she could slide her arms around him underneath his jacket. Mary rubbed her forehead against his shoulder and cried, and his T-shirt got wet, and he was pretty sure her running nose was coating him with snot, but Gordon didn't care. He had never felt happier. "It's okay. Don't cry. (Please, Jesus, let her cry until her eyeballs fall out because if she stops I'll have to let her go.) Just forget it. (I won't. I won't forget it for a thousand years.) He's a creep."

"Stay away from him, Gordon," she snuffled, her voice hitching, the crying jag at last under control. "Stay away from all of them. They're bad, but Lancer is the worst. Promise me. No fighting because of tonight. I mean if you have to defend yourself that's one thing, but no looking for it because of what he said about me."

Gordon had lied twice that day. He could have made it an even three, for there was nothing so clear and bright and perfect in his mind at that moment as the thought of revenge. Instead, he said, "I promise." He meant it.

And then Mary kissed him. It was a long, slow kiss of infinite sweetness, something with which she sealed the pact he had just made with her. At first Gordon was too surprised to kiss her back. They came up for air and the next kiss was his. The blood that was flooding into his penis was speaking to him in a voice that was hard to ignore. *Touch her, Gordon. Kiss her hard and use your tongue and you can touch her if you want. She wants it. She as much as said so back there.* But he did ignore it. Well, mostly. He kissed her with as much passion as he dared, stroking her back and pressing her hard against his chest.

"Mmm. That was nice," she whispered. "That's what I hoped it would be like. My first *real* kiss." *Real*, she said to herself firmly. *What Lancer did wasn't the real thing. But I can't think about that.*

"Real kiss?" Gordon's penis was killing him. Penises weren't designed to be bent double in tight jeans. "Was there a fake kiss?" he kissed her again, ignoring the penile agony.

"My cousin under the mistletoe when I was seven." She kissed Gordon lightly and touched the back of his neck. "Thomas White when a bunch of us were eight and playing spin the bottle. That was *oogy*, like Stan says." *And Lancer at the party.*

She kissed him harder then, blocking out the unsavory memory of that whiskey-tainted kiss, her mouth slightly open and Gordon felt his crotch expand to about the size of a prizewinning zucchini. *What would James Dean do?* he thought wildly.

"Hey there. Cough. Cough. Calling all Lakers. Cease the lip lock you lucky boy and girl; the brewmaster has arrived."

It was Frank carrying the six-pack; with him were David and Tony. Gordon's zucchini shrank within seconds. Part of him was grateful and part of him a little pissed off, but there was none of the anger he had felt when Lancer had assailed them. These were The Lakers. If you couldn't handle being razzed by your buddies, then you couldn't handle much.

"Beer, Mare?" asked Frank, waving a sweating bottle in her face.

Mary hesitated, the vivid memory of the last time she had drunk beer, which chiefly was the memory of the taste of her own vomit, clear in her mind. "Thanks, but I'll just sip from Gordon's."

"Beer, Tony?" Frank asked.

"There'll be a lotta shakin', rattlin', and rollin' taking place if I don't get one soon!" warned Tony.

"David?" Frank dangled a beer in front of him.

"You bet, man!"

Frank held one out to Gordon. "Need I ask?"

"Not really, but since beer is proof that God loves us and wants us to be happy," said Gordon, "I'd have to say yes. I will accept a cold one." There was an instant of stunned silence and then all The Lakers screeched in laughter.

"Where'd that come from?" asked Frank, taking a brew for himself.

"Something Joely told me," Gordon answered, opening his bottle. "Indian stuff." *Indian wisdom*, he had been about to say, but then he hadn't. He wasn't positive, but he kind of suspected that he was the only one with whom Joely shared the Indian wisdom things, and for a reason he could not define, it seemed better to keep that to himself. *Wonder what old Joely's doing right now?* he thought absently, sipping from the bottle. Then he handed it to Mary, and like the ghostly smoke of spent fireworks in the night wind's tide, the thought was gone.

■■■

The beers were savored slowly. Mary took fewer than a half dozen tiny sips from Gordon's bottle after first making sure he had spearmint gum to mask the smell on her breath. Gordon doubted that the Davidsons would be able to smell a pair of dead skunks had they been dropped in their laps after imbibing his father's martinis all evening, but Mary was taking no chances. They sipped and talked quietly and the hands of Gordon's wristwatch began once again to spin with maddening speed. At ten-thirty, with the cursed curfew approaching, they all decided to walk back to where David had parked his dad's car along the beach. He would drop Mary and Gordon off a few houses away from Brierly to avoid parental scandal, and then head home with the other guys.

No one locked a car door unless there was something valuable in it. You just didn't bother. David's dad's car contained nothing except a couple of towels, some empty Coke bottles, and a beach blanket, so it was unlocked.

So was Lancer Caldwell's car.

It was standing alone and empty, windows rolled down a few inches to let in the cool night air, paint gleaming, white walls spotless. It was begging to be despoiled.

"Well, well, well," mused David.

"Well, well, well, well, well," added Gordon.

"You touch that car and he will know it was you," warned Mary. "Don't you touch that car."

"*Moi?*" Gordon's was the voice of innocence. "*I'm* not touching that car." His eyes moved to Tony. "Tony, it's all yours."

Tony had not only consumed the healthy lunch and three of Denison's sauerkraut-laced hot dogs during the day, he had gone home to a dinner of his father's specialty: pigs' feet and beans with side orders of pickled eggs and fresh green onions. Tony was primed and loaded. He opened the Dodge's passenger door and rolled up the window. He climbed into the driver's seat and rolled up the window. He gripped the steering wheel, closed his eyes and let 'er rip. The car shivered on its chassis, the interior fogged. Gordon was amazed that the windows didn't shatter. Tony leaped out and slammed the door.

"You are all disgusting," said Mary. "I love it."

They had to drive Gordon and Mary back with the windows of David's father's car rolled down and Tony had to practically incinerate his clothing the next day, but those were minor considerations. For the following week, rain or shine, Lancer Caldwell drove the streets of Erie

View with six pine-tree air fresheners hanging from his rearview mirror and the windows rolled down.

Revenge was sweet. Unlike the interior of Lancer's car.

"Work saves us from three great evils: boredom, vice and need."

— Amos Littlebird, Odawa Sachem

Gordon was suffering. Partly he was suffering because Mary and her parents were gone to their Muskoka cottage for ten days or so, a place that had no telephone, and all he had was the memory of those delicious kisses to get him through until she returned.

"Don't you dare kiss anyone else," she warned him the night before she departed for the north. "I'll know if you've kissed anyone else."

"I won't." He had been kissing her goodbye when she came out with that one.

"Promise," she breathed.

There seemed to be a lot of promises involved in "going with" Mary. There was also a lot of walking. They weren't dating exactly; neither was allowed to date, and

Mary still wasn't allowed to be in Gordon's car alone with him, but she *was* allowed to walk with him. The logic of that defied him. Maybe Mrs. Davidson thought they couldn't get up to anything while they were walking. (Man, did he ever hope to prove that theory wrong.) Gordon figured they had walked maybe as far as Toronto and back during the evenings since the week following the fireworks, and they had kissed on every square foot of the beach. He had also promised Mary everything but his firstborn child.

"Promise," she said a little more firmly. "You better promise, Gordon."

"I promise." That got him another long, deep kiss. No tongue. He hadn't worked up to that yet, and he wasn't sure how he would. For now it was enough that he could hold her and kiss her and feel her breasts against his chest. God, it was killing him!

Gordon had promised, and he was suffering serious Mary withdrawal. But he was also suffering because he was cleaning chickens. Gordon and David both had landed summer jobs at Floyd's Market. They delivered the grocery orders that people called in from Monday to Saturday, using two of the most decrepit bicycles on the face of the earth. They could have used The Chief, but it would have meant paying for the gasoline themselves, since Tom Floyd wouldn't spring for gas. So they rode his bikes and hauled groceries all over town.

On Friday afternoons, a huge order of half frozen chickens was dropped off by Old Man Richmond, a local chicken farmer. The chickens were plucked, thank God, but they were never eviscerated. It was David and Gordon's job to cut open the chickens – which was what they were doing right now – and remove the innards.

Gordon's hands were blue with cold, although they were normally smooth and pink. He did have a writer's callus on the middle finger of his right hand, and there was a small line of calluses at the base of each finger, made from clutching bicycle handle grips. Not a single hair grew out of Gordon's palms. If the rumors he had heard when he was in grade school had actually been true, Gordon's palms would have been hairier than Lassie's butt. Even his brain might be hairy, because he was think-ing about sex and Mary. Sex in all its glorious shapes and forms was almost always in his thoughts. There were days when his brain was more of a movie screen, one not unlike that of The Palace's. Only instead of Rocketman, a steamy Academy-Award-winner, starring Gordon and Mary, was the feature film. If nothing else, it was keeping his mind off the pain in his hands, which was a good thing, because Gordon was sure they were ready to break off at the wrists.

"I hate these damned chickens," said David dismally. They were in the back room where the butcher blocks stood. His hands were just as blue as Gordon's.

"It's ten bucks, man," Gordon reminded him. "Just keep saying that to yourself. Ten bucks."

"There have to be better jobs than this."

"Not for ten bucks. Here. Have another chicken. Anyway, my dad would kill me if I quit after his getting me this job. And your dad would kill you."

"Probably. But I could kill you for talking me into this."

Mark Floyd leaned in the doorway. Mark, a big, soft-looking pudding of a guy was Tom Floyd's imbecilic son. He wasn't really an imbecile; he just looked like one, which Gordon knew he couldn't help. Mark, with his wavy blond hair, was convinced that he looked like Gorgeous George, the wrestler. He was always smoothing and combing his hair as he studied his reflection in a small pocket mirror. Gordon thought Mark looked more like Liberace than Gorgeous George, but he couldn't say *that* out loud.

The thing was, Mark acted like an imbecile, which was something Gordon knew he could help. Mark swaggered and bragged. He was his father's assistant butcher and one day he would inherit the business, as he was always pointing out to Gordon and David. *Someday this will all be mine, boys.* He was only two years older than they were and he still called them boys, which made Gordon practically nuts, but he was the boss's son, so what could they do?

"Yer leavin' too much lungs in them chickens, boys," he said, examining a carcass with a practiced, professional eye. "Too much lungs, boys. Get them lung bits out. Someday this will all be mine and I don't want no lung bits in my chickens." Then he wandered off.

"The imbeciles shall inherit the market," whispered Gordon.

"Not the lung bits, though, boy. No siree," whispered David. Which got them laughing so hard that *Tom* Floyd looked in.

"You nearly finished? There's five orders of groceries each to be delivered." Unlike Mark, Tom Floyd was a hard, slab-muscled man with a brush cut, a veteran who had been a butcher in the army during the war. He didn't swagger or brag. He didn't need to.

"Nearly, sir. We're getting out the lung bits now," said Gordon with a straight face.

"Lung bits? What the hell? Wash your hands and deliver the groceries, for chrissake." He exited the back room, shaking his head and muttering about lung bits.

Gordon and David washed up and each got their first load of groceries. There was neither rhyme nor reason to how they were assigned the deliveries, but at least Mr. Floyd made sure they rode out to the farthest destinations first so that they weren't half-dead by the time they got to the last houses.

"This load's for Mrs. Williams." He handed the bill to David. "Watch them eggs. This goes to the Fournuts, Gord." Gordon groaned inwardly. "Watch them eggs."

David was able to carry out Mrs. William's modest order to his waiting bicycle in one trip, but it took three trips for Gordon to load up the Fournuts' groceries, even with David helping him.

"Bad luck, man," said David.

"No kidding. Four nuts, three testicles, two balls –"

"– and a wank!" finished David. "Man, I would *definitely* change my last name."

Gordon and David parted company, each pedaling off in different directions. Gordon eased into the traffic on Main, keeping an eye out for homicidal drivers in the bicycle's scabrous mirror. He turned north onto Sunset with a sigh of relief. He would have to ride out for nearly three miles, but the traffic was always light on Sunset, especially as you neared the dead end where the Fournuts lived.

The Fournuts would never change their name because they were bizarre. There were also about twenty of them living in the big old farmhouse set down in a ravine. They weren't poor – Mr. Fournuts raised pigs and there was good money in pigs, Gordon's father had told him – but they looked poor, and the kids were always absolutely filthy.

Today there were seven children playing in the dirt with a small pig. Gordon was pretty sure the kids were girls, since they were wearing dresses, but you couldn't be sure with the Fournuts, because all of them wore their hair brutally short. And eight-year-old Brian Fournuts (who mercifully was *not* one of Stan's friends) had occasionally been seen in a dress. The pig was also wearing a dress. It did not look happy.

"We playin' house," announced one of the children. "Dis our baby."

"That's great," said Gordon as he got off his bike and walked it to the porch. He carefully set the bike's kickstand and was taking out two bags of groceries, when Mrs. Fournuts, a tall thin woman with gray hair an inch long, flung open the screen door.

"You kids get that dress off that pig!" she yelled. "That pig's not no doll. That pig's a pig. Hi, Gordon. Just set 'em on the table."

"Hi, Mrs. Fournuts. Sure thing."

"You kids get that dress off that pig! Your dad see a dress on a pig and there'll be hell to pay. Where's my bill, Gordon?"

"Right here." He handed her the slip. "I'll just get the rest of the groceries, ma'am." He carried them in as quickly as he could, wondering if weirdness was contagious.

"You hear that, you kids? Manners. He's got manners. Not playin' in the dirt with a dressed up pig." She paused long enough to pull a man's wallet from the pocket of her housedress and count out the money. "And a dime for you, Gordon. 'Cause he's got manners!" she screamed.

The pig made a mad dash for freedom as Gordon was pedaling away. It shot across the yard in its dress, with the

Fournuts brood in ruthless pursuit. Gordon heard cries of "Lookit dat baby run!" and "You kids get that dress off that pig!" echoing behind him. He pedaled past the lumberyard and rode in to get a bag of sawdust for cleanup, then rode back to the market.

The rest of Gordon's deliveries were less interesting. There was a trip out to the Clark house (normal children who would not have played with a pig on a bet), and one to Mr. Smyth, who was a confirmed bachelor (no children, pigs, *or* women), and then finally, a delivery to Garside's Pawnshop.

A bell tinkled when he opened the door and entered with a single bag of groceries. Gordon loved the pawnshop nearly as much as he loved Kitchie's Pool Hall. He wouldn't have been surprised to see a pig there either; Leonard Garside had everything under the sun in that place. There were musical instruments of all descriptions, cameras, jewelry, telescopes, service medals, books, tools, and clocks. Everything.

Mr. Garside, a frail-looking widower with hair as fine and white as cottonwood fluff, a man who favored bow ties, was sitting in an armchair behind one of the display cases, reading. He looked up over his wire rimmed glasses and smiled when he saw Gordon.

"Well, I won't starve after all, will I?" he said with feigned relief. "Not when you're on the job."

"Sorry, sir. I had to go out to the Fournuts' place first

and there were two other drop offs. Mr. Floyd kept you for last. Sorry."

"Good God, lad. The Fournuts! And you're still sane? That calls for a soda."

Mr. Garside took his groceries to the back of the store where he lived in a small apartment. Better to keep an eye on his goods, he always said. Much more convenient than the house these days. Gordon suspected it was also less depressing than facing an empty home every evening, one in which he had lived with his wife until her death a year ago. When he returned with two bottles of Vernors, Gordon was examining the case that held the medals.

"Anything new?" he asked, accepting the soda and taking a swig. "What's available?" Since it was a pawn-shop, you could only buy an item if it went unclaimed for a year. Not that Stan ever had any money; he spent his allowance on candy. But he always asked Gordon to look, especially if there might be new medals for his collection.

"Nothing special in the medal department, I fear. Couple of WWI service medals came in; one yesterday and the other last week, but Stan has one of those in his collection, if I recall correctly."

"Yeah. My grandfather's." Gordon laughed and shook his head. "A collection with one medal in it."

"But, as you have told me, he treasures that medal and that's the important thing. I believe that your brother honors your grandfather by wearing it."

Gordon knew that Mr. Garside didn't think much of anyone who pawned their medals. He also knew – this was from his father – that to own a pawnshop was a bit like being a minister or a priest. You did the business, but you didn't pass judgment, and so Mr. Garside took the medals when they came his way.

"Any more deliveries?" asked Mr. Garside, smoothing back his fluffy hair. Years later Gordon would see The Ten Commandments, take one gawk at Charlton Heston portraying Moses with his hair standing on end, stone tablets in hand and think, *Whoa! It's Mr. Garside, leader of The Chosen People!*

"No. Just have to take the bicycle back to Floyd's and I'm done." Gordon finished his soda and set the bottle on the display case's glass with a small clink. "Thanks for the soda."

"Anytime, Gordon, anytime. And say hello to your dad for me."

"Sure thing, Mr. Garside."

Back on the bike, Gordon pedaled like a maniac, leaning over the handlebars – hoping he didn't look too much like Rocketman – hurtling down the streets back to Floyd's. It was only 5:15; if he burned bicycle rubber and then Chief rubber, he would be able to get home, relax, and work on his tan before dinner.

Wrong again.

"One more delivery got called in," said Mr. Floyd from around a cigar he was gripping in his big, yellow teeth. It smelled like he was smoking a roll of smoldering pubic hair, and drove Gordon right to the edge of his olfactory limit. And yes, indeed; Gordon, after a reckless evening lighting farts with The Lakers when in their early teens, knew *exactly* what flaming pubic hair smelled like. "Kitchie's."

Gordon washed his sweaty face and dirty hands in Floyd's small washroom, ignoring Mark who was checking his profile over Gordon's shoulder. He was going to Kitchie's and he couldn't look anything but cool in Kitchie's. He combed his hair, checked his teeth for foreign objects (bits of hot dog, gum, chips? No, the Gordonian ivories were perfect), and then headed out.

■■■

Injun Joely was just finishing up the cleaning of a fedora when Gordon walked in. Joely let his eyes lift for a moment, a slight smile touched his lips, and then he returned his attention to the task. It might only be cleaning and blocking a hat, but it would be done correctly. Gordon knew that Joely didn't like to be interrupted no matter what he was doing, so he carried the box filled with rolls of toilet paper, a bottle of bleach, and packages of hand soap over to the counter. He settled up with Mr. Kitchie, who was drinking beer out of a coffee cup (he drank coffee for a nightcap), then he strolled back to where Injun Joely was giving the fedora a few last flicks with his brush. Joely grunted in satisfaction and set it on the shelf.

"Going to shoot some balls, Gordon?" Joely asked. "Practice up?" He put away his brushes and cloths with the grace of a dancer. Everything about Joely was precise, from the way he always buttoned his shirt to the throat, to the way he made up the cot he kept under a pool table, to the exact way he clipped his fingernails.

"No, not today."

Joely stared unblinkingly at Gordon and then smiled. "Probably a good decision. No sense in letting this place corrupt you on a daily basis." He cleared his throat a little, a most un-Joely-like act. "I was proud of you the other night. When you stood up for your friend. And when you stood up for me. It is a pitiful thing to live life with no respect for anyone, but you, Gordon, have been well schooled by your family, and so you understand the meaning of respect and of friendship. Could be you are on your way to learning the first of the three songs."

Oh, cripes. More Indian wisdom, thought Gordon. "Songs?"

"The Odawa people sing when they pray; to us a prayer and a song are much the same thing, you see." He looked out the front window of Kitchie's, a dreamy expression on his face. "When I was a boy about your age, my grandfather spoke to me of the 'Three Songs for Courage.' There is the song one sings when victory is clear, and the song you sing when defeat's bitter taste is in your mouth. I think by standing up for your friend and for me, you saw only victory. Victory was the only possibility. I think perhaps you have begun to understand the first song."

"Three. You said there were three."

"Ah, yes; the third song? *That* each person must learn alone." He smiled his slow, warm smile. "Had enough Indian wisdom for one afternoon?"

Jeez! The guy can read minds, said Gordon to himself, as he pedaled briskly back to Floyd's. The thought also occurred that he was pretty glad he hadn't been born an Indian. From all he could see, being an Indian was a very serious business. Unlike being a Westley *and* a Laker, which were both cool. *Lone Ranger to Tonto: Hey Tonto! Let's saddle up Silver and Scout and check out the action, have a few beers, maybe get laid at the Main Street Riding Academy. Wadda ya say? Tonto to Lone Ranger: No can do, Kimosabi. Must sit next to campfire and try to figure out Third Song for Courage. Lone Ranger to Tonto: Screw off. Tonto to Lone Ranger: You screw off. You're not the boss of me. Lone Ranger to Tonto: You're cruisin' for a bruisin', daddy-o.*

Gordon was just at the part where the Lone Ranger and Tonto were singing the Third Song for Courage with

Roy Rogers and Trigger: "Happy Trails to You!" when he arrived, yet again, at Floyd's. Which was just as well, because by then he was starting to get the guilts about making fun of Joely, even in his head. No laughs in the guilts, and so he turned his musings to Mary and how things would be when she got home. And just like that, his steamy mind-movie began to roll again.

chapter 9

"Of all noises, I think music is
the least disagreeable."

           - Amos Littlebird, Odawa Sachem

Mary and her parents returned from their cottage with
Mary's maternal grandmother in tow. Edith Warner, who
spent her summers at the family cottage and her winters
in Florida, looked like a Galapagos tortoise in drag. She
was possibly the most tanned, wrinkly, pouched, saggy
female that Gordon had ever seen. According to Mary, her
grandmother was only in her mid sixties, but to say that
she hadn't aged well was an understatement; it was like
saying that Jackie Gleason needed to lose a teensy bit of
weight. Gordon's grandfather didn't look much better,
but Mrs. Warner was a *woman*, for the love of God. How
those loins had spawned something like Mary's mother
was entirely beyond Gordon; even thinking about it gave
him the shivers. It was easy to only see the warts (literally),

until Edith Warner smiled. Then, behind the ravages of time, was the ghost of the lovely girl she had once been. And she still had her own teeth.

It hadn't taken Gordon very long to decide that he absolutely loved Mary's grandmother. But he didn't love her for her smile or the ghost of the lovely girl; he loved her because she was MODERN. He loved her because she was PROGRESSIVE. He loved her because she thought that it would be okay if Gordon and Mary started DATING! Under supervision, naturally, since she was modern but neither insane nor naive.

"Of course it's okay if they date, Myra; at least this sort of dating. I'll be keeping my peepers on them, so don't you worry. What are ya, Gordon? Eighteen? Nineteen? Sixteen! Oh, you kid!"

Her nanna had been a flapper, Mary had told Gordon. (He wondered if it had anything to with the manner in which the undersides of Mrs. Warner's upper arms wobbled around, but he didn't articulate that theory.) Instead, he looked up flapper in the dictionary. "A young woman in the twenties who flaunted her unconventional conduct and dress." Well, that was Nanna, even more than thirty years later.

She wore her white hair in a bob that had been fashionable in 1926; she was spry and loud and pushy. A gin and tonic in one hand, cigarette holder in the other, she liked to sit on the Davidson's front porch and listen to what she called HER MUSIC. Songs like, "Ain't We Got Fun," "The Black Bottom," and "The Varsity Drag." It drove Mrs. Davidson absolutely nuts when Nanna did the Charleston on the front porch. Gordon thought it was extremely funny, but then it wasn't *his* front porch.

One of the reasons that Gordon was going on a date with Mary (face it Gord, it's the ONLY reason you're going on a so-called date with her), was that Edith Warner was going on a date. With Gordon's grandfather, whom she had met two days ago. John Stanford was experiencing his lengthiest period of calm since World War I. Nevertheless, he was still moody and very unpredictable, so when Mary's grandmother walked out onto the Westleys' back porch, approached the rocking chair, held out her hand, and said, "Hi. I'm Edith Warner. Aren't you the cat's pajamas, you sheik!" Gordon had been certain his grandfather would flip out. (Headlines: OLD MAN SHOWS FLAPPER WHAT'S O'CLOCK)

It hadn't happened.

Perhaps it had been Edith's smile. Perhaps it had been that they were both old. Gordon didn't care. For him it was a miracle, because tonight he was going out with Mary.

■ ■ ■

"You're going on a double date with your *GRANDFATHER*? Oh, man!" David was collapsed across Gordon's bed and laughing so hard that he had barely been able to get out the words. He was tired and slaphappy – both he and Gordon had delivered groceries until seven o'clock tonight. The double date from hell would have been funny at any time, but right now, it was a scream.

"Look." Gordon gently touched his pompadour and drew the comb slowly along the right side of his head. "I'd go on a double date with Mr. Ligonier and Naomi Innagadda if it would get me out with Mary." He pocketed the comb and waited until David had stopped laughing and was only groaning and holding his gut. "And anyway, they're both acting as chaperones for us. Chaperones! I feel like I'm in *Gone With the Wind* or something."

"Maybe you guys are the chaperones. I can hear it now. 'Lawzy, Miz Scarlett! I don' know nothin' about babysittin' no ol' peoples! What we gon' do if dem two ol' peoples starts a-making out in da backseat a da car? Lawzy, lawzy, lawzy.'"

"Lawzy your ass, Molonovitch. Very funny. This is serious, old people or no old people. This is our first date! I want it to be the best."

"It will be. You'll do fine!" He slapped Gordon's shoulders and exited the bedroom, stopping only long enough to swing back into the open doorway and yell, "Kiss Mary for me. Better yet, kiss her grandmother!"

Listening to the thunder of David's feet on the stairs, Gordon turned back to the mirror and smoothed his hair yet again. *My first night out with her*, he thought for the hundredth time. *It's going to be the coolest!*

■■■

Gordon had not been inside the Sand Club since the summer after his father had returned home from Europe. He had at first thought it was the most wonderful place he had ever been inside. With its 25,000 square foot maple dance floor, a *floating* floor that could bear up under the weight of hundreds of dancing people, it was a titan among dance clubs. Large Chinese lanterns lit the cavernous building, shining down upon the wicker furniture. And there was a mirrored globe! A spinning mirrored globe that had spangled him and everyone else with moving dots of light. But a spinning globe can only cut so much mustard with a little boy, and Gordon quickly became bored, then restless, then cranky, then unconscious – asleep under the table. He had never wanted to go back.

And now he was back, and there was nowhere he would rather have been.

Nanna honed in on an empty table and led the way across the crowded dance floor. On the way over in The Chief (they HAD sat in the backseat together!), Gordon had learned that Edith Warner's musical tastes spanned several decades.

"I love this stuff," she shouted to a rather bemused John Stanford. "Some days music was all that kept me sane what with four kids in the house. Merciful heavens, that Myra was a handful, even as an infant."

Gordon tried to imagine Mrs. Davidson as a baby. She probably had been born wearing a tiny crinoline and high heels. Probably her first words were "DEEP SAND." Probably –

"Dance with my granddaughter, if you know what's good for you, toots," shouted Nanna. "John, I am parched and we haven't even started dancing."

"Would you like a beer, Edith?" asked Grandpa hopefully.

"Hell no! I'd as soon drink horse pee as drink beer. We'll have martinis!" Grandpa disappeared into the crowd and Gordon was wondering if he would ever come back, when Mary's grandmother leaned over and commanded, "Dance with my granddaughter, kiddo. This is her first date. Don't spoil it by being a wallflower."

"To this? How can we dance to this?"

THIS was Geraldine Pinkwater and Her All Big-Girl Band, one of the lesser of the big bands, but a big band nonetheless. All sixteen of the women were huge. Not fat huge, but HUGE huge, tall, and muscular. Gordon had seen a picture of them in *The Globe and Mail*, and because his father had read the article aloud, he knew their

history. Every one of them was a war widow. The original five-piece combo, a group of women who played for
fun, had lost their factory jobs when the men (not their
men; their men lay buried or scattered in little pieces all
over France) returned home from the war. Geraldine had
run an ad in *The Globe*: WANTED: War widows with
musical abilities. Must be at least six feet tall, blonde or
willing to become blonde, and be willing to travel. No
previous experience necessary.

Geraldine hadn't exactly been flooded with tow-
headed Amazons armed with trombones or saxophones,
but the response hadn't been too shabby either. Within
three months, she had gathered from various parts of the
country, eleven more women who were sick to death of
being alone, of being dependent upon the largess of
family, church or neighbors, who were still young and
wanted a chance at life. A few had children; most did
not, their married lives having been severed abruptly by
the war.

"Come on, Gordon," said Mary. "On your feet."

"We can't dance to this! My mom listens to this stuff."
Gordon knew the tune *and* its name, since his mother
only played the record about thirty times a week. It was
"Begin the Beguine."

"Well, it's what they're playing," said Mary over the
music, and a tiny frown line appeared between her brows.

"Okay, okay. Just a minute." He led her by the hand, weaving through the dancers, passing his grandfather who was dourly returning with ONE martini and a beer, right to the edge of the stage where, mercifully for Gordon, the beguine was not beginning, but ending. "Excuse me, ma'am!" he shouted through cupped hands. "Mrs. Pinkwater?"

"What can I do for you, young man?" Geraldine Pinkwater might have been big (no kidding; up close she looked like she could take Mrs. Thibodaux *and* John Wayne with one hand), she might once have been a munitions plant worker because she felt the need to serve her country, and she might have been, like all the Big-Girls, dressed in a pink suit so LOUD that it could make your eyes bleed. But she was, above all, a lady. "Do you have a request?"

"Yes."

Geraldine waited. She waited some more. "Yes? What's the request?"

"Something . . . something . . . current!"

"'Cherry Pink and Apple Blossom White,' 'Mister Sandman,' 'It's a Sin to Tell a Lie?'"

Gordon was just about ready to tell a lie and say he was having an attack of galloping brain tumors, anything to get away from Geraldine Pinkwater, AKA Mrs. Hit Parade, when one of the Girls called out, "He means rock and roll, Geraldine, for Pete's sake." Then under her breath, since Geraldine tolerated no unladylike behavior, "Jeez Louise."

"Why didn't you say so? Ladies? Rock and roll it is."

It sounded a bit odd, since there were only brass instruments and no guitars, but it was definitely "Rock Around the Clock." There was only one dance that suited that particular song, and that was the Lindy Hop, the Swing, what Gordon's parents called the Jitterbug. It was a dance based on tension and give – sort of like Gordon and Mary's relationship at the moment. They broke away and came together, broke away and came together, letting the beat carry them. Sometimes only Mary's hand was in Gordon's, then the length of her would be against him (Thank you Lord!) and then she was gone, hand in his, her hair all sparkly under the revolving globe, her eyes shining, her laughter ringing out above the music.

The band finished the piece and then swung into "Shake Rattle and Roll," accelerating the tempo. Gordon's heart was pounding; his T-shirt was growing damp, but nothing on earth could have made him let go of Mary. He spun her around and pulled her into his arms, shrieking with laughter, just as the band played the last bars of the song and slowed things down with "Unchained Melody."

There were hundreds of people around them as they danced, his cheek against hers, the heat of their bodies mingling. This is what it would be like, thought Gordon. AFTER. After we've done IT. This is surely what it would be like (minus the three hundred dancers), both of us hot and sweaty, both of us still breathing hard, me holding her close like this (minus the clothing, natch; Wesser only does it in the buff), both of us wanting more (one mind, one lust, one goal: COP. YOU. LAY. SHUN), each reaching passionately for the other's –

"Cut quite the rug, there, Gordon," shouted Nanna right into Gordon's ear. She was dancing with Grandpa, who actually looked like he was enjoying himself. Grandpa had on his face what Gordon called his happy crap smile. (Any day you take a crap at my age is a happy day, Gordon. Enjoy crapping. Crap any chance you get, any place you can, since when you get to be my age, that stuff'll retreat so far up your alimentary system they'll need a plumber's snake to find it. Take my word for it. I probably have crap in there that a museum would be proud to display.)

"What about you two? Look at you!" laughed Mary. Then, lifting her hair off of her neck, "I'm sweating to death. Can we get some air? Gordon and I are going to get some air, Nanna."

"Uh-huh. I'll give you about a half hour's worth of air and then we come looking. This is a date, not a Roman orgy," said Edith. Watching them walk out hand in hand, she shook her head. "Air. Uh-huh. She better not come back in here with her skirt tucked into her underpants."

"Edith," said John Stanford. "Are you suggesting my grandson is not a gentleman?"

"Nope. I'm suggesting that my granddaughter is the spitting image of what I was like at that age, and *my* skirt was stuck in *my* underpants more than once."

"You shock me, Edith."

"Hubba–hubba."

There was only the slightest of breezes. Gordon and Mary walked over to some picnic tables that were set out about fifty yards from the Club. Choosing the one that was the least spattered with seagull droppings, they sat down. Mary studied the sky, but Gordon couldn't take his eyes off of her. The way a small smile was parting her lips, the way she was giving herself over to the wind's light touch; she was so . . . Mary. The desire that he had managed to hold in check all evening came roaring through him.

"I have to tinkle."

"What?" asked Gordon.

"Tinkle. Wee-wee. Go bathroom." She dropped a kiss on his cheek and sprinted back to the Club calling, "Be right back."

Gordon sat alone on the picnic table, planning his next move. He wanted it to be just right, cool and sexy, but not too sexy, just the right amount of James Dean sex appeal, so that maybe he could move beyond level one of his agenda.

He was lost in revising the schedule of seduction when someone said, "Hey there, Westley." It was Lancer

(*Jesus! Not again*, thought Gordon!) with Dutch and Eddie standing behind him. Lancer's eyes were slightly glazed. "Just the guy I was hoping to find. And all alone. Nice." Lancer's speech wasn't too clear. A six-pack and half a bottle of rye tended to do that to a fella.

Gordon rose to his feet. He didn't want those bastards here when Mary came back. "Get the hell lost, Caldwell."

A pained expression came over Lancer's face. "Gordy, Gordy, Gordy. Is that any way to talk to your elders? I think you need to be taught a lesson, pretty boy. Hold him, guys." In a flash, The Sultans were on Gordon, who struggled wildly. Lancer punched him in the stomach as hard as he could. "I said hold him!" Lancer unbuckled Gordon's belt, undid the button of his jeans and with elaborate slowness, unzipped them and tugged them down over his hips. He pulled a switchblade from his pocket and flicked it open. "You circumcised, Gordy? If you aren't, you will be in a few minutes and if you are, well, guess I'll have to cut you a new one."

Gordon began to thrash about like a madman.

"Let him go!" screamed Mary. She ran across the sand and skidded to a stop a few feet away.

"Mary, get out of here!" cried Gordon. "Run!"

"No; that's okay, doll." Lancer pressed the tip of the switchblade to Gordon's throat and a bead of blood tracked slowly down his neck. "You can watch. Don't run now, baby, 'cause if you run, my hand might slip and then we'd have blood all over Gordy-Wordy's nice, clean clothes. Ever seen his little dick?" Lancer punched Gordon in the stomach again for all he was worth and Gordon went limp, his face ashen. Then Lancer leaned close and said, "Let's show Little Miss Davidson your tiny dick, Gordy."

"Leave him alone!" Mary rushed forward and grabbed Lancer's arm.

"Oh, baby," he moaned. "I can feel the heat from here. I know you want me, but you gotta be patient and let me take care of business first. Then we will adjourn to my chariot and I'll give you what you want. We'll even bring Gordy. You don't mind if he watches us while we do it, do you, baby?"

Gordon gasped, "Mary, get away from him! Don't you touch her, *Francis*, you goddamed pig!"

An ugly red climbed up Lancer's neck and into his face. He shook off Mary's hand. "Not smart. Not smart at all, Westley. Okay, let's just soften up your old sack first before I get to work on your weenie. Ten, nine, eight . . ." Lancer began the countdown and took a step back, ready to dropkick Gordon's scrotum and testicles into the next county, when three things happened: Gordon, reeling with pain and not wanting to see his scrotum become airborne, closed his eyes. David, tire iron in hand, came charging from the direction of Walnut Street, a wordless roar coming from him. AAAAAAAAAAAAARRRRRRRGGGGGH-HHH! Mary quickly scooped up two handfuls of sand and threw them in Lancer's face. The dropkick countdown ceased as Lancer clawed at his eyes, cutting his *own* cheek with his *own* switchblade. "Fuck!" he cried.

Dutch and Eddie might have been bullies, but they weren't stupid. They were afraid enough of Lancer to do pretty much whatever he told them to do. But now there was not one, but two witnesses. What if a cop car came by? The Accordion could turn up anywhere, anytime, and there would be pure hell to pay if he turned up now.

"Come on," said Dutch. "We're outa here." He and Eddie each took one of Lancer's arms and hauled him away.

"You're the walking dead, Westley. You hear me?" roared Lancer. "The walking dead! She's my girl; not yours, you little pissant!"

David slowed to a walk and stood over Gordon, who was on his hands and knees in the sand, Mary kneeling next to him. He brandished the tire iron. "Get out of here, Caldwell!"

Gordon, incapable of speech, raised his head and shot Lancer a look so filled with venomous hatred that Lancer felt a small, unfamiliar twinge of something akin to fear. (Nah. Couldn't be.) Lancer spat in the sand; the three Sultans turned and melted into the shadows. Gordon tried to pull up his jeans, but the pain in his abdomen wouldn't let him and he fell over on his side moaning. (Nope! says Mr. Gut Pain. You get to let Mary, the love of your life, get an up-close look at your underpants, which you have probably crapped. That'll get her hot and bothered!)

"Turn around and let me help him," said David, feeling Gordon's mortification as though it were his own.

"For God's sake, David, it's only underwear," said Mary shakily. "I do have a father, you know. I *have* seen men's underwear." But David wasn't budging, so with a furious huff, she turned around and stood there, her hands on her hips, tapping the toe of one saddleshoe in the sand.

"Come on, man," said David. "I know it hurts, but you can't lie here in your Stanfields all night."

It hurt all right, but with David's help, Gordon was able to get to his knees and pull up his jeans. He zipped and buttoned them with shaking hands and buckled his belt.

"Are you *decent?*" asked Mary, who when he answered yes, turned around and rushed to Gordon's side. "What were you doing here?" She was talking to David, but focused on Gordon, stroking back his hair, studying his face. "I mean, thank God you were here, but talk about a coincidence!"

"I, uh, I borrowed my dad's car and drove over because I, uh, just wanted to see . . ."

"The double date?" finished Gordon hoarsely. His hand was on his stomach. He wanted to rub it, but he couldn't let Mary know how much it hurt.

David knew that Gordon's humiliation in front of Mary was being made much worse by his presence. He paused a moment, not wanting to take any chances with The Sultans, but Gordon's Adam's apple, bobbing like a fishing float, forced David's decision. "Look. I told my dad I wouldn't be long; I better get going." They heard the sound of a car engine starting and in seconds, Lancer's coupe rolled slowly past the Sand Club. It paused, Butch and Eddie shot them the finger, and then it screamed down Walnut. "I better get home," he repeated. "I doubt Lancer and his buddies will be back, but maybe you guys should go inside to be on the safe side. Seeing how Mary is so helpless and delicate and everything."

Gordon tried to laugh, which hurt his gut like anything. "Gotcha." Then, the laughter gone, "Thanks, David."

"Hey, man! No problem," said David, blowing on the fingernails of his right hand and polishing them on his T-shirt as though he attacked The Sultans with a tire iron on a daily basis. He looked sideways at Mary. "Couldn't let anything happen to the old Westley plumbing, could I?" David grinned and then walked away, the tire iron over his shoulder. "See you later, guys," he shouted without turning around. "Don't do anything I wouldn't do!"

"You okay?" Mary set her hand on his belly. Gordon silently cursed Lancer. It was the most intimate place on which she had ever put her hand, and it was because that asshole had punched him.

"I don't care about myself; it was what he was saying about . . . doing . . . to you," whispered Gordon furiously. "I could kill him for that!"

She put her fingers over his lips and tried to keep her tone light, tried to keep even a hint of angry tears from starting. "Don't even think anything like that much less say it. Lancer's crazy."

Gordon shook his head as though he hadn't heard her. "I don't know where he's getting that crap about you being his girl." He searched her face and laughed a little uncertainly. "Weird, eh?"

"Yes. Weird and stupid." Her eyes, wide and filled with as much guileless confusion as she could manage, locked on his. "Why are you asking me this?"

Part of him wanted to say "Because if it's anything I excel at, it's lying, Mare. I am a connoisseur of the art of stretching the truth, of the innocent, blank look. Maybe you aren't lying, but you sure aren't telling me everything." Then, because Gordon definitely did *not* want to know everything, because suddenly it was more important than anything else that Mary remain untouched until it was *him* doing the touching, he said quietly, "Those guys can't even fight fair."

Her breath, the breath she had been holding like a shield against his probing, came out in a whoosh. "Exactly. And it was three against one, Gordon. If you're having any stupid thoughts about being unmanly or something, put them out of your head. *Three against one.* Typical Lancer. He's a bully, but I'm not afraid of him." But she was, just the idea of getting caught alone with Lancer made her feel ill.

"He'd better stop even thinking about you," said Gordon. He put his hand over hers so that she wouldn't pull it away. With his free arm he pulled her close and kissed her, a long kiss that almost overcame the pain. Almost. "And it was three against three." *But I didn't defend her. I couldn't. But I will next time. Lancer would do more than lay a hand on her if he ever got a chance, but he'll never get a chance; not while I'm around.*

"And we beat them," said Mary, freeing her hand and winding her arms around Gordon.

He kissed her again and then whispered against her lips, "Yup."

"Can we go up the beach where it's quiet?" she breathed into his ear. "Let's just go up the beach and get away from here."

The Chief was parked nearby. They both took off their shoes and socks and put them in the trunk from which Gordon got some towels for them to sit on. Hand in hand they strolled up the beach at the waterline, the wavelets washing over their feet, the sound of music coming from the Sand Club fading. Gordon tied to concentrate on

Mary and the quiet, but Lancer's sneering face was right there in his mind's eye.

"Do you think we should go to the police?" asked Mary. She felt him stiffen and knew it had been the wrong question.

Great, thought Gordon, *she's thinking about it too. Great.* "And tell them what? That Caldwell pulled down my jeans? Yeah. They'd fill out a warrant for his arrest within seconds."

"That Caldwell assaulted you and threatened you with a switchblade and actually cut you! And that he said he wanted to . . . you know. To do things with me."

"It would be their word against ours. The cops wouldn't do a thing. He would have even more of a reason to hate my guts than he already does, and no, I am not afraid of him (not of him, but of what he was going to do to me, to kick my nuts and then cut me; I have never been so scared in my life). What good would it do me to be afraid of him? What he said about you? That's different. That'll never happen; not while I'm in the picture." Realizing his voice had risen, Gordon said more quietly. "Come on. We'll just avoid him."

"Like tonight? He's crazy. He really is going to kill somebody someday, and I don't want it to be you."

He squeezed her hand. "It won't be me, Mare." Then, desperate to change the subject, "What about here?" he asked her. There were no houses or cottages; a small poplar wood rose above the edge of the beach. Gordon spread the towels and sat. Mary's rear end had barely made contact with the terrycloth when he pulled her into his arms and kissed her.

Yes! she thought. Mary was now entirely in love with Gordon. She had asked her mother a hundred times how she was supposed to know when she really loved someone, and her mother's cryptic reply had always been the same: you'll know. Well, she knew. Gordon was the one. That she was only sixteen years old didn't factor into the emotional equation; neither did the detail that he was her first love, the only boy she had *willingly* allowed to kiss her and hold her. She had no comparison at all, but Mary knew that Gordon was the best kisser in the world. He didn't try to French kiss – at least he hadn't yet – and she wasn't sure what she would do if and when he did.

She loved making out with him. His initial tentative kisses had been gentle and restrained, which seemed right. When kisses turned to necking, that changed – the heavier breathing, his damp palms, the way he whispered her name – it frightened her a little at first, but then she began to have a sense of her power over him. Mary had tried to tone things down, but then there was another shift in the balance. Gordon wasn't the only one breathing heavily. She knew she should be very careful so that they didn't go too far, but the way he made her feel! And the big problem was that she enjoyed feeling . . . aroused, because it was Gordon and she loved Gordon. But then he was squeezing her too tightly and kissing her too hard.

This is the thing, Gordon was thinking. *This is the best way to forget everything.* He needed to forget The Sultans and how mortified he had been to have Mary see him in his underwear, and how much he hated that bastard Lancer, and how he was going to get him back for it if it was the last thing he ever did! The pain! Man, he would make *Francis* suffer! The night sky had become overcast so he couldn't see Mary's face too clearly, but he sure as hell could feel the way she stiffened and then pulled away a little. "What's wrong?" he asked.

"If you are thinking about Caldwell while you're kissing me, I will strangle you." She took his face between her hands and said in her baby-sitter voice, "Don't you dare lie to me, Gordon Westley. Were you thinking about him?"

"About what he said; yeah. And what he did to me . . . what you saw. . . ."

"Gordon. I saw your underwear. Your underpants! The guy threatens to cut off part of your penis (she is talking about MY penis, referring to MY penis; it was almost worth it all to hear her talking about it!) and all you can think of is that I saw your underwear?"

Gordon knew that Mary had a temper. He had come to learn that she was spoiled and impulsive, but when she said, "I saw your underwear. Okay, fine; you can see mine!" he nearly had a stroke. He wanted to see her underwear, her panties and bra. He would rather have seen them in a little pile on the sand than on her body, but he would settle for them remaining on her body. Would he ever. "Are you sure?" he asked.

"How else are we going to go swimming?"

"Swimming?"

Mary pulled her blouse over her head, dropped it to the sand, and then unbuttoned and unzipped her skirt. It puddled around her feet and she stepped out of it. "Okay. Fine. Now you've had a look at my underwear." Then she bolted for the water.

Gordon stood there, unable to believe what he had just seen. Well, sort of seen, since it was pretty dark. He had never in his wildest, most erotic imaginings about Mary considered the possibility of them swimming together in their underwear. Would James Dean swim in his underwear? (Oh, man, I'm getting a hard-on. I can't take off my jeans. What if she sees it? What if it's too big and she passes out and drowns? What if it's too small and she passes out and drowns? What if —)

"You'd better get in here, Gordon! I mean it!"

Gordon stripped to his shorts and ran to the lake, praying to God that the water would be cold enough to chill his penis back to its ordinary dimensions. Lake Erie didn't disappoint him. By the time he reached Mary, he was boneless, but he was taking no chances. He stayed low in the water so that only his head showed.

"What on earth are you doing? Crawling?" laughed Mary. "Gordon, are you shy?"

"I'm not shy. I'm in my underwear."

"Which covers you pretty much the same as a bathing suit does. Good Lord; we skinny-dip at the cottage all the time when my girlfriends are up."

That revelation caused Gordon's penis (AKA Lazarus) to rise up and sing ALLELUIA! Well, it twitched a bit, thought better of it, and retreated. (You're on your own, Gordo; if you want to have sex with her, you're going to have to use something else, because no way am I coming out.)

"Doesn't this feel nice?" asked Mary.

"It feels like I peed myself."

"Oh, for God's sake!" Tired of trying to cheer him up, to make him forget the scene on the beach, and keep it out of her own mind as well, Mary stood, water streaming off of her body, just as the moon came out from behind a raft of clouds. Her first instinct, in spite of her bravado, was to drop back down. She forced herself to stand there in water that came up to just above her pubic bone, though, while Gordon stared.

She is so beautiful, he thought. Her underthings were white cotton, heavy enough that even when wet he couldn't see through them. But he could see her bare midriff and the hint of her ribs and her navel. It was the navel that undid him. He knew in theory that Mary had a navel (Of course she has a navel, you dimwit; do you think she was brought by the stork?), but to actually *see* it made his knees weak. But not too weak to stand and wade to her.

Gordon took her in his arms and kissed her. Even after having been in the water, she was warm. He ran his hands along her bare back and pulled her closer. Mary, her palms on his chest, slid them down and around his waist. He kissed her again, wanting to crush her to him. *I love her*, thought Gordon. She trusts me so much to do this, to let me hold her when she's half-dressed. I can't ever betray that trust. Which might have qualified as his second entirely adult thought, except for the fact that it only lasted a millisecond (since old Lazarus was rising again in Gordon's shorts).

"Nanna said half an hour," murmured Mary against his chest. "And I think I've had just about as much excitement as I can stand."

"Me too." Knowing he would have loved *a lot* more excitement, but not wanting to push his luck (not yet, at least) he waded with her back to shore, arm in arm, separating only when they reached their clothing on the beach. Once dry (even James Dean wouldn't be able to dry his underwear with a towel), they struggled into their clothing, Gordon having a far worse time of it in his jeans. *Now I really feel like I pissed myself*, he thought, exceedingly uncomfortable in the wet shorts. *I'll probably get all chapped and get crotch-rot and my boners will kill me even worse than they do now when I'm around her. Doesn't matter. That was just great and not even that ass wipe Caldwell can do anything to ruin the rest of our date! And may the rest of* Lancer's *night be truly and entirely fubarred!*

But the rest of Lancer's evening wasn't going to be fubarred at all. He had dropped off Eddie and Dutch in front of their houses, and then driven slowly back down Walnut Street. A few houses short of the Westleys' he had parked his car, gotten out and quietly walked down the sidewalk, hoping luck would be with him.

Lancer truly believed that he didn't have anything in particular against animals. They had their uses and in fact, could be vastly entertaining. He had learned that as a boy when he and his mother were left entirely on their own, his asshole of a father having managed to get himself killed in a bar fight. Yes, indeed. Lancer had learned that it sometimes took a squirrel hours to die if you hit it in just the right spot with your BB gun. Same with a rabbit; even better with a rabbit, because they made that cool baby squealing noise. A rabbit could keep that up for a long, long time. The way they sort of crawled with their hind legs dragging if you shot them just so in the spine.

And dogs? You had to wonder why they called them man's best friend, since you'd have thought that man might have wanted something a little smarter than a dog for a best friend. Dog's were slow learners and they were all the same. If Lancer drove down a country road past a farmhouse once, and there was a car-chasing dog in residence, the stupid thing would chase his coupe, snapping away at the tires. If he drove by a dozen times, the dog would chase him a dozen times. Until the time he drove by with a rag tied to the car's hubcap. The would be the last time Mr. Rover would chase any car ever again, because when Mr. Rover grabbed the rag with his teeth, it was an instant spin out, a broken neck, and a one way ticket to Doggie Paradise.

Cats were interesting, too, which was why Lancer was hoping that maybe the Westleys were the sort who put their cat out for the night, and that their cat just might be hanging around the spot he had seen it the afternoon he had flicked his butt on Gordy's piece of junk car. Maybe Lady Luck, that elusive whore, would be with him tonight.

She was.

Old Dougie was snoozing under the mailbox, one of his favorite spots for a catnap after a good feed. He had partaken not only of his own cat food, but of his nightly feast of human contraband, courtesy of Grandpa, who surreptitiously fed him bits off his own plate. Dougie had also eaten a number of olives fished out of various martini glasses over the course of the evening, a cicada, countless fish flies, and the head of a day-old dead carp. Dougie was stuffed to his kitty-cat gills and in full snooze mode, so he didn't protest at all when the nice man picked him up and started scratching him under the chin. He didn't protest when the man carried him down the street, or when the man put him into a car. Heck no! The only thing Dougie liked more than nibbling on decomposing carp heads was a ride in a car.

And he didn't make a fuss when the man tied the string around his neck. Old Dougie didn't know string from Shineola or he would have realized that what Lancer had tied around his neck was fishing line, twenty pound test, to be exact. Dougie uttered not a mew when the nice man stopped the car, opened the door and carried him out onto what he *did* recognize as the place that went over the water, Dougie's lexis being limited to words such as milkies, foodies, and outies rather than lift-bridge, long drop, and deep river. He didn't fuss when the man put him down and tied the end of the string to the bridge's railing and he only gave a single small *oof* when the man picked him up once more.

"Aloha, you little bastard" didn't translate to anything within Dougie's small and trusting brain. Lancer threw him off the bridge and although he did manage one desperate swipe to hold onto the man, the cat plunged into space, the line snapped tight and Dougie's head was ripped from his body.

Lancer heard the splashes when the pieces hit the river's surface. *Now* you're *fish food, you little fish-eating turd,* he thought. *Maybe your parts will wash up on the beach at old Gordy's house. Man, I'd love to be there to see that.*

Lancer didn't think about Dougie again that night. No scenes of feline murder haunted his rest, no softly padded footfalls walked the dark, twisting corridors of his mind. He slept the sleep of the righteous, the sleep of a man in love, and when he did dream, he dreamed of Mary.

■■■

Temporarily assuming his alter ego of Stan Westley, Superman had come upstairs to pee. Normally he would have just peed in the lake, but Lois Lane (better known as Marlene Cheyenne) and Jimmy Olson (Robbie Colons by night; boy reporter by day) were out on the beach building the Fortress of Solitude out of lawn furniture and pails of damp sand, so Superman had thought it best to drain his bladder in his own bathroom.

Bladder empty, Superman had flown down the hall to his parents' bedroom where he now stood, wearing only wrinkled swimming trunks, a large beach towel, and his braces. He was holding his SECRET WEAPON in his hands. There were more secret weapons (commonly known as guns) in Erie View than there had been at the Alamo. Rifles, shotguns, handguns of every make and description – you name it and it could be found somewhere in town, especially if the man of the house was a veteran. Gordon's father had a Luger pistol that he had brought back from France as a trophy. Neither Gordon nor Stan were supposed to know the location of the Luger, which was at the back of Louise Westley's brassiere drawer.

How his mother felt about having a handgun keeping company with her unmentionables was a complete mystery to Gordon, who had discovered the gun one day when he was seven years old and searching for hidden Christmas presents. When his questing fingers came into contact with cold, slightly oily metal, Gordon had nearly crapped his pants. He had pushed aside the brassieres and stared openmouthed at the gun. He had no desire at all to pick it up. Last year a kid named Paul McCain had blown off his right big toe when he was fooling around with *his* dad's pistol. Gordon liked having ten toes. He didn't want to be a nine-toe wonder like Paul. If he picked it up, maybe he would lose something worse than a toe. Maybe he would blow off one of his nuts or accidentally shoot himself in the brain, since if he picked up the gun, he knew in his innocent heart of hearts that it would suddenly come to life. So the gun remained untouched and to this day Gordon knew that he had made the right choice.

Gordon supposed that Stan knew about the gun. He himself had long ago ceased scrounging around in his parents' bedroom each December, having passed that Yuletide baton on to an eager and resolute Stan. What Gordon wasn't aware of, was that not only did Stan *know* about the gun, he had touched it, picked it up, clomped around the house with it stuck through his belt, aimed at himself in a mirror, and shown it to Robbie Colons just a few days ago. Only the hiding place had remained a secret. Robbie had told Marlene Cheyenne about the gun, who had told her big sister Charlene about the gun, who had passed it on to Henry Morton (he of the teensy, weensy penis), when she was making out with him, who had repeated the information to his cousin Eddie Morton, who was waiting for just the right moment to share the tidbit with Lancer.

All of which meant absolutely nothing to the oblivious Superman, who had secreted the weapon away, and who was now standing outside of Gordon's bedroom. Stan was exerting all his super powers, and including his X-ray vision, to entice Gordon to open his bedroom door. Stan had seen his brother a number of times during the day, but he hadn't been able to get him alone for an interrogation. Lex Luthor, The Prankster, and Mr. MXYZPTLK (Stan's parents and grandfather had no idea of their status as the archenemies of Superman) had been skulking around Metropolis. Oddly enough, Krypto (okay, Krypto *was* a dog in the comic and all they had was a cat, so Old Dougie was always Krypto) had been in seclusion.

Stan extended his arms, closed his eyes, and concentrated. He was focusing so hard that he didn't realize that

Gordon — who had heard the rattling of Stan's braces and was of the opinion that Stan was about as sneaky as a B-52 — had very quietly opened his bedroom door. Gordon took one look at Superman, (whose plaid swim trunks were hanging from his protruding hip bones and whose eyeglasses were speckled with sand and dead gnats), leaned down, and yelled, "GERONIMO-O-O-O!"

Stan's scream surpassed anything he had ever produced during the Spider Sweeper sorties, and he would have wet his pants had he not just relieved himself. An ordinary kid might have lost his temper. An ordinary kid might have had a tantrum or struck out, shamed to his core, but Stan? Stan's eyes popped open and he shouted, "Good one, Gordo! Got me good!"

"Gotcha good, Superman. Now move. I got places to go and things to do." Gordon smoothed back the sides of his hair and added, "The night and The Lakers wait for no man." He headed down the hallway and descended the stairs, Stan rattling away behind him.

"Wait up, Gordo!"

Gordon felt the slightest twinge of irritation. He had spent most of the day engaged in helping his father clean out the garage, which had barely left him enough time to spiff up The Chief as well as himself. Then his mother had managed to think of maybe two hundred more things for him to do before she and his father went out for dinner

with the Davidsons. He didn't have three hours for one of
Stan's conversations, so not only did he not slow down, he
sped up.

So did Stan. There was a god-awful clatter as he
slipped and pitched forward. Gordon, whose hand was on
the knob of the front door, whirled around, saw Stan
plunging toward him, cape streaming out. He didn't even
think; he just threw himself toward his brother. The colli-
sion was impressive when Stan, all fifty-six pounds of
him, hit Gordon and knocked him flat on his back. They
were lying there in the foyer, slightly stunned, with Stan's
towel flipped up over both of their heads, when Grandpa
walked in from the kitchen, a wooden spoon in his hand,
Edith Warner at his side with a tall, sweating glass in hand.

"You see that, Nanna? You see me, Grandpa?" yelled
Stan, untangling himself from Gordon. "See that? The
cape worked. Woulda been a massacre if I wasn't wearing
my cape. Right, Gordo?"

"And they call me crazy," Grandpa said, with resigned
hopelessness. "You kids seen Dougie? I'm cooking up our
favorite sardine omelet dinner."

"And if I survive it, I'll probably live to be two
hundred," said Nanna. She sipped at her G&T. "More
quinine can't hurt. Remember that when you're a geezer,
Gordon."

Grandpa shook his head and stalked away, Edith trail-
ing behind. "Get up off the floor, Stan," he shouted from

the kitchen. "Act decent. You'll get piles sitting on the floor. Piles, I'm telling you!"

Gordon climbed to his feet, his shirt half out of his jeans, his duck's ass a mess, ready to verbally slaughter Stan for being so stupid. Stan's smile wavered and then disappeared. He hated it when Gordon got mad at him. He could take his mother's scolding and his father's quick and unrelenting discipline and even Grandpa's Army Retard Game, but not his brother's derision. "You mad?" he asked softly.

Gordon's anger disappeared. Something he didn't quite like, something a little too close to pity took its place, and an unbidden series of thoughts: *what kind of life is he ever going to have; who except his creepy friends are ever going to want to hang out with him when he's older; why does he have to be like this* flashed guiltily through his mind. He pulled out his comb and slicked it through his hair. "I'm not mad, but jeez, Stan, will you be more careful? Use your head, will you? What if I hadn't been there to catch you?"

Stan let out his breath in a whoosh. "Don't be dumb; you'll always be here to catch me, Gordo. Boy! I thought you were gonna kill me there, but you can't kill Superman, so I shouldn't a been worried, should I of?"

"Should I have. SHOULD I HAVE. Superman doesn't talk like a feeb." He pocketed the comb. "Go get Marlene and Robbie and find Dougie for Grandpa, will you? Can't let that delicious sardine omelet go to waste."

Stan made a gagging sound. "Will if you tell me."

"Tell you what?" Man, he was so late!

"You kiss her?"

"That's none of your business. You kiss Lois Lane?"

"None of *your* business!" shouted Stan, his face coloring suspiciously.

"Yeah, well, get your super rear end in gear and find the cat."

"Gordo?"

Gordon, his hand yet again on the doorknob, smothered an inpatient sigh and asked, "What?"

"Can I be a Laker? I mean, when I'm old enough to?"

Gordon looked back at Stan and a pang of love as sharp as a dagger twisted through him. "Sure," he said quietly. "You'll be a great Laker. Now go find Dougie." And with that he hurriedly left the house, blinking hard a few times (must be sand or something or maybe ragweed), as he ran across the yard toward The Chief. Hoping the stench of the sardine omelet, something redolent of cat food left out in the sun for a week, wasn't clinging to his clothing, he set out.

David was standing outside his house, hands in his pockets when Gordon pulled up to the curb. Once inside the car he asked, "How they hangin', Wesser?" That was it. He didn't say anything about The Sultans, he didn't ask about Mary, he didn't mention what had nearly happened to Gordon's penis. He just sat there smiling.

Gordon, who for the millionth time in his life was wondering what he had ever done to deserve David's friendship said, "Hangin' low and easy, Ace. Low and easy."

David leaned back and put his hands behind his head. "Drive on, Watson, my good man!"

"We're motivatin', Sherlock!"

The Chief picked up speed because Chuck Berry's "Maybellene" was starting on the radio. When "Maybellene" was playing, Wesser didn't drive, he motivated. Speed was involved in motivating (as well as a lot of finger snapping), so Wesser arrived at Frank's house during the second verse. Frank and Tony were sitting on the front porch. Motivating did NOT involve parking the car, so Wesser just kept driving.

Tony said, "Gotta be 'Maybellene.'"

"Yup," said Frank. "He's motivatin'."

Since the song was only about two minutes long, Wesser motivated up to the curb in front of Frank's house just as Chuck was interrogating Maybellene as to why she couldn't possibly be faithful. By the time he turned the engine off, the song was over, the question unanswered.

"Ready, guys?" asked Gordon, still snapping his fingers. "What's our destination? Nothing's open, really."

"Denison's will be," said Tony when they were in the car. "Denison's is always open."

"And tell us about your date with Mary. Tell it all, man," said Frank. Both he and Tony leaned forward in anticipation of the details.

Unlike when Stan had queried him, Gordon suffered a slight testosterone assault. There was a part of him that wanted to tell his friends about what had happened on the beach, to maybe even embellish it, describe her breasts, her body, how she had wanted him. But then, the sudden need for privacy (that was between us and it was pretty personal) took precedence over the adolescent male instinct to brag about all things carnal. "Sorry," he said loftily. "Wesser does not kiss and tell." But he thought about Mary the whole time he was driving, testosterone percolating through his blood, an erotic octane booster.

Denison's Fries, Franks, and Foam was a long, low drive-in restaurant on the beach east of the Sand Club across the street from Victoria Park. A waitress could take your order and you could eat in your car, or you could partake of the delicacies inside the building. Denison's was painted pale yellow, the color symbolizing the famous lemonade that had been made there since 1926. The hamburgers and hot dogs were excellent, the fries always crispy, and the lemonade very good; not as good as beer, but still good. When Gordon pulled up, the sandy parking lot was already filled with vehicles, and Constable O'Driscoll's squad car was sitting at one end. O'Driscoll would be inside on the pretext of making certain the peace was not being disturbed, but in reality he would be scarfing down hot dogs to maintain what Gordon thought of as his *Girlish Accordion Figure*.

"What'll it be boys?" asked Mr. Denison. Strangely, he was the only adult Gordon knew who liked rock and roll. He had the best jukebox in Erie View: a Wurlitzer 1015 with polished walnut sides and bubbling columns that was a work of art. Right now, there were three couples dancing in front of it to Karl Perkins's rendition of "Blue Suede Shoes." Constable O'Driscoll, who had just consumed his regulation four hot dogs, was sipping a lemonade and trying to ignore the music.

"I'll have three hamburgers, a large fries – no make that two large fries – and a large Coke," said Gordon.

"Thanks for buying, Gord!" said Tony.

"Most generous," said David.

"You guys have had dinner. I did NOT have dinner because dinner was a sardine omelet," said Gordon. "Have you ever gotten a whiff of a sardine omelet? It makes Dougie and his litter box smell like a dozen roses. I am starving to death."

"We could be your food tasters," David suggested, waggling his eyebrows.

"Uh-uh," said Gordon. He paid for his meal, pocketed the change, and picked up his tray. "Come on. Order; I'll get a table."

"All right. All right. We buy our own, guys," said David with deep regret in his voice. "You're not even going to share with Mary, are you? Poor Mary; she looks like she's dying of hunger."

Gordon's head whipped around. There she was, standing in the doorway near the big glass windows with Laura Crane. Mary's head was tilted to one side, and she was listening to something Laura was saying. The corners of her lovely mouth were lifted in a slight smile. She threw back her head and laughed, shaking her head. Her cheeks filled with color when she saw Gordon.

"You're excused, man," said Tony, pulling out his wallet. "The Lakers can't stand in the way of true love."

"Catch you later, guys," said Gordon, his attention fixed on Mary as he crossed the room.

Gordon inhaled two hamburgers and the better part of a carton of fries and then slowed down. He consumed the last burger, took a long swig of Coke, belched softly, and groaned in contented repletion. "That was good."

"Are you too full to move?" asked Mary sweetly.

"Maybe," said Gordon, knowing full well what she wanted. He rubbed his flat belly, pushing it out. "Man, I guess I am awfully full."

"Gordon," she warned. "Come on."

"Okay. Okay." He stood, took her hand, and led her out onto the dance floor; there were more than twenty people dancing now.

"Wonder what's the matter with *her*?" whispered Mary.

"Got me," said Gordon.

Her was Lila Box. Diane Bender and Lila were sitting at a table; Diane was comforting Lila, who was crying. Both were big-breasted girls, both dyed their hair platinum blonde and wore it so ratted, that there very well could have been hungry ferrets living in there. And they wore enough makeup to paint an army of clowns. Both girls had terrible reputations and their necks always sported hickeys. Their names and telephone numbers were written on the walls of every rest room in Erie View, which didn't necessarily mean much, Gordon knew. In some rest rooms, the walls resembled telephone books or dissertations penned by demented philosophers. (*For a good time call Patty Norman at Whitehall 3-2044. Richard Peck loves Sandy Dean. People who write on shithouse walls, should roll their shit in little balls. And those who read these words of wit, should eat those little balls of shit.*) Gordon, who couldn't conceive of taking a dump and writing poetry while some guy next to him was farting loud enough to shatter the toilet bowl AND the tank, thought it bizarre.

Lila, not only had a bad rep, she was considered to be a little bit nuts. That was because she had been dating Lancer Caldwell off and on this summer; Caldwell, whose idea of a date, it was rumored, didn't include flowers and chocolates, but rough sex and the use of enough condoms in one evening to equip the Royal Navy.

Gordon's father had said many times that you shouldn't judge unless you knew from personal experience. Lila's virtue, or lack of, was destined to become an UNSOLVED MYSTERY, since the idea of screwing her held about as much appeal as sticking his penis into a Mix Master. On the other hand, even if she wasn't a slut, she sure did a good imitation of one. (Tonight at the Ed Sullivan Theater, we have a *rrrreally big shoo*. Straight from Romania, we have a waiter balancing spinning plates on sticks. We have the most *borrrrring* opera singer in the world, *and* we have Erie View, Ontario's own LILA BOX doing her impersonation of a slut. For a *rrrreally big screw*, call LILA BOX at Whitehall 3-2209.)

Frank was at the jukebox punching in five songs for the quarter he had deposited. The record was flipped onto the turntable and in a few seconds, Haley's "See You Later Alligator" was playing. All The Lakers were dancing – David with Laura, Frank with Charlene Cheyenne, Tony with Susan Welch, and Gordon with Mary. Everybody was doing The Lindy Hop, since the rhythm was too brisk for The Stroll. The song finished; they waited for the next record to start playing (Gordon taking advantage of the pause to hold Mary in his arms). It was "See You Later Alligator" again. By the time it had played a grand total of five times, every person including Mr. Denison, was ready to garrote Frank.

"I'm never going to get that stupid thing out of my head!" Mary complained as they passed Lila and Diane.

Lila sobbed, "That was our song. 'See You Later Alligator.' That was our song."

"Get this, man," said David, as he and Laura slid into the booth. He pointed at Lila with his chin. "I just heard something. You're gonna love it! Lila Box? The reason she's crying? She and Lancer broke up for good this time. You'd think she'd be celebrating that she didn't have to scr– uh, date him anymore. The word is, he's on the prowl for a new girl."

"God," said Laura, rolling her eyes. "What an opportunity. Who's the lucky babe who's got him in her future? Hey! Maybe we should take a shot at him, Mary. Wouldn't that be a scream?"

"A real scream," said Mary flatly, and there was something in her voice, her lowered eyes, the sudden stiffness of her posture that Gordon didn't much care for. She sat there, picking at a small loose thread in the hem of her shorts, staring at it. Then she slid out of the booth. "He's disgusting. I don't even want to talk about him, okay? And as a matter of fact, I think I'd just like to go home."

"Fine with me," said Gordon, shrugging his shoulders, but in the back of his mind in a dark room of suspicion, an unpleasant little voice was whispering, *Liar, liar, pants on fire. Mary has a secret, Mary has a secret. There's more to this than she's telling you, Gord, ask her, ask her.*

But Gordon didn't ask her anything, and assuring The Lakers that he wouldn't be too long, followed her to the door of Denison's where Mary shrieked, "Oh, God!" her hands flapping around her face. "I hate these things!" She made a run for The Chief through a fish fly hatch worthy of "Ripley's Believe It Or Not" that had in essence taken over Erie View. Thousands of swooping insects were swarming around the streetlights or clinging to every surface. An inch of them lay dead on Walnut Street, turning driving conditions into a slimy, smelly mess. Gordon reached out to open The Chief's passenger door as Mary picked fish flies off of herself, and just as he put his hand on the door, he heard the roar of a powerful engine.

Gordon knew that sound. It was a '55 Chev Bel Air convertible, Dutch Batting's father's Bel Air convertible, which Dutch occasionally borrowed, something that caused Gordon to doubt Mr. Batting's sanity. The Bel Air, its top down, pulled up to the curb and stopped. There was Dutch, all right, but he was in the passenger seat and it was Lancer who was driving.

Lancer took a swig from the mickey he had tucked in his lap and shouted, "Want a drink, baby? You like rye, don't you? Come an' have a drinky-poo with old Lancer."

"Get in the car," said Gordon shortly, and Mary, who disliked being ordered around and who normally would have taken her sweet time getting in The Chief if she had gotten in at all, slipped inside without a word.

"Aw, come on, baby! You're breakin' my heart, here!" moaned Lancer. He drained the bottle, hurled it at The Chief, missed, cursed, and slammed his foot down on the Bel Air's gas pedal. Gordon heard Dutch's wail of "Take it easy for chrissake!" as the convertible careered down the street. Actually, it was more of an uncontrolled slide. The wheels spun, the rear end began to fishtail through the fish flies, mashed insects spraying everywhere. There was a thump when the Bel Air hit the curb and slid sideways into Victoria Park. It might have slid a good deal farther, had the park's dominant feature, an enormous seagull dropping spattered statue of Queen Victoria, not been in the way. The Chev hit the statue's pedestal broadside with a tremendous thunk, Queen Victoria broke off at the waist and tumbled down in a shower of marble chunks, doing a somersault that would have earned her a 9.3 at the British Empire and Commonwealth Games, landing upright in the backseat of the Chev.

Denison's emptied in seconds, Constable O'Driscoll leading the pack. "Merciful Mother o' God, what's goin' on out here?" he bellowed.

Gordon poked his thumb in the direction of the crime scene. "Lancer Caldwell is kidnapping the queen, sir," he announced as the Chev rolled ponderously out of the park, its rear end weighted down by a ton of British royalty. Both rear tires were now flat, and the warped wheel rims were grinding against the fender wells, giving the distinct impression that Queen Victoria was yodeling.

The Accordion drew his gun and strode out into the street, planting himself in Lancer's path. "You're under arrest, you little gobshites!" he shouted. "Outa the car, you worthless arseholes!"

Gordon wasted no time, and neither did the other Lakers, as they crammed into The Chief. Gordon started the engine and drove away from Denison's before they could somehow be implicated. He ignored Lancer and Dutch as he passed by them, standing in the street, their hands braced against the ruined hulk of the Chev, while O'Driscoll patted them down under the mild gaze of the truncated monarch. But he couldn't ignore Lancer's enraged shout of, "You're dead meat, Westley! I shit you not! Dead meat!"

The Lakers made a lot of lame jokes about exactly what sort of dead meat Gordon might be – the hot dog variety was too simple; he was more of a cutlet or maybe a *filet mignon* – but Mary didn't joke. She simply sat there as Gordon dropped off each of his friends. She didn't utter a peep even when they were alone, and not a sound escaped her lips when he pulled up in front of her house and parked, the engine idling quietly.

Gordon took a deep breath and asked, "You going to tell me what's wrong or are you going to make me guess?"

"What do you mean?" she asked him.

"Why is he after you? Where did he get the idea you're his girl?" Gordon saw her throat move. He felt cold shoot into the pit of his belly. *Not Mary! Not my Mary!* "What happened?" Then, the hardest thing he had ever said in his life, "What did he do to you?" praying that she would say that NOTHING had been done to her.

"You'll hate me."

His heart nearly broke. "I could never hate you." *Liar, liar*, sang the little voice.

Out it came. May 24th weekend, a party at Laura Crane's when Laura's parents were gone, beer, rye, funny how fast it had gone to her head, funny how it made you do things you might not do otherwise, funny how even when The Sultans had crashed the party she hadn't been scared. At least not until Lancer Caldwell had pulled her into the backyard and got her up against the side of the house.

"He kissed me. That's all. I never would have let him do it, but it just happened so fast. He was so fast."

"Did he touch you?"

"What do you mean, touch?"

"You know what I mean. Did he . . . did he touch you?"

"No." Even in the shadowed car he could see the blush rise in her face. "No. And it was all over in a second because some guy came out and started throwing up." She

faced him then, her head held high, but he could see the
glint of tears in her eyes. "You hate me, right? You think
I'm no better than Lila Box. I didn't kiss him back, you
know. *He* kissed *me* and there's a big diff—"

But she couldn't complete her sentence because
Gordon was kissing her and she was *definitely* kissing *him*
back. There were whispers of how he didn't hate her, how
he could never hate her no matter what, of how she was
his girl and how she didn't ever have to worry about
anyone else trying to kiss her again. All very sweet and
romantic and nicely tinged with passion, but inside
Gordon the little voice was saying, *You realize that this
means war, don't you?* Gordon had to agree with the voice.
From now on it was war.

chapter 10

"A handful of patience is worth more
than a bushel of brains."

— Amos Littlebird, Odawa Sachem

1:58 a.m. Gordon couldn't sleep. He lay in his underpants on his back on top of the bedspread, sweating, raging, abandoning plan after vengeful plan. That Lancer had probably been arrested and definitely had been publicly humiliated wasn't enough. Caldwell was going to suffer; somehow he was going to suffer for that stolen kiss, for even laying a finger on Mary, who was, thank God, safely asleep in her own bed.

But Mary wasn't sleeping at all. She was sitting up, her knees drawn to her chest, her damp hair stuck to the back of her neck. The dream. She had had the dream again, the dream where Lancer was kissing her, her wrists held behind her back, his body molded against hers. And she wasn't kissing him back; she had never kissed him back!

She had loathed every second of that kiss and yet it had wakened something in her that even now she didn't dare think about. Because if she thought about how she'd broken free to stand, panting and sweaty, if she thought about the victory in Lancer's eyes, then she was no better than Lila Box. And that just could not be true. Gordon would never want her if she was like Lila. Never. Mary lay back down and stared at the ceiling. She slammed the door shut on the sordid dream in much the same way that Gordon was slamming his mental door shut on thoughts of vengeance, since if he didn't get some sleep, he wouldn't be able to avenge squat.

And Lancer wasn't sleeping either. He and Eddie Moron were in a blind pig just outside of Erie View, where, in the company of half a dozen alcoholic insomniacs, they were drinking beer. The beer, Eddie had noticed, wasn't doing much to improve Lancer's mood, which was a lethal combination of wrath, blood-lust, and just plain lust. Hoping against all hope to direct the high beams of Lancer's simmering rage away from himself, Eddie offered up his small gem of information.

"Lancer. Lancer! Listen to this. Gordon Westley's old man has a machine gun in his house. Smuggled it back from Germany. I have this on the best authority. Man, I would sure like to fire a machine gun. *Ack-ack-ack-ack-ack-unk!*" The *unk* had interrupted the *ack-acks* when Lancer drove his elbow into Eddie's side hard enough to cave in his rib cage. Not only did Eddie stop *ack-acking*, he stopped breathing for a minute.

"Thanks for the tip," Lancer said in the same tone of voice that he would have said "eat shit and die."

"Anytime," Eddie gasped, certain that the machine gun would be forgotten.

He was incorrect. Lancer simply took another sip of beer and filed the gem away in the foul and cankerous part of his brain that he thought of as "things to do."

chapter 11

"Fear not death, for the sooner we die,
the longer we shall be immortal."
— Amos Littlebird, Odawa Sachem

Stan Westley died on a warm Saturday night at the end of July, a night fragrant with the scent of roses and the watery tang of a slight breeze coming in off the lake. It would have been a tragedy of enormous proportions in any case, but Stan was just beginning to live what passed as a normal life for him. Up until a few days ago, he had been a chronic bed wetter. No matter how often he bathed, a slight hint of urine always hung about his body. (Pee-Pee Pants Stan was the cruel nickname with which some of the kids at school tortured him.)

The permanent removal of his braces caused some sort of a bizarre chain reaction: he stopped making sand porcupines (sand angels were still on his agenda, though), he suffered more patiently as the victim of *The Army*

Retard Game, and he stopped wetting the bed. It was as though some urinary nocturnal guardian spirit had turned off a spigot in his small penis. That's how quickly he stopped. And so, on this night he had been accorded the unheard-of privilege of a sleepover at Robbie Colons', which was an A-1 miracle, since he had gotten himself into deep trouble just yesterday for attempting to ride his scooter down the staircase during a rousing game of *Superman vs. Flash Gordon*.

And so, the last hours of his life were spent in the company of Robbie. At Stan's suggestion, they carried two ladder back chairs from a spare room into Robbie's Tinker Toy- and Dinky car-strewn bedroom, their parents downstairs playing bridge and drinking Manhattans, oblivious to the construction project. Then they took some extra blankets that were kept folded on the top shelf of Robbie's closet and made a crude tent by draping the blankets over the chair backs and weighing the corners down with books, which in Robbie's opinion was the best use to which the books had ever been put. Robbie didn't like to read books; he only liked to read *comic* books.

Robbie had lots of comic books. Stan figured that if you piled all of them up they would make a stack twenty feet high. Maybe thirty. They had tried it once, but didn't get much past five feet, because it was at that point the stack had fallen over. Unfortunately, the Colons' Pomeranian, Buffy, an animal that to Mrs. Colons' intense irritation her son called Barfy (Mom! Barfy's puked up a ball of dog food the size of British Columbia and it's *on the good rug!*), was strolling past. Mrs. Colons had seen her beloved Buffy disappear under an avalanche of comics and subjected the boys to a severe scolding. Which was minor league compared to *The Army Retard Game*, as far as Stan was concerned.

There they were in the makeshift tent with a bowl of buttered popcorn, bottles of Coke, two flashlights, and a pile of comic books. Robbie was reading *All Hero*, Captain Marvel being his favorite of all the heroes. Stan, who was wearing his Superman cape over his pajamas, was just starting *Blitzkrieg, Searing Battle Sagas of WWII As Seen Through Enemy Eyes!* It had a particularly lurid cover, one in which a terrified woman (who looked like Marilyn Monroe in a bib apron) and her daughter were cowering in a doorway. One German soldier was holding a handgun and screaming in his talking balloon, "DO NOT SHOOT, HUGO!" The other German, one armed with a machine gun, was screaming in *his* talking balloon, "ORDERS ARE ORDERS! They are the enemy . . . AND THIS IS WAR!"

"Look at these Nazi swine," said Stan. It sounded more like *ooka ees awzee ine*, because his mouth was stuffed to maximum capacity with popcorn.

"Cool," said Robbie, "but how can you tell they're Nazis?"

Stan swallowed, took a slug of Coke, belched, and said, "'Cause only Nazis would kill Marilyn Monroe and her daughter. They do *oogy* stuff. See, there are all kinds of Germans. Nazi Swine Germans, soldier Germans, good Germans, and *oogy* Germans."

"No kidding?"

"No kidding! My dad told me all about it. You know Mr. Diefendorf, the tinker? Well, he was a German soldier in the war. Same one my grandpa was in. Dad says he's just like Grandpa, even if he is German and Grandpa is from England, because both of them still act like the war is going on. But Mr. Diefendorf isn't a Nazi, because Nazis hadn't been invented yet."

Robbie started picking his nose, which seemed like a good idea to Stan, so he jammed a finger in the old noserino. "That *oogy* poop Hitler hadn't invented them yet," said Robbie.

Now, when either of them brought up the name Hitler, it was *de rigueur* that they sing THE SONG to the tune of "Whistle While You Work." It went:

Whistle while you work.
Hitler is a jerk.
Mussolini bit his weeny.
Now it doesn't work!

Then for good measure they sang three verses of something Stan's grandfather had taught them, the tune of which – "The Colonel Bogey March" – would in time be forever associated with the film *Bridge over the River Kwai*.

Hitler has only got one ball.
Göring has two but very small.
Himler has something sim'lar.
But poor old Goebbels has no balls at all!

Hitler has only got one ball.
The other is in the Albert Hall.
His mother, the dirty bugger
Cut it off when he was small!

She threw it into a great big tree.
It fell into the deep blue sea.
The fishes grabbed their dishes
And ate scallops and bollocks for tea!

Then of course, they burst into manic laughter the same way they always did, bubbles of snot popping out of their noses, Stan snorting and gasping, Robbie quacking his brains out, sounding like a flock of migrating mallards.

Once recovered, his nose having been wiped on his pajama sleeve, Stan stuck up a more or less clean finger. "I knew I forgot something. My medal. Gonna sneak back home and get it. Door'll be unlocked."

"Why sneak?" asked Robbie.

"Because, crap for brains, sneaking is better," explained Stan, exiting the tent.

Robbie parted the blankets. "Butt wipe."

"Dick wad."

"Whale poop."

"Hurry back, penis face. This is too fun."

"Okay, farthead."

Stan crept out of the bedroom, down the hall, and down the stairs with the ease of a veteran sneaker. Down another hall and into the kitchen, a soundless opening and closing of the Colons' back door. Then a sprint across the fenceless backyards that separated the two houses, keeping an eye out for Dougie. There had been some furtive whispering at home about how Old Dougie had gone off to die somewhere, which had made no sense at all to Stan, who was convinced that Dougie was just on vacation. He'd be back any day now. No way Old Dougie was dead!

The back door was unlocked, but just in case Grandpa was awake, Stan stole into the house very quietly. Grandpa, hard of hearing anyway, slept like the ever-loving departed, but there was no sense in eliciting an evening rendition of *The Army Retard Game*. Stan passed his scooter where it was parked against the newel post and stroked it lovingly.

He tiptoed up the long, steep staircase, entered his dark room, and retrieved the medal from the cigar box on his nightstand. He noiselessly retraced his steps, but he only made it to the top of the staircase.

Where Lancer Caldwell was standing.

Stan was terrified of Lancer in the first place. Lancer was worse than the bogeyman, the Creature From the Black Lagoon, and King Kong all rolled into one, as far as Stan was concerned. But to see Erie View's Prince of Darkness standing right there in the flesh (ohmygod! Ohmygod! OHMYGOD!) was too much. Stan simultaneously wet his pants, the hot urine flooding down his goose pimpled legs, and took a deep breath so that he could scream his guts out. Lancer, who was running on pure instinct, nerves, a deeply rooted fear of incarceration, two shots of rye, and the pills he had taken an hour ago, shoved Stan as hard as he could. Stan didn't touch a step. His bare foot caught the handle of his scooter, toppling it over just as he hit the hardwood floor with a dull crack.

Lancer stared at the unmoving boy, never letting his attention leave Stan for a moment as he slowly descended the stairs with the menace of a drugged-out black mamba. The kid's eyes were wide open, which bothered Lancer, because if the kid's eyes were open, it could mean that he was alive, and if he was alive it *definitely* meant that something would have to be done about that slight problem. But once Lancer was standing over Stan, whose arms were spread out, palms up, some stupid towel bunched up under him, there was no doubt in his mind that the little shit had checked out. Him and his fucking cat, together in heaven forever. Good stuff!

"Louise? Gordon? That you, Ben? Stan?"

The voice was from upstairs and the other end of the house, but a white-hot surge of adrenaline laced with terror shot through Lancer, who had been positive the place was empty. Yet greed overcame fear; he might not have the gun, but no way in hell was he leaving this dump empty-handed. Lancer swooped down and snatched the medal from Stan's open palm with his gloved hand. Then he quickly left the Westley residence, without even a single glance back.

■■■

Gordon pulled The Chief over to the side of Main when a police car, red lights flashing, sirens screaming, appeared in his rearview mirror.

"Whoa!" cried Frank, leaning out the back window. "They were going sixty, at least. I'm gonna be a cop when I grow up so *I* can drive down Main Street at sixty miles an hour."

"Whaddya mean *when* you grow up, daddy-o?" asked Tony. He punched Frank's shoulder. "Shouldn't that be *if*?"

"Holy shit!" yelled David, eyes riveted to the rearview mirror. "Here come two more!" The pair of squad cars raced by. "Something must have happened."

Frank slapped his forehead. "Ace, you genius! Something must have happened!"

"Maybe somebody drowned," said Gordon thoughtfully, as he pulled back out into traffic and hunched over the wheel once more. He glanced at his wristwatch; it was 9:05, which gave them enough time to check out the action, maybe get a burger at Gertson's, putting them in an oh-so-prime position for a few games of pool.

Gordon undraped himself and lit his first cigarette of the night. He couldn't smoke and drape and hunch at the same time (he had set his pompadour on fire once doing that), so he leaned back in the seat and let his head tilt and sort of fall over to one side. And then to the other side. And then back to the other side; he looked like a teenage metronome managing to hold on to a little sneer. (Just a little one that probably wouldn't cause too much of a cramp.)

"Your theme song, Ace!" shouted Gordon. "Turn it up, man!"

They all had theme songs. Tony's was "Tutti Fruiti," Gordon's was "The Great Pretender," Frank's was – could it have been anything else? – "You Ain't Nothin' But a Hound Dog."

And David, poor, pitiful persona-less David? His personal favorite was Gene Vincent's new hit, "Be-Bop-a-
Lula." He was beating out the rhythm on The Chief's
dashboard and singing along with possibly the most terrible voice in all of North America. Gordon's grandfather
had once described it as "worse than a gut-shot hyena in
heat." Gordon had never heard a hyena in heat, much less
a gut-shot one, but he knew REALLY BAD when he heard
it. David's singing sounded like what you might hear if
someone was being castrated with a potato masher. But
nothing lasts forever (thank the little Lord Jesus!) and
neither did "Be-Bop-A-Lula." His ears ringing, Gordon
pulled alongside the curb and parked The Chief a few
storefronts up from Gertson's.

Inside, The Lakers were able to get their favorite
booth: the one near the jukebox. They ordered burgers,
fries, and Cokes when the waitress came. It was crowded,
so she took forever getting to them, and then it took
another eternity for the food to come, but at least it was
hot. David interrupted his meal to examine the record
labels currently on the jukebox. Gordon was praying to
God and hoping against hope that "Be-Bop-A-Lula"
wasn't among them, when he heard the wheezing breath
and stentorian footfalls of none other than Constable
O'Driscoll.

"Young Westley," O'Driscoll said.

"Yes, sir (that's my name; don't wear it out)," answered Gordon.

"You'd best come with me. Young Molonovitch, there? You'll drive your friends home and then bring young Westley's car back to his residence."

Gordon's face reddened. "What have I done? Have I parked in the wrong place? I can move my car. What are you arresting me for?"

"Not arresting you, lad. You're needed at home, is all. Come along, now."

For several defiant seconds Gordon remained seated. Then he stood and handed his keys over to David who whispered, "I'll be fast, Gord."

"Hope everything is okay, Gord," said Frank and Tony simultaneously.

Constable O'Driscoll said nothing. Not when he ushered Gordon into the passenger seat of his squad car, not as he pulled out onto Main, not as he drove the side streets and onto Walnut, all the while Gordon's fear growing and growing until it was an ocean of fear from which normalcy was disappearing with the relentlessness of an outgoing tide. Only when he parked the squad car in front of Gordon's house and turned off the engine (of course he has to park in front because there are already TWO squad cars AND Doctor Henderson's car in the driveway) did he utter a syllable.

"You'll have to be very brave now, young Westley."

"Who is it? I can't go in there not knowing. It's Grandpa, isn't it? He's had a heart attack, hasn't he?" said Gordon shakily.

"There's been an accident."

"WHO IS IT?" Gordon shouted.

O'Driscoll sighed. "It's your brother, lad."

Gordon opened the door and was out of the squad car and across the front yard before O'Driscoll could stop him. He flung open the front door to find the two policemen and his father, who had aged fifteen years since Gordon had last seen him, standing in the foyer.

"Where's Stan?" asked Gordon. There was a high ringing in his head and icy, rank sweat broke on every inch of him. "Stan's okay, isn't he, Dad?"

"He's gone, Gordon."

"Gone?" (Gone as in gone from the room, right? Gone as in gone for a walk, right? Gone as in gone up to bed, right?) "Dad?"

"Stan is dead, Gordon."

■■■

The night when someone you love dies, especially if you have never before been stroked by death's wintry finger, is the longest night of your life. It's one of those nights you will always remember, no matter how old you become. An unwelcome specter, the memory will tuck itself away in your mind, sleeping, waiting patiently, and when you least expect it, rise up and slash at your heart with its claws.

You don't sleep the night your SOMEONE dies. How can you sleep when your brother is lying in a hospital morgue, when your mom and grandfather are zoned out on the shots Doctor Henderson has given them, when your dad – YOUR DAD! THE TOUGHEST MAN IN THE WORLD! – is sitting at the foot of the stairs, crying like a little boy? That the cops and the doctor finally go away, doesn't help. That your father drinks down a water glass filled with Glenlivet maybe helps him, but it sure as hell doesn't help you. No. There was no mercy at all for Gordon on the night Stan died.

His mind numb, Gordon watched the sun come up from where he had spent the night sitting alone near a sand porcupine on the dark beach. I have to cry, he told himself. If I don't cry for Stan, it's wrong. But he hadn't been able to summon a single tear for his brother. It meant he was worse than dirt. His mother had started screaming again about an hour ago. He suspected that Doctor Henderson had returned and given her another shot, because the screaming had gradually reduced in volume and intensity until he could no longer hear it.

"Gord?" It was David. "Gord? The cops wouldn't let me come in last night. I parked The Chief out front. Here are the keys." He sat down next to Gordon and set the keys down on the sand with as much care as he would have had they been made of thin crystal. "Jesus, Gord. What happened?"

"Robbie said that Stan came home to get his medal. The cops think he was trying to ride his scooter down the stairs. Maybe playing Superman. It was dark. An accident."

"Jesus."

"Doctor Henderson says he didn't suffer; that it was quick."

"Jesus, Gord." *If it was quick, that's a good thing for Stan, but it sure isn't going to be quick for Gord and his family,* thought David. "How're your folks doing?"

"Not so good. Grandpa found . . . Stan. He ran to get Dad at the Colons' and Mrs. Colons called the cops. They tried to stop Mom but they couldn't. Stan was already . . . dead, but she wouldn't let go of him, I guess, and they had to drag her off. My dad . . . my dad . . ." Gordon put his hands over his face. "I can't cry, David. I can't cry and it's wrong because Stan was just a little kid, and he was my brother, and he shouldn't be dead. That's not right . . . I loved him, David. I did. Really."

David put his arms around Gordon, not just around his shoulders, but entirely around him. Gordon wept then. For the kindness and goodness of his friend, for the loss of his little brother, for his own misery, but mostly just for Stan.

chapter 12

"When one man dies, one chapter is not torn out of the book, but translated into a better language."

                – Amos Littlebird, Odawa Sachem

At 2:30 that afternoon, Louise Westley floated out the door of her home on her husband's arm, leaving Gordon with his grandfather, who was prone with grief, at the house. Not that they were alone; Mrs. Davidson, Mrs. Colons with a pale and despondent Robbie in tow, and Mrs. Molonovitch were there organizing the food (after the next few days, Gordon would never again be able to eat a casserole of any sort) that had been dropped off by sympathetic neighbors and friends. Yes; she just sort of floated out the door on a cloud of tranquilizers. Destination? Rose's Funeral Home to oversee Stan's funeral arrangements. Gordon retreated to his room where he wept again, great hoarse sobs that left him shaken and empty. Exhausted, he slept, and when he woke, it was to the shrill tones of his mother's cries and the thud of something hitting the wall.

"Where is it? I have to find it! Goddamn you, Ben! Let me go!"

She was in Stan's bedroom, struggling to escape the grip of his father's powerful hands. The contents of the cigar box – Indian head nickels, baseball cards, BBs, the desiccated foot of a chicken, marbles – had been dumped out on the floor. The white chenille bedspread, sheets, and pillows were on the floor. So were the contents of all of Stan's dresser drawers. The thought that the mess and chaos would have greatly impressed his brother flickered like heat lightning across the dazed surface of Gordon's consciousness, and was instantly replaced by sorrow so all-consuming that he nearly vomited. *I forgot he is dead. Oh, God. How could I forget that he is dead?*

"I can't find it, Gordon." She was sobbing now, limp in his father's arms, her hair wild, both nylon stockings laddered. Louise Westley looked up at her son with eyes slitted by hours of weeping. "His medal. He has to be buried with his medal and I can't find it."

"But he always kept it in the box if he wasn't wearing it," said Gordon softly. "He never kept it anywhere else. Could it be at the Colons'?"

It was not at the Colons'. Nor was it in any of the closets, drawers, pockets, cups, bowls, toy boxes, waste-paper baskets, garbage pails, or trunks at the Westleys'. It had disappeared, vanished, departed. Much like Stan.

Louise Westley, inconsolable at the death of her son, was now nearly insane with grief. She latched onto Gordon with the mindless determination of a leech; latched on and screamed and screamed that he was all she had left, he was all she had left, he was all she had left. Gordon, at first terrified of this mutation that death had wrought (no straight nylon seams now, uh–uh, no resemblance at *all* to Grace Kelly), finally let himself be swept away by the current of her anguish. Dr. Henderson was yet again summoned to sedate her, but not before she had clawed her face until it bled and ripped out several chunks of her own hair.

"I'm not certain she should attend the viewing, Ben," Gordon heard Dr. Henderson say as he descended the stairs, battered medical bag in hand, once Louise had been drugged into a stupor. Gordon saw Dr. Henderson speaking. He had to be speaking because his lips were moving, but Gordon wasn't hearing. He had heard only *one* word of Dr. Henderson's recitation, and it was a word so infused with horror that his skin began to crawl, and a cold fist knotted itself around his gut. VIEWING.

■ ■ ■

I will not look. I will keep my eyes on this shitty oriental carpet and I will not look. No one can make me look. No one can pull my eyeballs out of my head and focus them like binoculars. Not the prime minister, not the president of the United States, not the queen, not God. I am walking up there with Dad; he can look all he wants, but I DON'T HAVE TO LOOK if I don't want to, and I don't want to. I will not look.

Gordon looked.

His first thought was that Stan was alive, because this wasn't Stan. This *thing* was sort of flat, a deflated version of something that looked a little bit like Stan, maybe, (it was wearing a suit exactly like the one Stan owned), except that Stan didn't wear makeup and this *thing* was definitely wearing makeup. Pancake on the cheeks and forehead, a little bit of pale pink lipstick, powder. (A real Halloween getup! BOO!) But the illusion was slipping away as when you wake up from a dream and can't hold onto it, can't keep it within the nebulous limitations of your mind, until the illusion was gone and all that Gordon had left was the corpse of his little brother.

Then his father said softly, "You've done a good job, Karl. Thank you."

"Louise will be fine when she sees him," said Mr. Rose, his hands clasped behind his back, his entire bearing oozing with funereal pride. He was a big, jolly looking man who looked like he should trade places with Mr. Ligonier and run the Palace. "It's the best way to make peace with losing a loved one, Ben. The best way."

Gordon's father leaned down, put his hands over those of his dead son and squeezed gently. "Stan, my baby boy.

My sweet, sweet boy." He kissed Stan's cool lips and stroked back his dry, blond hair. "It will be a closed casket, Karl. I want Louise to remember him as he was when he was alive. Not like this. Not like this." Tears were streaming down his cheeks. "Do you want to say goodbye to your brother, Gordon?"

Stan would want me to do this, thought Gordon. *I don't know how I know it, but I do.* Gordon squeezed his brother's shoulder, feeling the light bones beneath Stan's jacket. He could barely see for the tears that were filling his eyes. He hadn't kissed Stan since his brother had been a baby. Gordon still kissed his mother, and sometimes he hugged his dad or Grandpa, but he hadn't kissed Stan for years. If he didn't kiss Stan now, though, then he would *never* kiss him again, because the casket lid would be closing in a few minutes. He leaned down and pressed his lips to Stan's powdery forehead. "Bye, Stan," he whispered, his throat thick with tears. "Bye."

"Best wait out in the hallway while I do this," Rose said gently, and so Ben obediently led his son out of the viewing room. It wasn't carelessness that caused Karl Rose to miss a small detail as he tucked the mortal remains of Stanley Livingston Westley away for all eternity. (Rose was not a religious man. In spite of his platitudes, he had embalmed enough stinking bodies to believe only that dead was dead and no formaldehyde-pickled corpses would be rising up on the last day. They would just lie

there. Dead.) Rose was a professional. He worked quickly
and efficiently, and faster than you can say TOE TAG, the
Westley casket was closed. So, it wasn't carelessness.
Rather, it was his annoying far-sightedness that caused
him to miss seeing the single tear – one of Gordon's tears –
that had fallen onto Stan and was now slowly tracking
down his cheek. Gordon would never know it, but he had
left something far more important with his brother than
the lost medal that was haunting Louise Westley's med-
ically altered dreams. For what is a medal compared to a
brother's love?

■■■

By the morning of Stan's funeral service, Gordon had heard
enough crap at Rose's about *other* funerals to last him for
eight lifetimes. (Ernest looked so good. He looked *just* like
he was sleeping.) Ernest, whoever the hell he had been, had
probably looked like road kill à la Max Factor, but Ernest's
wife or mother or whore for all Gordon knew, didn't merit
insulting just because she was stupid and insensitive. Hell
no! She was only one of a mob of mindless imbeciles (Join
The Legion of Cretins and ruin a defenseless kid's wake!)
who had turned up to help his parents mourn their loss at
the funeral home. Gordon's anger, fueled by his heartache,
had smoldered until he was ready to beat someone to death
with a tasteful arrangement of lilies sent by Stan's last

teacher, Miss Evans. But Miss Evans's lilies hadn't deserved it and neither had Miss Evans, who had wept quietly while praying at Stan's coffin.

It was the sight of the other Lakers — accompanied by their respective parents — that had caused his rage to dwindle until all that was left was a bitter smear of anger. And then that was gone. They had said nothing except his name, each of them embracing him, David tall and elegant in finely cut jacket and trousers, Tony and Frank in cheap suits that smelled respectively of mothballs and cedar. With Gordon they had gone to Stan's casket, David bowing his head, Tony and Frank crossing themselves and praying. Then for the rest of the evening they had simply stood with him, an honor guard of his dearest friends. When Mary walked in with her mother and father, Gordon felt none of the sudden rush of sexual longing that always resulted when he saw her. He accepted her whispered condolences and the feathery brush of her cheek against his. In unspoken agreement, the other Lakers took her in charge. Frank, David, and Tony had sat together in the pew behind Gordon and his family during the service at St. Andrew's Anglican Church, and they were here with him now at the graveside.

Gordon glanced at his mother, who was strangely (drugged out of her skull) composed. She had insisted upon seeing Stan in private one last time before the funeral. His father had acquiesced and Gordon, who had

not wanted to see Stan one last time, had waited in the
hall. He glanced again. With her puffy, scratched face and
bloodshot eyes, she now looked like Grace Kelly's grandmother, but her black suit was pressed and her hair freshly
washed and curled. Gordon thought she might actually
get through it. The pallbearers — Mr. Davidson, Mr.
Colons, Constable O'Driscoll, Mr. Floyd, Mr. Garside,
and Mr. Kitchie — began to lower Stan's coffin into its
burial vault.

"No."

Gordon winced as though he had been slapped.

"No," repeated his mother a little louder. "Not yet."

"Steady, Louise," his father whispered. He put his arm
around her and pulled her close to his side, but she pulled
away. Gordon's grandfather stared straight ahead.

"It's my fault!" she wailed. "It was my idea to buy the
scooter!" She began to sob, her face buried in her hands.
"I killed him. I killed my little boy! My baby!"

A wave of hot shame flooded over Gordon. Not that
their friends and neighbors were witnessing his mother's
uncontrolled display, not that some of them were clearly
uncomfortable, but rather that neither his father nor he —
particularly he — could do anything to comfort her. It was,
in fact, his first entirely adult thought, one unmotivated
by his own needs.

Gordon put his arms around his sobbing mother; his
father put his arms around them both, so that she was held

between them. Grandpa continued to stare straight ahead, his attention fixed on something only he could see. "It just happened, Mama," said Gordon, and Louise cried harder than ever, for her son hadn't called her that in such a long, long time. "If it's anybody's fault, it was mine." *I didn't take care of him*, thought Gordon. *God, oh, God! I wasn't there to catch him*. "But, I'm here now for you, Mama. I'm here."

Men who had not cried in years felt their eyes well up. Women pulled handkerchiefs from purses or pockets. The pallbearers, all blinking hard, lowered Stan's coffin into the vault, the service proceeded, Gordon heard Father Elliot's voice and the responses of those present, there was the patter of soil as people tossed handfuls down upon the casket (don't think about it, he's in Heaven, he can't hear it, he's in Heaven), his grandfather saluted Stan's coffin with solemn dignity, and then his father was leading them away. Through the watery lens of his own tears, Gordon vaguely noticed Injun Joely standing some distance off, but then his mother was weeping again and all he could do was murmur, "I'm here, Mama. I'm here."

chapter 13

"There are some defeats more triumphant
than victories."

- Amos Littlebird, Odawa Sachem

The Westley home had been filled with people; cars were
parked all up and down Walnut Street, some in places
where it wasn't legal to park, but not a single parking
ticket would be written that day. Those were the orders of
Leonard Green, the Chief of Police, who had two consta-
bles making certain that no shit-eating, sonofabitchin'
beach crappers (his own rather inventive term) took
advantage of the Westleys' desolation to sunbathe or swim
while parked illegally.

Most of the visitors didn't stay too long. A quick sandwich, a coffee, a glass of wine, as though sips and bites
were the yardsticks of etiquette this afternoon. Gradually,
the house emptied. The Davidsons took Mary home; The
Lakers remained with Gordon – their parents having

driven back without them – until finally, even they called it quits and set out walking into the twilight.

Gordon's mother, who could bear no more, was resting (out cold from a mammoth shot of whatever Dr. Henderson had been pumping into her for the last few days), his father was nursing a beer and talking with Mr. Kitchie, Grandpa was out on the back porch ALONE, having loudly announced that anyone who violated his sanctum would be shown what's o'clock.

Gordon, not wanting to be shown what's o'clock or much of anything else, took off his suit coat, loosened his tie, and wandered through the house, out the front door, and onto the porch. Fireflies drifted about in the still air, tiny chips of brilliance against the shadowy bushes. It smelled of damp earth, and for a moment, Gordon's weary mind was dragged back to his brother's grave. He squeezed his eyes shut and willed the image away. Willed and lost.

Then he heard a soft cough.

Gordon's eyes opened. Someone was standing next to The Chief.

"It's me, Gordon," said Injun Joely. "Just me."

Gordon stepped off the porch and crossed the yard, his good leather shoes becoming slick with dew. The only thing about Joely that he recognized was the man's face. Joely was wearing an old suit of deep blue. A Windsor knotted tie was a dark exclamation point against the white of his shirt. Another time Gordon's jaw might have dropped. *He was wearing this in the cemetery when he was standing there by himself. I remember.*

"Thank you for coming today . . . to the cemetery," said Gordon. "I saw you, but I couldn't . . . my mom . . ."

Joely held up a hand. "You were doing what you had to do. What was necessary." He looked at the dark lake and then at Gordon. "Loss and grief can be the same as defeat if you let them overcome you. Today you rose above your own grief and did the right thing by your mother. I was proud of you yet again, Gordon."

"The second song," said Gordon faintly.

"Exactly so. The second song for courage. My grandfather used to say that grief teaches the steadiest minds to waver, but I do believe that it has begun to teach you a rather different lesson, Gordon."

"I guess. Maybe." He rubbed his forehead, which was beginning to ache. "There's still all kinds of food, Joely. You should come in and have something to eat. I mean, you were at the funeral and everything; you should come in."

Joely shook his head. "No wantum white man's little sandwiches, Kimosabi," and it hit Gordon so strangely that he laughed aloud, the sound of it shocking him.

Joely reached out and squeezed his arm. "It's okay to laugh, Gordon. It's okay." He let his hand fall away, turned and walked off into the darkness, only to pause in the pool of light cast by a streetlamp. Although pitched low, Joely's voice carried, as sound does over calm water. "I am truly sorry, Gordon." Then he was gone.

■ ■ ■

Within a week, it was clear that Louise Westley could not deal with being in her own home, not now anyway. She wouldn't let anyone touch a thing in the ruins of Stan's room. She couldn't walk anywhere near the place where Stan's body had sprawled at the foot of the stairs, keeping well away from it, a small glass of whiskey in her hand, her face averted. She herself made the decision to forgo most of the powerful sedatives Dr. Henderson had prescribed, preferring to experience the aftermath of Stan's death with nerves peeled raw and sluiced with alcohol. Gordon wondered if she was going crazy. He wondered if *he* was going crazy. But when his father announced that he and Louise were going away with the Davidsons to their cottage in Muskoka for a few weeks, and that Gordon would be left under the supervision of his GRANDFATHER, (how's that for a giant step in the nuthouse version of "Mother May I"?), he *knew* THEY had both gone crazy.

chapter 14

"Abandon all hope, ye who enter here."

— Amos Littlebird, Odawa Sachem

"Do it," Mary said. Gordon had phoned her as he did every night.

"Do you really think this is okay? What I'm doing? You know, with Stan and everything," he asked. "I mean, we haven't even gone out walking or anything since . . . since Stan. We've sat around your place or mine while Grandpa and your nanna talk, but —"

"Look. We can take in a show on Saturday if it feels right; Nanna says it's okay. And going out on the boat for the day with your friends doesn't mean you don't miss Stan," said Mary patiently. "It doesn't mean that you aren't respectful of the fact that your brother has died. Your parents went to our cottage with my parents, didn't they?"

"That's different."

185

"No it isn't. They needed to get away. *You* need to get out."

"You don't mind?"

"No." It was a little lie, she would have much rather that he be with her; so Mary was glad he couldn't see her face. "Just have fun. And be careful."

■■■

Gordon's father had a new boat, a 1955 Shepherd mahogany inboard with a nine-foot beam and twin 250 hp Chrysler V-8s. It was absolutely lovely, with a glossy, polished finish. He had always been very generous about letting Gordon take it out, largely because Gordon was as careful with the boat – which had been christened the *West Wind* – as he was with The Chief. And partly because they had always had some sort of boat; Gordon knew his way around them very well. Up until recently, he had been in possession of at least a little bit of common sense, common sense being essential if you were going to come back alive after boating. If Gordon had had a guardian angel, it would have been biting its nails right now, since its ward was planning a day of pandemonium on Lake Erie.

Ben Westley kept his boat at Hanson's Marina, which was situated on the west bank of Laurel Creek, well up past the Queen Victoria Lift Bridge. The building that housed the office of Hanson's Marina was a classic. They don't make offices like that anymore, thank the good Lord. Today people would scuttle their boats before they would enter an office like Hanson's. To get to Fred Hanson's desk (Gordon assumed there was a desk underneath all the french fry containers, greasy paper plates, coffee cups fringed with a coating of mold), you had to pass through THE WORKSHOP.

Once something was put down onto the floor or workbenches of the workshop, it was as though it grew little roots, because it never moved again. Unless, as in the case of an outboard motor, it was dismantled by Hanson and the parts strewn all over creation. Where they would grow more little roots. It was an outboard motor cemetery. THE LITTLE ENGINE THAT ONCE COULD, had metamorphosed into something that was ten feet long. Gordon thought of it as THE LITTLE ENGINE THAT WASN'T EVER GOING TO DO ANYTHING MORE THAN RUST. Aside from the engine parts, there were coils of stiff, aged line, cans filled with the dregs of bottom paint, dead batteries (another graveyard), crushed boat fenders, fly tapes resembling a jungle of insect-crusted lianas (Gordon didn't *ever* look up when he was in there), girlie magazines (Gordon *often* looked down when he passed *those*), cases of beer bottles, piles of Egyptian cotton sails so old that King Tut's lackeys had probably overseen the making of them, and something Gordon categorized as *stuff*, because he didn't have a clue what it was.

Besides working on engines, selling gasoline, and renting dock space, Fred Hanson also rented out one other thing. He rented out people's boats. Permission had not been granted for this enterprise, but Hanson never let a little thing like grand theft stand in his way. This service he provided early in the morning or at night for someone who just wanted to tear around the lake for a while, or who, perhaps lacking a vessel of their own, wanted to go fishing. Hanson had done exactly that with the *West Wind*, and by the time the leather-jacketed renter had brought her back in, there was less than a quarter tank of gasoline left, something that, sooner or later, would cause the Westleys aggravation and with any luck, would get one of them into very deep trouble.

Which was exactly what Lancer Caldwell had been counting on when he paid Hanson ten dollars the evening before. He had waited until around midnight, and then had taken the Shepherd out for a little spin. The urge to mar the boat's smooth varnish with his car keys for that extra touch was maddeningly strong. He wanted to drive the heels of his boots into the gauges, shattering them the same way he would someday smash in Gordon's face, the crunching of his cheekbones and nose making a beaut of a sound. He longed to cut up every one of the cockpit cushions, ripping at them with his switchblade, grunting out Westley's name with each savage slash. But Lancer was nothing if not entirely in control. *The day will come*, he thought. *The sweet, blessed day will come.* So in the end, he simply returned the Shepherd to its slip and had satisfied his longings with a luxurious piss against the boat's hull.

Gordon, unaware that the *West Wind* had been used as a urinal, planned to pick up the other Lakers around two. They would take the boat out on the lake, cruise around, fish, swim, watch the sunset, and then drink beer by moonlight. But then the plan had mutated. Now they would sleep on the *West Wind* – she had comfortable cockpit seats and a small cuddy cabin – then come back in around dawn. And how had they convinced those responsible for their welfare to allow such insanity? Simple. They hadn't. Gordon had told his grandfather he was spending the night with David, who told his parents he was spending the night with Gordon; Tony and Frank told the same semi-truth at home. They *were* spending the night together after all.

The engines purring, they cast off the *West Wind*'s lines at around three, having taken the time to wash her, then stock her with food and drink: chips, a dozen baloney sandwiches, pickles, cookies, Cokes – and contraband cigarettes and beer. It was a beautiful, *powerboat* sort of day, hot and still. There wasn't a breath of wind, not a hint, not a tap. The lake would be like glass.

Gordon kept to the center of the creek, motoring past boats with such names as *Mama's Mink* or *Lady G* or *Italian Galleon* immortalized on their sterns. He glanced down at the gauges, just as he would have had he been driving The Chief.

"What the hell?"

"Problem?" asked Frank who was already into the sandwiches.

"I don't think so, but I filled her up the day before yesterday and look at this thing." He snapped a finger against the fuel gauge, but it didn't budge. "Funny. Dad'll have to take a look at it when he gets back."

Gordon's guardian angel, had it been standing in the cockpit in deck shoes and a blue blazer – they know how to dress in heaven – would have been having an angelic fit. (Angel to Gordon! Angel to Gordon! Now hear this! Turn the boat around; the tank is not full. The tank is almost as empty as your head! Bah! Mortals!)

Gordon motored on, unaware. He took the *West Wind* under the lift bridge, past the fishing tugs that were tied along both sides of the cement seawall, past the two small lighthouses that marked the entrance to the outer harbor, and out onto Lake Erie. He turned sharply to starboard and opened her up, racing toward the beach, slowing down only when he reached the public swimming area and the series of small linked buoys that marked how close any boat could come to shore. Then the Shepherd just puttered along, not so that they could check out the action, but so that the action could check out The Lakers, who were in the nicest boat in Erie View.

"I wonder what the commoners are doing?" said Tony, his mouth stuffed with chips and baloney sandwich. Tony always said that, which was the only reason Gordon could understand him.

"One of them has his mouth crammed so full that he looks like Porky Pig," said David.

Gordon glanced at the gauge again. Had it dropped a little, or was it the same? Same. Definitely the same. By this time the guardian angel's hair *and* feathers would have been standing on end. Sparks would have been coming off its halo. (Use the eyes God gave you, you idiot! IT'S GOING DOWN!) Gordon throttled up, swung to port, and headed straight out onto the lake for about two miles and then he cut the engines. The boat slowly drifted to a stop.

For the next four hours they fished unsuccessfully, swam, ate, belched, waited until they wouldn't drown from stomach cramps, and then swam again, peed in the lake, farted thunderously in the lake (that was Tony; Gordon was surprised he hadn't seen entire schools of fish come floating to the surface belly up), and generally messed around. They also, naturally, talked about girls and doing the old horizontal cha-cha.

Being out in the *West Wind* always reminded Gordon of sex, which might have seemed odd, but did have a certain logic. In their pre-teens, The Lakers had discussed sex all the time, often when sitting together fishing in the creek. They didn't know what they were talking about, but that didn't stop them. Who else was there to talk about it with? Especially if the topic was masturbation and its side effects. By the age of twelve, none of them had gone blind. Their palms were not matted with hair, they were not incapable of fathering children, and they had not gone insane (the last was debatable). By the age of thirteen, the guilt had pretty well disappeared for Gordon and for David. Tony and Frank were in a different pickle, being Catholic.

"You're shitting me!" Gordon had said when Frank had explained. "You have to tell a priest every time you jerk off? Why would a priest want to hear *that*? What do you say?"

"Because it's a sin," Tony had told them, with the bleak resignation of the hopeless. "Catholics confess their sins. You have to confess impure thoughts and jerking off. You say, 'Bless me father, for I have sinned,' and then you recite the sins and tell him how many times you did each one. You say an Act of Contrition. It's a prayer where you sort of apologize and you do your penance. Good as new!"

"If you die with sins on your soul, though, see, and they're venial sins, minor league sins, you go to purgatory for a couple million years or something to pay for the sins. Catholics are very serious about payback. But if you die with *mortal* sins on your soul, big sins like masturbation, you're screwed. You go to hell forever."

"Just for playing with yourself?" Gordon had asked in amazement.

"Yup. Jack off, go to confession, jack off, go to confession. Say your penances. Sometimes it's the whole rosary *and* the Stations of the Cross, but sometimes you get off light with a couple of ejaculations."

"Wait a minute," said Gordon. "Ejaculations?"

"Yeah," explained Frank. "Ejaculations. They're little, short prayers."

"You say ejaculations for having ejaculated," Gordon had mused. "Think about it."

"I would go mental if I was a priest, having to listen to some kid talk about pulling on his dick," David had said. "Remind me never to become a Catholic."

"Do you think girls masturbate?" Frank had asked.

"Naw," Tony had answered. "How can they if they don't have dinks?"

Gordon recalled and would always recall *that* conversation, because the next day had been a Saturday and he had gone fishing with his dad in their old boat. Once well out on the lake, hooks baited, the boat bobbing gently, the sun shining, gulls crying, the morning had dissolved into a nightmare. Why? Because Gordon couldn't swim a quarter of a mile to dry land and escape his father who had chosen *this* day to explain THE FACTS OF LIFE to his son. Gordon had thought he knew at least a little about

sex, and he was right; he had known a little. By the time
Ben Westley was done — the information having been
relayed briskly, frankly, and not without a bit of amusement at the occasional choking sound coming from his
son — Gordon knew a *lot* and he definitely knew that
although girls possessed different equipment, they without
a doubt could masturbate. Which explained the hypo-
thetical link between the boat and solitary pleasure, but
couldn't explain Gordon's unease. For although he was
trying to keep Mary's words in mind and get some pleasure,
any sort of pleasure from the day, it just didn't feel right.

"I love it out here," said Frank. He toweled off with
one of the *West Wind*'s monogrammed towels and pulled
a T-shirt over his sunburned shoulders.

"It's so peaceful," agreed David. He was stretched
across the bow of the boat. "Maybe the sea is my calling.
Maybe I'll join the navy or become a sailor or a commer-
cial fisherman."

"If what you caught today is any indication of your
talent in that area," laughed Tony from the cockpit, "you'd
be in the poorhouse."

Only Gordon was still in the lake, treading water
easily about twenty feet from the boat. He took a deep
breath and dove, having decided to check out the props.

"What's that sound?" asked David. He sat up and
stared at the shore. "Oh. My. God."

Gordon swam toward the Shepherd, the water silky and cool against his skin; small bubbles rose around him and effervesced toward the surface. He was right there, right under the edge of her hull; he turned his head to look at the propellers when she heeled hard, smashing into his shoulder, driving him down. ("Swim!" his guardian angel would have been saying. "Swim or you and I are going to meet face to face sooner than we're supposed to!")

Gordon, his shoulder in agony – he'd have a spectacular bruise for the next two weeks – kicked his legs hard and burst from beneath the water. The sky had been clear only seconds before; now low, dark clouds scudded above them. Driven by the storm, the *West Wind* was turning her stern into the tremendous wind.

"Gord! Get on!" screamed David.

"Start the engines!" Tony shouted.

"Not with him in the water!" warned David. "Grab the swim ladder; Gord, grab the swim ladder!"

Gordon reached, stretched and missed, his fingers just brushing the chrome. "Throw me the life ring! Make it fast; tie it to something! It's in the cabin!" He began to swim after the *West Wind*, as Frank disappeared into the cuddy. "Start the engines! Leave it in neutral!" Gordon shouted. "I'm okay!" *God, please let Frank be quick*, he prayed. *Please. None of them can drive a boat in this. They'll run me over!* And he was bang on about that, because the small waves that the storm's onslaught had created were now one-foot swells and building. ("Hang on, Gordon," his guardian angel would have been saying as it hovered over him, untouched by the wind. "I have it on the most exalted of spiritual sources that the worst is over for now. You'll survive. But you really should pray more often, by the way; not just when you think you're drowning. Keep those lines of divine communication open.")

Frank threw the ring for all he was worth. It was a fight; waves were splashing onto Gordon's face, he could barely see, he was choking. The second his hand grabbed the ring, he could hear The Lakers cheering, screaming, roaring in victory. It was too rough to get the ring over his head, so he locked an arm around it and let himself go limp as they pulled him to the boat. *Thank you, God*, thought Gordon. (Now his guardian angel would have been saying "Isn't a Halleluiah, a *thank you* much nicer than praying about your bone – excuse me, Lord – about the state of your reproductive equipment?")

They helped him up the swim ladder with shouts of good going, Gord, The Lakers do it again, victory, guys!

"Get lifejackets for everybody, put everything inside, and then close up the cuddy!" Gordon shouted. He took the helm, put the gearshift levers into forward and turned the wheel so that the Shepherd was heading into the wind. When the other Lakers were wearing their life jackets, Gordon gave the wheel to David so that he could get his own on. "Stay low. You want to be down in the cockpit when the storm hits!" he shouted.

"What do you mean when it hits?" yelled Tony. "What is this, a breeze?"

"It's a strong blow, but it's not the storm. Those white clouds? That's the storm! This is just a warm-up."

He had been through the same thing with his father once. A low line of white that stretched across the sky was racing toward them. The wind began to moan, then shriek, and when it hit? That was when the *West Wind* ran out of gas.

■■■

The only good thing about a summer squall on Lake Erie, is that it often blows itself out in two or three hours. Three hours isn't a very long time unless your boat is riding every which way up and down waves with you clinging to it, and you are *this* close to being dumped out. It isn't a very long time unless you are vomiting, which they all were. But the three hours did pass, the storm speeding south and away, and very slowly the waves diminished until the lake was once again almost calm.

There are many varieties of seasick people. There is the SILENT SUFFERER, who makes his offerings to the lake gods and carries on; that was Gordon. In between bouts, he had tied each of them onto the Shepherd with line so that if they capsized, they might be able to hang on to the hull or at least stay close to it. There was THE MOANER; that was David. Even when he wasn't being sick, he was groaning and whining. There is HE WHO WISHES HE IS DEAD; that was Tony, who went on and on and on about it. And there is HE WHO *LOOKS* LIKE HE IS DEAD; that was Frank, who had just about dry heaved himself into a coma. It was *so* bad, that if Gordon *had* had a guardian angel, the thing would have been green and looking like an over-grown, winged leprechaun. (This is one of the times that I do *not* regret the lack of a digestive system, Lord.)

"How far offshore do you think we are?" asked Frank, who was finally able to sit up without having to lean over the side. "Very far?"

"I don't know. Pretty far," said Gordon, "but boats come out here all the time."

"Are there any paddles?" asked David. "We could paddle back."

"She doesn't paddle," Gordon told him. "We tried it once and you don't get anywhere but tired. There are flares, though." He went into the cuddy and brought out a flashlight, the flare gun, and a box of war surplus flares. He flicked the flashlight on and then off. "It's about 1:30. I'll shoot one off now and we'll shoot another one off every hour until dawn." *Or I can shoot two off tonight and two off tomorrow night because we are at least twenty miles offshore and this is a big lake. They think we're at each other's houses and won't miss us until sometime today.* He pulled the hammer back on the gun, raised his arm above his head, and squeezed the trigger. For a few seconds the sky was lit, and then darkness closed in again.

"That's it?" asked David.

"That's it," said Gordon, trying to sound like he was in command. "You can see them a long ways off." *What would James Dean do? Sorry JD, but SCREW YOU; what would my dad do?*

"I could have killed you when you wouldn't let us go into the cabin during the storm," said Tony. "I never thought I would want to strangle a fellow Laker."

"Yeah, well. If I had, the cuddy would be filled with vomit, and if we had capsized, we might not have been able to get out. I tried to explain that, but you weren't exactly listening."

"No," said Tony, "puking affects my hearing."

Gordon went back into the cuddy and called out, "My mom keeps throws – you know, blankets – in here for when we go out at night. There are . . . still . . . three sandwiches, two Cokes, and . . . the beers."

"We came out here to drink beer," said Frank. "I'm gonna have a beer, even if I hurl up my appendix."

Gordon, who didn't have many alarm bells, whose alarm system had almost entirely shut down since his parents' departure, felt a small twinge. It might have been caused by his theoretical guardian angel exerting all its celestial mental muscle. (Listen to me, you half-wit. You *don't* mix alcohol and boats. What do you think this is, the HMS WEDDING AT CANNA? Have you noticed that unlike a certain deity, you can't walk on water? No more teenage boys, God. That's all I ask. Get me out of the teenage boys' department and into one where what I have to look out for at least has a semblance of a brain.)

But in reality, Gordon was experiencing one of the last tenuous holds he had on any of the advice his father had given him; most of his father's rules having sifted out of his head since Stan's death, so much silica sand through a sieve. *Don't drink and drive, Gordon, and DON'T operate a boat while under the influence.* In a flash, his brain had devised a suitable syllogism.

Beer, which is meant to be drunk, is on the out-of-gas boat, which isn't going anywhere. Gordon likes beer. Therefore, Gordon will drink beer.

"Okay," he said, coming back out on deck. "We each have a half a sandwich and a beer. Then I'll stand watch for an hour and you guys can sleep in the cuddy. My dad's foul weather gear is in there. We'll take turns wearing it; gets pretty damp out here at night. And there are extra jackets if you want to sleep in one, but you have to leave your life jackets on. David will take the next watch, then Frank, then Tony. You good with that?"

They were good with it, and sat munching and sipping,

not talking until Tony said, "Nobody knows we're out here on the lake right now."

Gordon took a sip of beer. It wasn't very cold. "Someone will figure it out and come looking for us." *Oh, God, I hope Mary tries to call me tonight*, he thought. "In the meantime, we have one last sandwich and we can fish."

"What do we do; burn the boat so we can have a fish fry?" asked Frank. "I don't think so, man."

"I feel like I'm in that movie where those people are in that lifeboat. What's it called?" asked David, racking his weary brain.

"*Lifeboat*," said Gordon. He finished his beer; he had never enjoyed one less. "This is not a lifeboat, guys, it's one of the best boats made, and we're going to be fine. Now get some sleep."

■■■

The night was long, cold, and uncomfortable; Gordon shot off another flare around three o'clock but decided that would be it. If they had to spend another night on the lake, they would need flares. With David standing watch, he slept the sleep of a skipper: restless, listening, any sound waking him. Just before dawn, Gordon gave up. Putting on one of the foul weather jackets they kept for guests, he went on deck to find David sitting there in a heavy fog.

Great, he thought. *Just great.* But he whispered, "How they hangin' Dave?"

"They've shrunk to the size of peas; I'm so damned cold," David whispered back. "How are things in the dormitory?"

"They're asleep, I think. Once the sun comes up it'll burn this fog off. Want to go inside and warm up?"

"Nah. I like it when my balls are the size of peas and have crawled so far up into my body that they are talking to my tonsils."

"You don't have tonsils. We got them out at the same time, remember?"

"All I remember about that is the smell of that lousy ether. That, and the gorgeous nurse with the big tits."

"Get out. You were six years old. No way you were interested in tits when you were six years old."

"Wrong. I have always been interested in tits. Maybe I'll change my name to Mammary Man."

"That's not a very pretty image . . . what's that smell?" They both sniffed the air.

"It smells like a bus," said David. "What would smell like a bus?"

"Tony! Frank! Get up now! Get on deck NOW!"

"Okay, okay, Captain Bligh," muttered Tony as they came out. "Time for our morning flogging?"

"That smell is diesel, guys. A diesel engine. Quiet. Listen." Gordon could now hear it as well as smell it; the distant, low throb of a big engine. He reached into the cuddy and got a tin signal horn. "That could be a freighter." He blew a long, ear-splitting *blat*. "We may have drifted into the freighter lane. Maybe we haven't, but if we have and it's heading right at us — *blat* — we're going to have to jump and swim for it. It'll have to be at the last minute because we have to be sure — *blat*. Swim as hard as you can."

"It's getting louder!" said Frank. *Blat*. "Oh my God, I am heartily sorry for having offended Thee, — Tony's voice joined Frank's in an Act of Contrition — and I detest all my sins and dread the loss of heaven — *blat* — but most of all because they offend Thee my God, who are all good and deserving of my love."

Frank took the horn from Gordon. *Blat*. "Go ahead, Gord." The sound of the engine was very loud now.

It took Gordon a second to understand. "I don't know any prayers like that. I'm not Catholic."

"Yes, you do," said David softly. "We better stand up if we have to jump. Our Father, who art in heaven — *blat* — hallowed be Thy name."

The Lakers all stood and prayed, Frank joining in between *blat*s, the sound of a powerful diesel engine grew louder and louder, Gordon and then the others took off their foul-weather jackets, stepped up to the rail and each put one foot on it, ready to jump.

"I'm scared," said David. *Blat*. "My mom and dad . . . what'll they do if . . ."

"We're all scared," said Gordon. He took the horn from Frank. *Blat*.

"I'm terrified," said Frank. He took the horn back, blew it – *blat* – and passed it to Tony.

"I've never been this scared before," said Tony. *Blat*. "Never." He passed the horn to David.

"Well, at least I'm not alone," David said unsteadily, and he blew the horn. *Blat*.

"You're not alone," said Gordon, his eyes never leaving the fog. "You've got us. The Lakers." He dropped the horn to the deck. "It'll never be able to stop; it's too close. As soon as we see it, as soon as we're sure, we jump and swim like hell. We can do this. It's coming right from there." He stopped speaking then and just stared, strained to see through the fog. "Guys, I just want you to know that –"

"What the heck you kids doin' out here?" boomed Jack Porter as his fish tug the *Better B. Good* came creeping out of the fog. "Got a death wish or somethin'?"

Jack Porter and his triplet sons, Richard, Ken, and Teddie, made the Thibodauxs look like midgets. The triplets were silent but cheerful young men, who rarely spoke since they were excruciatingly shy. Unlike their father who was loud, forward, and seldom shut up. Jack Porter had "opinions" and it was his God-given duty to express them. He was a good man though, and very easy-going unless he had been drinking. When he had been drinking, not only did he believe it was his God-given duty to express his opinions, he felt it was his duty to convince you to take his side, something he did by punching the bejesus out of you.

Jack Porter loved to fight. In particular, he liked to fight in The Laurel Creek Hotel – popularly called the L.C. – the raunchiest of the waterfront bars in Erie View. He had broken more furniture, mirrors, and heads in the L.C. than any other fisherman in town. He was tougher than an entire hogshead of nails, incredibly strong, and had only one eye, having lost the other during the last war when his ship was under attack. When he was in one of the Erie View bars and had to use the men's room, he would take out his glass eye and put it into his drink, just so no one would take a sip from it. Jack Porter was as short on charm as he was on eyeballs.

The relief The Lakers felt was so palpable, it was so plastered all over their faces, that Porter could see it from fifty feet away, even in the fog. They all could have kissed Jack Porter's feet, even though his boots were covered in fish scales.

"We ran out of gas!" Gordon shouted. "Could you tow us in? Please?"

"Sure!" Porter called back. "Toss 'em some line, boys, and pull 'em alongside. You kids hungry?"

David and Tony caught the lines and tied them to cleats while Gordon rigged the fenders. Two of the Porter triplets hauled in the *West Wind*. When the Shepherd was alongside the fish tug and riding easily — the tug was moving very slowly in consideration of both the fog and the powerboat — Jack Porter said, "Come aboard. You look like cats that's been out in the rain all night." He peered closely at Gordon once The Lakers were on the tug, and one of the triplets was easing out the line so that the *West Wind* could be towed astern. "You're Ben Westley's kid, ain'tcha?"

"Yes, sir. I'm Gordon Westley and this is Frank Thibodaux; this is Tony De Salva. David Molonovitch."

"Your ole man does my books. Hell of an accountant. Come on into the galley. Coffee?"

None of The Lakers drank coffee, but at this moment in time, they would have downed hot *anything*, had it been offered. Fortified with milk and sugar, and shortly accompanied by fried egg and baloney sandwiches, it was going down pretty well. For once Jack Porter kept his mouth shut, and so all that could be heard was the rumble of the tug's engine and the occasional burps of The Lakers. Finally, unable to maintain such an unnatural silence, Porter burst out with, "So. Said you ran outa gas, eh?"

Gordon swallowed and said, "Yes. But I don't know why. I mean, we always keep the gas tank full, and I hadn't taken her out or anything."

"Keep 'er at Hanson's, doncha?" When Gordon nodded, Porter laughed shortly and said, "That explains it. Fred Hanson musta rented it out, the sumbitch. Got a key to it for so-called emergency, don't he?"

"WHAT!" Gordon just about choked on his bite of sandwich.

"Yup. See 'em out here alla time; mostly real early or late, mostly. That's what he musta done. Rented 'er out, the sumbitch." Porter was frowning now. "You was real close to the freighter channel. Real close. Coulda been killed, smashed to hell and nothin' ever found." His two oldest sons had been killed at Ortona in '43 and Porter did not look benevolently upon the thought of young lives wasted.

"Jeez," said David softly. "What a jerk."

"What are you going to do, Gord?" asked Frank, helping himself to another sandwich. "Say something to Hanson?"

"It won't do any good to say anything to Hanson," Tony said angrily. "He'll just lie."

"Oh, he's a lyin' sumbitch, that Fred Hanson. Way he keeps that shed a his would gag a maggot. I seen shit-houses looked better." He stopped frowning and smiled widely. "Tell ya what. Tie 'er up alongside my dock when we gets in. Your dad gets home from work, you tell 'im an' he can take it up with the asshole."

"My mom and dad are away for a while, Mr. Porter," said Gordon quietly. "I'm not sure when they'll be back. My mom needed to . . . rest and get away after . . ."

Porter slapped his forehead. "Sorry, son. Sorry for bringin' it up and sorry for your loss. Didn' know they was away." When Gordon nodded, his lips pressed tightly together, Porter said, "Don't matter if it's all summer. You tie 'er up on my dock an' no sumbitch'll touch 'er."

That was exactly what they did. Once the *Better B. Good* was tied at the long dock that served as its slip, the triplets walked the Shepherd around the tug, switched the fenders to the port, and secured the powerboat with lines from the tug.

"I'll get our lines and change them around, sir," said Gordon.

"No rush. No rush," Porter said mildly. "Take yer time. No rush."

"Thanks, Mr. Porter," said Gordon, the other Lakers thank you's following.

They walked back to the marina parking lot where Gordon had left The Chief, not saying much. Once inside the car and heading to Tony's, Frank asked, "Have you gone to confession lately, Tone?"

"No. You?"

"Naw. But maybe I will. I mean, that was close out there."

"Maybe I will, too."

"My mom's been bugging me to clean my room," said David absently. "Really gets to her because she keeps the rest of the house so nice. Guess I should."

"No kidding," said Tony. "It's starting to look like Hanson's office."

No one asked Gordon what he was going to do, what symbolic gesture he would make in thanksgiving for still being alive. It'll be something to do with Stan, though, thought David. I'd bet anything on that.

Good thing he didn't, because David would have lost.

And Fred Hanson? A few days later he would end up minus two front teeth in a spectacular bar fight with Jack Porter, one that Hanson had no clear recollection of starting. What he would always remember, but would never understand, were the words that Jack said just before he dealt the blow that floored him: an' this one's for the kids, you sumbitch.

■■■

The bell over the door of Garside's tinkled when Gordon entered it, the same way it always did, and Mr. Garside looked up from his book and smiled, the same way he always did.

"Hi, Mr. Garside," said Gordon. "How you doing?"

Leonard Garside put a bookmark in his book and closed it. He set it down on the counter and said, "Fair to middling, my boy. Fair to middling. Just a few service medals, if that's what you've come in for."

Just the mention of *those* medals sent a bolt through Gordon's gut. In spite of himself, he glanced down at the case that held them. *Stan*, he thought. "No. I haven't. I want to buy, that is, I want to look at jewelry. At . . ." He cleared his throat. "At rings."

"Well, I do have some nice men's rings here." Garside began to reach into one of the cases for a tray of rings.

"Uh . . . ladies' rings. A lady's ring. For a gift. For a . . . a . . . friend." *Jeez! I sound like I've just learned to talk!*

"Ah!" said Garside, nodding sagely. "A gift. For a friend." He moved to another display case, took out a tray of rings, and put it in front of Gordon.

"I don't know anything about rings, sir. I want something really nice, but I only have twenty dollars. Which are the twenty-dollar rings?"

Young love, thought Leonard Garside. *If I strain this old brain of mine, I can sometimes remember where I put my car keys or my wallet. But I will never, never forget what it was like to be in love with my sweet Margaret when we were just teenagers.* He sighed and said, "Why, for you Gordon, these are all twenty-dollar rings."

Gordon, who could see from the little price tags that they were *not* all twenty-dollar rings said, "I can't do that, sir. I want to pay the fair price."

An honest boy with scruples, thought Garside. *Don't come across those all the time.* He leaned forward and asked, "Do you understand the concept of markup, Gordon?"

"Not really, sir. Sort of, I guess."

"Well, I pay you for a ring. Say, ten dollars. Then I sell it for twenty if you don't claim it in a year; that's how I make a living. Markup."

"Markup?"

"Markup!"

"Okay," said Gordon, "that sounds fair."

"So all you have to do is decide upon a ring. What size is your friend's finger?"

"Her finger?" *Her finger!* he thought wildly. *I know the size of her breasts; they would fit right in the palms of my hands. Maybe I should buy her a brassiere instead of a ring. (I've changed my mind Mr. Garside. Why don't you show me the brassieres that women have pawned recently. Something in a nice shade of puce.)* "I don't know, sir."

"Well, take a guess. About the size of your little finger?"

"Probably."

"What are your friend's tastes in jewelry? What does she usually wear?"

She usually wears a virgin pin, but I can't say that! thought Gordon. "Sometimes a wristwatch. She almost always wears blue."

"What about this? You can't go wrong with pearls, my boy."

What he handed Gordon was an Edwardian ring with three pearls set lengthwise in a row. Gordon tried to get it on his little finger, but it would only go partway. "Are those diamonds?" he asked, squinting at the tiny stones that flanked the pearls.

"They are. Only mine cut and a low grade which lessens the value," fibbed Garside.

"I'll take it. I think she'd like it." *I hope she does*, Gordon thought.

Garside wrote up a receipt, took two ten-dollar bills, put the ring in a small ring box, and handed it to Gordon. "Enjoy, my friend."

"Thanks for your help, sir," said Gordon as he turned to go.

"You don't mind that I just lost over a hundred dollars, do you, Margaret?" Leonard Garside whispered. "Why am I even asking? I'd have to listen to your recriminations for all eternity, had I not sold that ring to that boy. For all eternity." He shook his head. "Young love, Margaret."

■■■

Gordon was just getting ready to leave Kitchie's and head home; he had delivered a load of groceries there and his workday was over. The pool hall was deserted. The only sound was that of the squeegee that Joely was using to wash the inside of the front window. The silence didn't last; a group of six guys that Gordon vaguely knew from school came in, noisy and excited.

"Put pool tables in circle, Kimosabi," Joely whispered. "The Cavalry has arrived."

"That doesn't make sense, Tonto. It's the wagon train guys who put the wagons in a circle when the Indians attack."

"Best Tonto could come up with on short notice." Dropping the stilted dialogue and his Tonto voice, Joely asked, "So. How you doing these days, Gordon?"

Gordon lifted his shoulders. "Okay. My parents are still away, so I'm pretty much on my own until they get back, I guess, but it's okay."

"What about your grandfather?"

"We're looking out for each other."

"That's good." Joely took a step back, examined the gleaming window critically and began to polish it with a cloth. "The elders are a treasure." He glanced at Gordon. "Got a big evening planned? It's Saturday night, after all."

"A movie with The Lakers." He paused and then said, "I'm taking Mary Davidson."

Joely took a rag from his bucket of soapy water, wrung it out, and began to wash the sill. "Very pretty girl, always dresses in blue, beautiful red hair?" He laughed a little at Gordon's surprised face. "This is a small town. She your girl?"

"Yes. Mary's my girl." He took the ring box from his pocket and popped it open. "I just bought this at Garside's. I'm going to give it to her tonight."

"That's a fine ring." Joely took the box from Gordon and turned it this way and that way, so the sunshine sparkled on the diamonds. He gave a low whistle. "She must be really special." He closed and gave back the box, saying, "I'm honored that you've shown it to me. Is she your friend as well as your girl? Can you laugh with her?"

"Why . . . yes, she is," said Gordon. *What weird questions*, he thought, though. "And yeah. We laugh. We have a great time together at the beach and stuff."

"Never took to it." Joely met Gordon's questioning look. "The beach. Swimming. Can't swim a stroke. I always liked to wade, sometimes I would fish with my grandfather in his canoe, but I always wore a life jacket. World's only landlubbing Odawa." He seemed to shiver a little. "That's good, though, that you can laugh together." Joely was washing the sill once more. "Friendship and laughter will outlast everything else in a relationship."

"Did your grandfather tell you that?" asked Gordon, wondering at the disjointed conversation. Swimming, not swimming, rings, laughing . . . jeez!

"No. I've learned that myself over the years. Have fun tonight, Gordon. It's okay to have fun."

■■■

Lancer Caldwell was entirely sober for the first time since he had taken care of the Westley brat. The better part of the last weeks had been spent in an alcohol-induced haze. Lancer did not know the word *ironic*. His circle of friends did not include *ironic* as part of their vocabulary. Something might be *fucking cool*, but it never would be *ironic*. If he had known and understood the word's meaning, and if he had been privy to the inner workings of the Westley household just after Stan's death, Lancer might have found it "ironic" that both he and Louise Westley had sought oblivion in the same manner. But he didn't.

Lancer was totally sober because the day before it had hit him that he had made a rather large error while under the influence. Not the killing; that was a minor point. There wasn't a single shred of evidence, not a solitary witness, not a hope in hell that he would ever be tied to the kid's death. The problem was the medal; he had pawned it at Garside's while drunker than an entire House of Lords. He most definitely had to do something about that, and fast.

■■■

Gordon was the only one of The Lakers who owned a car. David's mother flatly refused to let her husband buy him one. When David had miraculously turned up at the Sand Club, it had been his father's car, a 1955 Buick Roadmaster that he had borrowed. *Borrowed*. An unusual event among the wheelless Lakers. The three of them

stole their fathers' cars on a regular basis; they had had
their dads' keys copied so they wouldn't have to steal
those, too. You just waited until your parents were out for
the night in someone else's car, seeking entertainment
somewhere other than Erie View (nothing like running
into your parents when you and your friends were riding
around in their car), and then you took temporary possession of the vehicle. Simple.

Gordon, Mary's ring in his pocket, was at the moment,
a passenger in David's father's car, his parents having gone
to Yorktown with Mr. and Mrs. Colons to see a play. Part
of Gordon would have preferred to once again be with
Mary in The Chief, but it was important for him to
support David's larcenous endeavors, and so there he was,
on his way to The Palace where he would meet Mary,
who was walking over with Laura.

They were cruising Main, Ace in the driver's seat with
Beery next to him, Wesser and Breezy occupying the seats
behind them. The hellishly hot night meant that the
windows were all rolled down. They would have been
rolled down if The Lakers had been driving in a blizzard,
because Mr. Molonovitch didn't use the ashtray of his car.
He didn't even smoke in his car, and if the car should
happen to have the merest hint of nicotine about its faultless interior, the full force of his suspicion would be turned
upon his son. With good reason. David would be
grounded for the next century. So if you wanted to smoke

in the Buick, you did it with your arm held out the window at a forty-five-degree angle to the car, even if your arm went numb to the shoulder.

"*Godzilla Raids Again*," said David, once he had carefully parked his father's car. They were examining the movie's poster. There was Godzilla breathing his radioactive breath on something that looked like a cross between a gila monster and an enraged hedgehog.

"What is *that*?" asked Gordon.

"It's Angilas," explained Frank. He and Tony had seen the movie last night. "Very cool."

Gordon didn't care if Angilas was cool. He only cared that he had finally talked Mary — Laura would be there with David on their first secret date — into sitting in the balcony with him. The Lakers bought their tickets, Gordon and David buying two for the girls, the transactions going quickly, since it was Betty Williams with her ordinary, everyday breasts, who was in the booth. Frank and Tony went on ahead to secure six seats.

When Mary walked into the theater, it was as though the entire world blurred for Gordon. Sure, there were other people there, but it was only Mary who was clear and sharp-edged in his love-struck tunnel vision. When she smiled at him, his blood turned to something hot and thick, something that made his throat tighten. (Not a boner! Not in the lobby with two thousand people looking at it! Merciful Jesus, make it go away. Was there a patron saint for boners? St. Ralph the Limp?) It did *not* go away, and so Gordon walked toward Mary, hoping the damned thing would be concealed by his movement. When Mary's eyes flicked toward his crotch and then away, an action so quick it might not have happened (but it had), the blood left his loins and made a beeline for his face.

"You look great tonight," he fumbled. "I like that color."

"It's blue. I mostly wear blue; you know that," she laughed. Mary took his arm and leaned close. "You look great too. You know, that's the first time I've seen you in a sportshirt. Pretty sexy."

Gordon, who had only worn the shirt because he was entirely out of clean T-shirts, laundry being even less of a priority in his mother's absence, felt his blood beginning to drain south once more. SEXY. *She thinks I'm SEXY! I will never take off this shirt again!* He led Mary to the concession where David was already paying for his and Laura's popcorn and Coke. By the time Gordon had done the same for Mary and himself, his boner situation was more or less in hand, so to speak. (Thank you, Saint Ralph.)

The front row balcony seats were taken, but Frank and Tony had laid claim to six seats in the second row. Gordon glanced back at Sultan territory. Eddie was making out with Diane Bender and Lancer was, surprisingly, once again in the clutches of Lila Box; all four were going at it with the ardor of breeding minks. It was sort of funny until Lancer began to massage Lila's left breast and Lila gave Gordon a languorous smile, heavy with pleasure.

One that Mary, unfortunately, intercepted.

"Jeez," whispered Laura, in horrified fascination. "Why don't they practically do it in front of us? Jeez."

"They might," whispered David. "They're just getting started."

The lights dimmed and the screen suffered its nightly onslaught of popcorn boxes; they watched the cartoon (Tom and Jerry) and Rocketman (everyone was stunned into silence during *that*). Gordon whispered, "Weird, eh? Bet the movie is even weirder."

"The look she gave you!" Mary hadn't whispered; she had blurted it out. "Lila Box is a . . . a . . . pig!"

Please, Lord, Gordon thought, don't let anyone else have heard. I don't care about myself, but I've got Mary to think about here. He put his arm around her shoulders and whispered, "Forget it. Let's just enjoy the movie."

"SHUT UP DOWN THERE!" yelled Lancer.

"Yeah!" echoed Dutch. "Some people's tryin' to enjoy the show."

"Among other things," whispered Gordon. "Can you imagine making out with the King of the Gobberoonies?" He said it just loudly enough that only Mary and David could hear him. Mary's hands went to her mouth to hold back her laughter, and Gordon felt relief wash over him. It was a good thing the movie was starting, because David had passed Gordon's last remark to Laura, who had passed it to Frank, who had passed it to Tony, and all of them were giggling.

Gordon hoped that neither Tony nor Frank ever wanted to be film critics. The movie was too bad for words. The only good thing in it was when a group of criminals being transported through the city managed to escape. They had stolen a fuel truck and crashed it into an oil refinery. Godzilla, who loved bright lights, came stomping back and was, at the moment, fighting with Angilas, and they were effectively flattening the city. For some reason the action was sped up so that Angilas and Godzilla looked like the Keystone Kops.

But Gordon really didn't care, because about halfway into the movie, Mary snuggled up to him, her head on his shoulder. He wanted very much to kiss her. *Suck away on old Lila Box,* Francis. *Enjoy the lips that have worked their way through just about every guy in Erie View, while I kiss Mary. My Mary.* "Just a sec," he whispered. Mary moved away and Gordon leaned down to get rid of the pop and popcorn so he could hold her more comfortably, which was when a massive gob hit the back of the seat in front of him and Lancer bawled, "I TOLD YOU TO SHUT UP, SAILOR BOY!"

Gordon slowly rose to his feet. "You had better have been aiming for me, Batting," he said, ignoring Mary's pleas for him to sit. "But do it again and you'll wish you hadn't." She dragged him down, Gordon fighting his anger. *Sailor boy!* he thought.

Lancer elbowed Dutch and pointed at Gordon. Dutch began to draw up a wad of phlegm. This would be the mother of all gobberoonies, with enough weight, density and velocity to knock Westley's head off his shoulders. Up it came, Dutch sucking, urging it on. It was at the back of his throat, it was in his mouth, colossal and slick, a veritable Godzilla among gobberoonies. He took aim —

"I have had a complaint." It was Mr. Ligonier. "Spitting!" He descended the steps and examined the evidence, which was clinging to the back of the seat like a gelatinous, gray tree frog. Gordon could see that Mr. Ligonier wished he hadn't. He considered offering him his popcorn box so he could puke in it, but he didn't. "SPITTING IN MY THEATER! THE POLICE WILL BE CALLED! CHARGES WILL BE LAID!" He began the interrogation. "Was it YOU? Was it YOU?"

Gordon waited until Mr. Ligonier's back was turned and then whispered, "I hate to say this, but maybe we should go. He's going to be up there for the rest of the movie." They slipped out of their seats and quickly retreated. But not before Gordon caught sight of Mr. Ligonier screaming at Dutch. "ANSWER ME! Was it YOU?" Dutch appeared to be choking on something. He swallowed very, very hard, turned the color of sour milk, and croaked a small and faint, "No."

David was laughing so hard, tears running down his face, that they all but had to carry him out of the theater. "Can you imagine *swallowing* one of those things?" he asked as they walked to the car. "Can you imagine what they *taste* like?"

"Puhlease!" said Tony, holding up both hands. "My delicate stomach."

"Good thing Godzilla lives in Japan, Tony, because if he ever got a load of your house at Christmas he'd be in your front yard breathing his radioactive breath at it."

"Don't rank out my Christmas decorations," said Tony, trying to sound insulted. "What's wrong with a few lights?"

"A few?" shouted Gordon. "You must have the highest January hydro bill in the universe. I can see the glow at night from my place!"

"This conversation is making absolutely no sense!" laughed Mary.

"If you had lived in Bethlehem the night baby Jesus was born, the Three Wise Men would have ended up at your house!" said David.

"*Away in a manger no crib for a bed; the Little Lord Breezy is out of his head!*" sang Frank.

"I think Godzilla has bad breath and he needs some Ipana toothpaste. The next movie could be *Godzilla Versus Bucky Beaver*," said David thoughtfully.

"Are you guys always this nuts?" asked Laura, giggling when there was a resounding YES! "So how does the movie end? Do they kill Godzilla and that other thing?"

"Angilas," said Frank. "Godzilla horks out a gobberoonie that flattens Angilas, and then —" But he couldn't finish because he was overcome by his own wit.

That, and the fact that Laura stopped them all and asked, "Is this Lancer's car?" It was.

Mary held up a finger and said, "Just a minute." Digging around in her purse, she brought out a lipstick and pulled off the cover. It was a pale pink. Mary had stopped wearing lipstick when she had started kissing Gordon, since it was so messy, but she still carried it around.

Laura, who had not yet begun kissing David, was still wearing lipstick when out of her mother's sight. "If you're going to do what I think you're going to do, Mary, use mine." She took it out and uncapped the tube. "Red Fury."

Lancer's car was parked on a side street about a hundred feet back from where David had parked his father's car. It was deserted, but Gordon felt a distinct spasm of discomfort at the thought of what Mary was going to do. The Sultans might cut him or beat him to a pulp; what could be done to Mary if Lancer were *ever* to learn it had been her, was unthinkable. He took the lipstick from Laura and thought a moment. *Sailor boy? Shouldn't have said that,* Francis. *Think you can touch my dad's boat and get away with it?* He scrawled a message across the hood of the car, another on the windshield and with a flourish, returned the tube to Laura. Muffling their laughter as well as they could – Gordon wasn't laughing; he was now sure that it was because of Lancer that they had nearly been killed – they hurried away from the scene of the crime.

■■■

Eddie Morton couldn't read very well. He had spent three years in the eighth grade until they had finally passed him, just to get rid of him. Besides, the girls were terrified of a classmate who wore a black leather jacket and had a one o'clock shadow. But he was giving it the old college try to decipher the message on the hood.

"Fancies . . . no . . . France . . . no . . .FRANCIS! Sacks . . . no, sakes, nope, sucks. SUCKS! Francis sucks the big . . . the big . . . the big –"

"Twelve, you moron," said Diane.

Eddie started in on the windshield. "Poopy . . . no . . . poppy . . . no . . . POPEYE! Popeye Coldwills? CALD-WELL'S! Popeye Caldwell's . . . pens, pens, no, pennies, nope . . . penis, PENIS! Smalls – your dick ain't small, Lancer – smiles, no smells, SMELLS! Popeye Caldwell's dick smells – why's somebody callin' you Popeye? You ain't no sailor man."

Lancer, who had been slack-jawed with rage, couldn't stand it any more. To see that his penis smelled like a dead moose cock had been written on the windshield of his car was bad enough. That his car's hood had been similarly defiled was worse, but to have to listen to Eddie sounding out the message with all the skill of the world's largest grade oner was too much. "Shut up!" he snarled.

"Who would be stupid enough to do something like that?" asked Lila. "Gonna be a bitch to get off. Looks like Red Fury."

Lancer, himself in a red fury, was scrubbing at the windshield with his handkerchief, while Dutch and Eddie worked on the hood. *Somebody is gonna pay*, thought Lancer, *and I know exactly who*.

■ ■ ■

Laura sat in the front seat between Tony and David, who was so distracted by her closeness that he had nearly run a light. Gordon, his arm around Mary, was in the backseat with Frank. Something hit the rear bumper of the Buick. "Sonofabitch!" yelled David as five heads whipped around. He saw Lancer's coupe in the rearview mirror. Lancer gunned his engine and tapped the Buick again, a little harder. It was all David needed. He slammed his foot down on the gas and the car shot out into the traffic. "My dad'll kill me if he finds a mark on this car!" he shouted.

"Not if you kill us all first and save him the trouble!"
yelled Gordon. He turned around. Lancer had also run
the light and was in pursuit.

"How can he know you wrote on his car?" Mary
asked in horror. "Is he psychic or something?"

*Same way I know he burned The Chief and took out our
boat*, thought Gordon, but he only said, "He hates me and
the feeling is mutual. Step on it, Ace; lose him!"

The Buick picked up speed and so Lancer picked up
speed. That was just about when – doing fifty-five miles
per hour – they passed Constable O'Driscoll, who was
sitting peacefully in his squad car. Lights flashing and siren
howling, O'Driscoll joined the parade.

"Turn the corner and douse the lights! TURN THE
CORNER AND DOUSE THE LIGHTS!" shouted Frank. Laura
screamed in utter terror as the Buick went around the
corner on two wheels and David turned off the headlights.

"He's still on us!" shouted Gordon. "Another corner,
Ace! Another corner and quick!"

"It's kind of hard to see," said David, but he gamely
whipped the wheel over and two-tired it from Sunset to
Chestnut, his own street, and headed for the barn. The
barn in this case, was Mr. Bennett's garage. David's house
didn't have a garage, so his dad rented the one next door
from Mr. Bennett.

Herman Bennett was a shop teacher at the Erie View

District Collegiate Institute. Herman Bennett had been
stealing wood from the Board of Education for about
ninety years. There were planks of oak, maple, cedar, and
pine, enough wood to build a good-sized schooner, and it
was all neatly stacked away in the rafters of the garage.
David turned the wheel with a vengeance and spun into
the garage, but without headlights, it was a bit difficult to
judge exactly where the end wall could be. The Buick
found it unerringly. Just as Lancer and Constable
O'Driscoll screamed past, it smashed into the wall, and
what sounded like about a ton of lumber crashed down
upon it. No one said anything. All that could be heard was
the ticking of the Buick's engine and the occasional
woody creak as a board shifted.

David broke the silence with a weak, "Cripes."

It took ten minutes to get *out* of the car, and it took
The Lakers a half hour to get the lumber back up into the
rafters while Mary and Laura rubbed and polished the
Buick with their handkerchiefs. Someone in the big
parking garage in the sky must have been watching over
them that night, because the Buick hadn't a mark on it;
not one that couldn't be polished out by Mary's and
Laura's hands, anyway.

"I think your father's car should stay put for the rest of
the night," said Gordon. "I think we've just about used up
our good luck."

"Thanks, man," said David, clearly relieved that he didn't have to take the Buick out again. "Come on, Laura. I'll walk you home."

"Walk?" said Frank to Tony. "I don't think I remember how to walk. Do you remember how to walk, Tone?"

"Listen," Gordon said to Mary, once they were alone and strolling down Chestnut. "It's not late, really. Why don't we go over to my place and get The Chief? We can take a drive."

"Do you really think it's a good idea to drive around town after what just happened?" asked Mary doubtfully.

"We don't have to drive around town. We could drive somewhere else." He was trying to sound very blasé, very cool, very *Wesser*.

"What do you have in mind?" asked Mary. "I have to be home by eleven."

"How about Hawk Point?"

chapter 15

"Love is composed of a single soul
inhabiting two bodies."

— Amos Littlebird, Odawa Sachem

Hawk Point wasn't really a point; it was a cliff. In the
spring and fall dozens of birdwatchers, some of them
armed with telescopes powerful enough to see other
galaxies, would gather there. Why anybody would go to
all that trouble and expense to look at something called
the *parasitic jaegar*, was entirely beyond Gordon. Sometimes he and The Lakers would go to Hawk Point just to
watch the Erie View Royal Ornithological Society.

The birdwatchers — Mr. Ligonier was the president
of what Gordon thought of as THE ERIE VIEW BIRD-
BRAINS AND ROYAL PAINS — had no idea how entertaining they were. They had a dress code. Gordon would
have loved to know where they bought their getups just
so that he could avoid shopping there. If he ever got a

gift certificate and went into the store and saw it was filled with the crap the birdwatchers wore, he would garrote the giver.

The birdwatchers dressed like they were on safari; Mr. Ligonier was too charming for words in shorts, knee socks, a vest with enough pockets to hold the contents of a dime store. And a pith helmet. All they needed was African bearers carrying ivory tusks or maybe boxes of popcorn on their heads.

So, Gordon had been to Hawk Point with The Lakers lots of times – during the day. He had never been at night, because you didn't go to Hawk Point at night with your buddies; you went with your girl, because Hawk Point was where you went to park and make out.

Mary stopped on the sidewalk. "Hawk Point?" She knew exactly what went on there. A small thrill, a mix of anticipation and fear, shot through her. "Okay," she said slowly, "but I do have to be home by eleven."

They walked so briskly, that they were nearly running. All the lights except the front porch light were out at Gordon's house; he knew they would be, since Grandpa was over at Mary's playing checkers with Nanna. He opened The Chief's passenger door for Mary, helped her in, and shut it. Taking a deep breath (I can't believe she said yes!), he got in behind the steering wheel and started the engine.

On a weekend, Hawk Point was filled with cars; in cooler weather when windows were rolled up, it looked like a steamy-windowed used car lot. There were a dozen or so vehicles there, windows rolled down, since the night was still warm. His hands slick with perspiration, Gordon parked as far away from the other cars as he could. He turned off the engine, but left the radio playing softly and just sat there. Suddenly he didn't have a clue what to do. He didn't want to just grab her. Well, he did want to grab her, but he didn't want to seem like a sex fiend.

Mary wiped her palms on her skirt as unobtrusively as she could. Why was he just sitting there? She didn't want to scoot over. She did want to, but she didn't want him to think she was loose. All of a sudden, this seemed like a very bad idea. But then, Gordon, nearly desperate for physical contact, reached out and put his hand on her cheek. Mary put her hand over his.

"I love you," he whispered and realized with absolute certainty that he did.

Everybody knows guys will say that when they want to get into your pants, thought Mary. *Everybody. It's like, rule number one of making out.* But this wasn't a guy; this was her Gordon, and she knew he meant it. "I love you, too."

Gently, very gently, he pulled her into his arms and kissed her, at first feeling only tenderness and something that so completely filled the chasm of loneliness that

Gordon's soul had become, that he could have wept. She opened her mouth, her soft, soft mouth just a little and he did the same. Without thought, he let his tongue touch hers. So warm. He couldn't kiss her anymore, then. He could only hold her because he wanted to do far more than kissing.

Gordon gulped hard. "I want so much to . . . to touch you, Mary." He cupped his hand over her breast. "I won't hurt you. I swear to God, I wouldn't ever hurt you."

She put her hand over his and drew back, staring at him, her eyes shining with emotion, "I know that." Mary looked away, her face flaming. "I know that." She faced him now, and it was perhaps the most difficult thing she had ever done, because she could lose him in an instant. If she didn't let him, some other girl would let him. "I'm scared."

"I won't hurt you."

"I'm scared because I want you to touch me. I love everything you do to me, the way you make me feel. . . ." She took a deep breath. "If we do much more, I know I won't be able to stop. It won't just be touching. It's not only guys who want sex, Gordon. It isn't that I don't want you. I do, but I'm scared. Can we just go slower?"

Every sexual inanity he had ever heard spoken ran through Gordon's brain; it was a ticker tape machine of truisms – I'll respect you tomorrow; I'll wear a safe (I don't even *have* a safe; I have never even *owned* a safe). You won't get pregnant; I'll pull out before I cum, (right; I have the self-control of a billy goat). If you won't let me, it means you don't really love me (I am making myself sick, here), if you don't let me I'll be in horrible pain, that's how much I need it. (I am already in horrible pain; can a boner kill you?) He was no longer himself. He was nothing more than his penis and testicles, which were aching so badly, he felt faint. His first impulse was to grab Mary's other breast, no matter what she was asking of him. (That's why you have *two* hands, Gordon, because she has *two* breasts.)

But, then Gordon did something that perhaps no other teenage boy in history had ever done or would do. It was an act so unique in young male sexuality, that it was beyond time and space. If it was ever discovered by, and recorded by future anthropologists, they would win the Nobel Prize for Implausibility and get their own stars on the Sexual Walk of Fame.

Gordon took his hand away.

He loved her that much, and he was that afraid of losing her. Gordon could not imagine getting through a night without the sweet and perfect knowledge that Mary was his girl. That's how much he loved her.

"Okay," he said hoarsely. "We go slower. I can still kiss you, can't I?" Gordon didn't wait for an answer. He pulled her into his arms and kissed her with a passion that left them both breathless. "Better get out of here before I change my mind."

"You! What about me?"

"Slower, right? Just slower?"

"Yes. Just slower."

"Wait!" said Gordon. In the ardor of the moment he had nearly forgotten. "I have something for you."

"Uh-huh. I bet," said Mary with a short laugh. "You did say slower."

"No. Really." He took the ring box out of the pocket of his jeans and gave it to her. "I . . . just wanted to give you something. Just something nice." He waited, palms sweating, while she slowly opened it and then just sat there. "If you don't like it . . . I mean, I didn't know for sure –"

"Oh, God! I love it!" She took the ring from the box and handed it to Gordon. "You should put it on my finger, though," she insisted, holding out her left hand.

Gordon slipped the ring on her finger – it fit perfectly – and without even planning to, asked her, "Will you go steady with me, Mare?"

"Yes. I'll go steady with you; how can I not? And look; it's a perfect fit. It's beautiful. Thank you." She put her arms around him and kissed him deeply. *He gave me this because he loves me*, she thought, *not because he wants to get into my pants. I love him back; maybe I've been wrong. Maybe it would be okay to go a little further – not all the way, but just a little further – if we're careful.*

With that she gave herself over to Gordon and he could feel the difference. Within a few minutes all of their senses were focused on nothing except what they were doing. They didn't hear the low and menacing rumble of a car engine or the thunk of its door when it was carefully opened and then shut. They didn't hear the slow, measured bootsteps or the popping of his knee joints when Lancer crouched down next to The Chief. But Lancer heard, and when Mary moaned out Gordon's name, his fingers froze on the valve stem of the right rear tire, and he squeezed it so hard that his fingers bled. His anger, fed by the lipsticked insults, distilled into something close to a madness that would have made it very easy to push the Pontiac toward the edge of the cliff and over it. But no. Not tonight. Tonight he would settle for flattening a couple of Sailor Boy's tires.

■■■

Much later in his room, Gordon lay in bed balanced on the soft cusp between wakefulness and sleep, definitely leaning toward sleep, but not yet ready to give up. Not wanting to, he started to think about the flat tires and how he had been able to change only one of them. Of how the front right tire was now destroyed from driving on it, and of how he couldn't get the idea out of his head that Lancer was somehow involved, because if it was bad, it involved that asshole.

He pushed Lancer to the darkest corner of his mind (actually, he pushed him right out the second storey so that the creep did a pratfall) and concentrated on Mary and what they had done tonight. God, it had been wonderful. He turned on his side, yawned, and gave in to his weariness. *What a day. She loved the ring. Have to tell Mr. Garside that. Tired.* His breathing began to slow. His conscious and unconscious minds flowed across each other, water and oil mingling for an instant. He saw Garside's. The glass display case. The medals, two service medals, one with deep scratches.

His eyes opened and Gordon sat straight up in bed. Had that been Stan's medal? Had it been scratched or was he *willing* it to have been scratched? And if it was Stan's medal, how had it got into that display case? He hadn't a clue, but he knew who could tell him.

■■■

"This is an unexpected pleasure, Gordon. Two visits in two days. Did I order groceries and forget about it?" asked Mr. Garside. It was Sunday, so the pawnshop wasn't open for business, but it was *open*. Mr. Garside liked the company.

"No, sir. I just came to look at the WWI service medals."

"Medal. There is only one."

Gordon refused to give in to the way his spirits wanted to plummet. (Sorry, guys; plummet without me; I'm on a mission here.) "But there were two yesterday morning. I'm sure there were two." (I'm not sure; I have never been less sure of anything in my life, but please God, let there have been two.)

"Yes. There were two."

"Who redeemed the other one?"

"No harm, I suppose. Lancer Caldwell. He said it was his grandfather's and he deeply regretted having gotten drunk and pawning it at all. So badly scratched as it is, it isn't worth much, except for the personal value it has for Lancer. Some say he's a thug, but I have to admire him for his sentiments."

It was at that moment that Gordon knew Lancer had killed Stan. He didn't suspect it, he didn't have a theory; he knew it. There was no point in telling his parents when they came back, neither was there any point in confiding in the police. No one would believe him, since there wasn't any evidence. Even if the medal could be produced, there was no way to prove it was his grandfather's, what with Grandpa having filed his name off. None of that lessened Gordon's certainty. Lancer had killed Stan and for that, Lancer was going to die.

chapter 16

"Practice, the master of all things."

— Amos Littlebird, Odawa Sachem

Gordon was a crack shot. He'd had a BB gun at the age of seven; Stan had inherited the BB gun at the same age, Gordon having graduated to a pellet gun some years before. He and David hunted for rabbits and pheasants in the fall, and for squirrels in the winter on sunny days when they were out of their nests; during the rest of the time the gun was in a case on the top shelf of his closet. You could kill small game birds with a pellet gun; you could take down a good-sized cottontail and maybe even a jackrabbit. (They didn't kill jacks; you couldn't eat a jackrabbit because they were too stringy, and they only shot what they could eat.) But you couldn't kill a person with a pellet gun unless maybe you were very close and you shot him in the eye.

But you could kill someone with a Luger.

Gordon, having made sure Grandpa was asleep in his rocker on the back porch, sat on the edge of his parents' bed, his father's Luger in his hands. When he had been in the fifth grade, he had done a report in history with his father's help; it had been a comparative study of the Luger, the handgun used by German officers, and the Browning Hi-Power; what the Canadians had used. It was the only D he had ever scored and *that* was because of his teacher, Mr. Logan. James Logan, a quiet bachelor, had been an airman. In 1944, courtesy of Adolph Hitler, he and sixty-seven other airmen, twenty-five of them Canadians, had spent four months in Buchenwald, a camp for social misfits. Although none of the misfits — Jews, Jehovah's Witnesses, homosexuals — were spared the inventiveness of Nazi atrocities, it was his memories of the children and their violated, mutilated childhoods there that plagued Mr. Logan. It was why he drank himself into a stupor most nights; for James Logan it wasn't lights out but rather, pass out.

James Logan did not take kindly to anything or anyone German. Gordon's report had been objective and had favored neither weapon, but the very fact that he had written about a Luger had earned him a D. Gordon's father had gone to school to talk to Mr. Logan. His father never told him what had been said, but Mr. Logan regraded the report. C minus.

His father had also shown Gordon an old copy of *Life* magazine, one that contained a pictorial titled *The Living Dead of Buchenwald*. What he saw – piles of bodies, people so emaciated that they looked like walking skeletons – haunted Gordon's dreams for weeks. Nothing was haunting James Logan's dreams these days. He had committed suicide four years ago.

Gordon remembered how to fire the gun, but he needed a refresher. Not that he *had* ever fired it, but his mother kept *everything* he and Stan did at school. She had shelves of special boxes, some for him and some for Stan; in fact, she had already bought the boxes for this coming school year. That Stan's would remain forever empty, brought a hard lump to Gordon's throat. It was in his grade five box that he had found the infamous and excruciatingly detailed report. He went over it and felt the old drill slip into place. Then he loaded the Luger.

"To load," he read aloud, "first press the magazine release button on the left beside the trigger." He did it. "Pull the empty magazine out and hold it firmly in your left hand." Done. "Pull down the stud attached to the magazine platform. Insert the cartridges one at a time." The gun loaded, he chambered a round and held it in his right hand, his arm extended.

When the telephone on the nightstand rang, it scared Gordon so badly that he fumbled the Luger – he looked like he was on the *Ed Sullivan Show* juggling it — and nearly dropped the gun, something that elicited a flashback to the first time he had touched the Luger, convinced it would come to life and blow his brains out if he handled it. Gordon pulled down the Luger's safety lever, set the gun on the nightstand and picked up the phone.

"Hello?"

"Gordon, it's me." It was his dad.

"Where are you?"

"Huntsville. Your mom wanted to go to church this morning, so we all came in."

"How is she, Dad?"

"Coming along, son." *Drinking* way *too much, using language she's never before used in her life, has lost fifteen pounds, can't sleep unless she goes to bed with half a bottle of whiskey in her*, thought Ben Westley. "Not so bad, really. We're going to come home this Friday. Labor Day weekend and everything; your mom wants to be there when you start school."

"Okay." *I know what happened, Dad. It wasn't an accident. Lancer Caldwell killed Stan and took his medal. So, you just stay up there, Dad; stay up there as loooong as you want and don't worry about a thing, because I will take care of everything.* "I'll tell Grandpa."

"How's he doing, son?"

"He's okay, Dad. He's pretty much hanging out with Mrs. Warner every night."

"Good God!"

"She's pretty nice, actually." *Nice enough to let me date Mary.*

"And how are you doing, son?" *He'll lie*, thought his father. *He won't be able to admit missing his brother.*

"I really miss him, Dad."

"Me too," said Ben Westley, shaken by his son's honesty. "Me too."

"Don't worry about me, Dad. Just take care of Mom." *And I'll take care of Lancer.*

His voice thick, unable to go on, his father mumbled a goodbye and hung up.

"Bye, Dad," said Gordon to the dead telephone.

He hung it up and put the Luger back into his mother's brassiere drawer. If he was going to do this – and he was – he had to have a plan. He couldn't carry the Luger in a holster and he couldn't keep it permanently in the glove box of The Chief. He wasn't concerned about being caught with the Luger; he was concerned about being caught with the Luger and having it *taken away*, which would mean he wouldn't be able to kill Lancer with it. So, he had to have a plan, a foolproof plan for catching Lancer alone. Until then, the Luger would remain where it was.

chapter 17

"If you wish success in life, make perseverance your bosom friend, experience
your wise counselor, caution your elder
brother, and hope your guardian genius."

— Amos Littlebird, Odawa Sachem

That Friday, the still air an unwelcome blanket against his sweating skin, Gordon untangled himself from the sheets and crawled out of bed. A pair of swim trunks lay on the floor keeping company with much of the rest of his summer wardrobe. He pulled them on and then made his way through the silent house and onto the beach.

The quiet here was different. Incomplete. You thought it was silence at first, and then came the soft whoosh of small waves, a single gull's mournful cry, the insistent morning song of robins. Not that it was morning yet; the sun wasn't up, but already the clouds, large cumulus clouds riding low on the horizon, were beginning to glow as though heating up.

For about a half hour Gordon walked west, facing a day that would surely be a nightmare. His father's phone call had rasped away at the thin nacre that had formed around his waking moments, leaving him exposed to what his parents' return (his mother's intense and naked grief) might bring.

And he wasn't sure how well he could deal with that.

A light breeze skittered across the lake's surface, raising patches of tiny cat's-paws. Gordon's skin pimpled with goose bumps and the hair on his forearms lifted, but it wasn't because of the coolness of the morning or its teasing breeze. It was a sound, a distant singing or moaning or something. He couldn't be certain what it was.

Just ahead where the beach curved into a small bay, a huge uprooted poplar lay half in and half out of the water. You either had to climb over it, or wade out and around the branches. Gordon slowly and soundlessly waded out, the water rising up to his knees, then to his thighs. That's when he stopped, because not only did he hear the sound again, he could see what, or rather, *who* was making it. About fifty yards away was a man, one whom Gordon did not recognize at first because the familiar backdrop of pool tables, spittoons, soiled fedoras, and *Eau de Kitchie's* was absent.

It was Injun Joely.

His back was to Gordon, his arms were raised, his legs were apart; his head thrown back, he was a human X backlit by the molten sunrise. And he was praying. At least Gordon thought that was what he was doing, even though he couldn't make out any words. Although he couldn't put a mental finger on why, he was pretty sure that Joely would not want anyone to see him here. It looked so lonely. *He* looked so lonely.

Gordon carefully waded backwards until Joely's silhouette was once again hidden by the downed poplar. He walked back up the beach, staying close to the waterline, his footprints disappearing as waves washed up and over them. Once home, Gordon stopped and looked back. An odd twinge rippled through him. *Stan*, he thought. *Stan looked like that when he used to sprawl on the sand, his arms and legs spread out, making sand angels.* Gordon squeezed his eyes tightly shut. *No. Put it away. Think of something else. Think of Mom and Dad. Get that old Westley brain under control, man*, he thought, as he went over the list of chores he had to do.

But Gordon was no more the master of his brain than he was the master of any other part of his body. His brain just chugged right along, and all morning the X-shaped images of Stan and Joely – one dark and alone, one sunlit and laughing – rose in his mind as he worked.

Gordon spent four hours cleaning the outside of the house that day. He hadn't touched the spider sweeper since Stan's death. There were a thousand things that reminded him of his brother: the occasional marble he

had found under a chair, the stupid TV shows that Stan
had favored. Where Stan and Robbie, if he had been over,
would watch "The Mickey Mouse Club" wearing their
Mickey Mouse hats. (You look like the world's largest
rodents, guys; want some cheese?) "The Howdy Doody
Show" whose grotesque marionettes resembled escapees
from "Pinocchio Meets Frankenstein." (DOODYVILLE,
Stan; when are you and Robbie moving there? Sounds
like the land of turds and farts to me, Stan. And FLUB-A-
DUB. What the hell *is* that thing? Then there's old MR.
DOODY himself, Stan. Look at those teeth! I bet he could
chew through a wall.)

It was the spider sweeper, for some strange reason, that
elicited the most painful memories. It wasn't that Gordon
regretted teasing his brother so enthusiastically; it was that
he would never be able to tease him again. And so the
spider sweeper had simply hung there, the spiders running
busily rampant until the house looked like it was haunted,
which, in a sense it was. Stan's presence lingered everywhere. Gordon couldn't protect his mother from *that*, but
he could do his best to make certain the house looked as
normal as possible for her return.

Gordon did not realize how much he had missed his
parents until, standing on the front porch that afternoon,
he saw Ben help Louise out of the car. Until he saw her
enormous eyes in the pale, thin, oval of her face. His
parents had grown smaller, somehow. They had lost

weight, but there was something else missing: they were diminished, as though Stan's death had leached an indefinable substance from their very bones.

His mother hugged him. It was not the desperate clinging he had feared. (Please God, don't let her still be like that.) Instead, he could feel in her embrace a calmness he had not expected at all.

They – his father, mother, and grandfather – wept. Gordon did not. Crying just ripped the scab off the very deep and unhealing wound of his loss and poured salt onto it. The next tears he cried would not *be* for Stan, they would be on Stan's *behalf*. The next tears he cried would be tears of joy when Lancer lay dead at his feet.

■■■

Late that night, Gordon lay on Stan's bed, as he had done many nights during the last weeks, stretched out on top of the covers, his hand on Stan's battered old Teddy bear. Most nights he would get up and go back to his own bed after a while. Sometimes he fell asleep, only to wake in the morning, disoriented and gritty-eyed, the Teddy bear in his arms. No. He didn't cry anymore. Crying was for weaklings; crying wouldn't bring Stan back. Crying wasn't part of the superb act of revenge that rarely left his mind.

If Gordon had been able to have an out-of-body experience just then, if he had been able to float over the

bed, as some say the soul does upon leaving behind its
corporal husk, he would have seen himself curled on his
side, asleep, the Teddy bear clutched to his chest. He
would have seen a young face profoundly etched with
sorrow. And he would have seen the tears that each night
he unknowingly wept for Stan.

chapter 18

"All good things must come to an end."

— Amos Littlebird, Odawa Sachem

"So, this is it, Gordon," said Injun Joely. He was brushing a pool table that really didn't need brushing, just on the principle of the thing, sweeping up because he liked to keep busy. His brush whooshed along the felt, a soft accompaniment to the clacking of pool balls.

"Yeah," answered Gordon with disgust. The incongruous image of Joely on the beach flashed through his memory. He chalked his cue and blew on it. "This is it and it is definitely the worst."

After today — Labor Day — Gordon's summer life would be shelved for yet another year. Back to school. No more weekday evenings out. How he would survive without even the possibility of being with Mary each night was beyond him, but he was letting nothing spoil

today. This would be their last date of the summer, and he
wanted it to be superb.

"Labor Day was the worst when I was a kid, Gordon.
It will always be the worst."

"Well, I'm making the best of it. A few games of pool
with the guys, then an afternoon at the beach." No
boating, though. Gordon's father had been furious when
he heard about the *West Wind*. Gordon could have taken
the boat out, since his father's anger had been for Hanson
alone, but the memory of that escapade was still very
much with him. "It's a great day out there, even if it is
Labor Day. We'll swim and later on, have a hot dog roast."

"Swimming," said Joely. "Not for me."

"That's right. Tonto can't stand to get feet wet."

"You got it, Kimosabi. Dry land's the place for this
wagon burner."

Tony finished racking the red balls and Frank had
spotted the coloreds. The Lakers stared at the pool table
with the intensity of soldiers eyeing a battlefield. Gordon
was going to break. Hand on the wooden edge, pool cue
balanced on his knuckle, he concentrated, drew back the
cue, broke the balls, and made a complete disaster of it,
since he hadn't played all that much pool recently. David
and the other Lakers howled with joy at the mess.

"Off my game, I guess," Gordon said sheepishly.

"True love'll do it every time," said Tony, squinting at
the balls. "Complicate your life. Screw up your game."

"Gotta play it cool," advised Frank, leaning on his cue. "That's me. Cool is my middle name."

"Right. This red in the side pocket," laughed David, taking the next shot and missing. "Shit. You're about as cool as those long-legged underpants they sell for old ladies."

"My man, I'm so cool, I could walk on lava if I wanted to," said Frank. "I'm so cool that I don't sweat, so cool that Elvis would beg to wash my car. And what have you been up to recently, David, if you're an expert on old-lady underwear?"

"You don't have a car," Tony reminded Frank. "Red ball in the number one pocket." In it went. "Black ball in the corner pocket. Shit."

"Minor point. I'm so cool that if I wasn't me, I would sincerely wish I was. I would pay to be me."

"Hey!" said Tony. "I finally made up a punch line for my secret password knock-knock joke. Okay. Knock-knock."

"Whore's there?" asked David.

"Ubangi," answered Tony.

"Ubangi who?" asked Frank.

"Ubangi? YOU BETCHA!" said Tony triumphantly.

"That is so bad, man," groaned David, slapping his forehead. "That is so-o-o-o bad."

Gordon listened to his friends' good-natured teasing, punctuated by muttered expletives from other tables, and

the occasional *ping* when an older man used a spittoon.
Joely walked by him, a full spittoon in his hands, heading
to the bathroom to empty and rinse it. How could he
stand emptying those things? In fact, how could he stand
living in a pool hall? How could he stand cleaning other
guys' hats, the bands all greasy and rank? Gordon hoped
he never had to live like Joely did, a thought that made
him ashamed of himself, because Joely, on his way back
with the clean spittoon, was giving him an unanticipated
smile. Gordon blushed like a girl.

"Thinking of Mary! Thinking of Mary!" chanted
Frank.

"Beats thinking about Charlene Cheyenne," said
Gordon, trying to recover his lost poise.

"Best bone –" Frank glanced at Mr. Kitchie, thought
better of commenting on the fact that Charlene was the
best boner material in Erie View, and finished with, "I like
Charlene. Meeting her at the beach today, matter of fact.
Refreshments courtesy of our fine froggy friends from
Quebec."

"Great!" said David, saluting the world with his bottle
of Coke.

"Gonna be some party! Look, I gotta split," said
Gordon. He paid Mr. Kitchie for his part of the game.
"Have to get home for lunch."

Gordon returned his cue to Joely, who examined the

tip, found it just met his standards, and placed it back in the rack. "Nothing like good lunch, Kimosabi," he said. "Unless it good breakfast."

"Tonto, if you had been eating what Kimosabi had been eating up until his parents came back . . ." Gordon faltered. He sounded pathetic. Joely hadn't had a home-cooked meal in years, probably. Not even a sardine omelet. "I promised my mom I would be home for lunch," he said quietly.

"Gordon," said Joely. "You're a good kid. Don't be ashamed of it. My grandfather used to say that the Creator could not be everywhere, and so He made mothers. I can't remember my mother; you always will. You'll always have the memories of those you love."

For a moment, Gordon didn't know what to say. It was the only personal thing Joely had ever told him, except for the grandfather Indian wisdom stuff. And it was getting dangerously close to the subject of Stan. "I thought you were going to tell me about the third song there, Joely."

Joely smiled. "Kimosabi's on his own for that one. Indian sidekick no can help."

Gordon laughed, relieved that the conversation had shifted into safer territory. "What good are you, anyway, Tonto? Better tell quick; Kimosabi must mount up and ride into the sunset."

"Some days bear eat Tonto; some days Tonto eat bear. Most days Tonto prefer ham on rye."

■ ■ ■

At home, The Chief parked in the shade, Gordon walked around the house to the back porch. His dad and grandfather were sitting there, each with a plate — sandwiches, deviled eggs, and pickles — on their laps. They had their mouths full, so they only nodded a greeting as he passed them and went into the house.

His mother, who was seated at the kitchen table, stood when he came in. Louise Westley gave her son an unsteady smile and said over-brightly, "There you are!" When Gordon leaned down to kiss her cheek, he found himself locked in a hug. "There you are!" she said again.

"Here I am!" he said gamely, the horrific memory of his mother screaming, "You are all I have left!" bright and painful in his mind.

"It's okay, Mom." He hugged her hard. "Hey. This looks really good. You're eating too, aren't you? I mean, you're not gonna make me eat alone, are you?"

"I'm not very hungry, dear," said his mother.

"I'm not eating alone," said Gordon quietly. *She's so thin*, he thought. *She barely eats anymore.* "You have to have something."

His mother picked at an egg salad sandwich, watching Gordon who was trying not to wolf his down. He probably could have stuffed the whole thing in his mouth and she wouldn't have said a thing. Stan's death had dissolved a brittle layer from his mother's personality, a layer he had not ever really noticed until it was gone. His dad had told him that he believed his mother had simply taken stock of what she had left – they both had. The golf club wasn't important, the house wasn't important; only their family was important. It would take time for all of them to come to terms with Stan's death, but they could do it if they stuck together. Gordon was trying very hard to live with that stocktaking, but the intensity of his parents' love was, at times, entirely overwhelming. What had been sometimes absently sprinkled on him, his grandfather, and Stan, was now poured over him until there were days he felt he was drowning in affection.

"I thought you might like a picnic, so I made one for you," she said. "I assume you're picking up Mary. Do you have money?"

Neither Gordon's parents nor the Davidsons had the slightest clue of what had gone on between the two of them during the last weeks. It was with a bit of guilt – but not much – that he had asked his mother and father for permission to speak to the Davidsons about starting to date Mary. They had agreed; he knew they would (Dad,

can I borrow your car and drive it off the cliff at Hawk
Point into the lake? Why sure, son. Just be home by
11:00.), since they were giving him anything he asked for
these days. Not that he was abusing it. *That* would really
have created guilt.

And Mary's parents, Mrs. Davidson a bit grudgingly,
had agreed, since Nanna had assured them that Gordon
was a fine, young gentleman. To Gordon, with Mary
standing next to him in mute horror, Edith Warner had
later said, "Good thing she didn't come back from getting
air that night at the Sand Club with her skirt stuck in her
underpants. You would have been snookered, kiddo."

"Yes. I'm picking her and David and Laura up. And I
have money for Denison's. I won't be home for dinner.
Remember? We're staying for the fireworks and cooking
hot dogs."

"I remember. It makes me think of that day you took
Stan and Robbie to the beach," she said wistfully.
Gordon's eyes shot to his mother's face, but there were no
tears. "He was so excited."

"We had a good time that day."

She put a hand over her eyes; when she took it away,
Gordon saw that the tears were coming now. He reached
across the table and held both her hands.

"I just wish I had been able to find his medal for him,
Gordon. That I could have done that one last thing for
Stan. If I could find it now . . ." Her voice fell away.

"I know," he said gently. *I am going to take care of that, for you, Mom*, he thought. *I just know that Lancer has Stan's medal, and before I kill him, I'll make him tell me where it is. I'll get it for you, Mom. For Stan.*

Louise Westley wiped her eyes, sighed shakily, and tried a smile. "Well! You just finish eating your sandwich and I'll pack up the picnic basket luncheon!"

"Is it a *healthy* lunch, Mom?" The words were out of his mouth before he could really think of what effect they might have, but his mother surprised him.

"Of course it's healthy." She stood and lifted her chin. "I'm your mother, dear. I am incapable of making you an unhealthy lunch, no matter what."

That's my mom, thought Gordon. Maybe things would be okay again in time. Maybe.

■■■

Mary was in the change house adjusting the straps of her new bathing suit, one that her mother would never have allowed her to buy, much less wear. But her mother didn't need to know everything. She took a deep breath and picked up her beach bag. "I wonder what Gordon will think?" she said under her breath.

What Gordon thought, was that Mary had lost her mind and was in her underwear. It took a few seconds for his astounded and hormone-driven brain (Dear God! She has gone crazy, but she looks so good!) to register what he was seeing.

"You bought it!" squealed Laura.

It was a two-piece white number that although perfectly modest, showed far more than Gordon had seen of Mary's body. *That's cleavage*, he thought wildly. *Cleavage! And could it be . . . yes; praise the Lord and pass the Coca-Cola! A little bit of breast tops! And her navel! In the sunlight, breast tops and her navel!* Mary had acquired a light tan over the course of the summer, but the tops of her breasts and her midriff hadn't had the benefits of sunning. They were creamy and pale. It struck Gordon that he was seeing what color the unrevealed portions of her body actually were. Just about the same time it struck him, that everybody *else* was seeing it too.

"Do you like it, Gordon?" she asked. *He doesn't like it.*

"I like it. I really like it!" said Gordon enthusiastically. *I hate it*, he thought. *If I was alone with her I would ADORE it. But I'm not, and I HATE it that everybody else is seeing what I've been wanting to see when we are alone.*

"It's a bikini, right?" asked Gordon.

"No. It's just a two-piece. That? What Marla Jenkins is wearing? *That's* a bikini."

Butsy Lane had all but fallen off his lifeguard chair. Dutch Batting and Eddie Morton, who looked like beached whales in *their* bathing suits – or sartorial vegetables, since they were wearing leather jackets over them — were practically slobbering. Gordon had never been so thankful for the existence of Marla's tits in his whole life. Encased in a beige, crosshatched fabric bikini top, they resembled massive ice-cream cones. They were truly bizarre. BUT! Marla's cones had diverted most of the attention from Mary. And so, Gordon allowed himself the luxury of liking Mary's suit.

"You look great," he said. "That color looks good on you."

"White?" She flicked off a few grains of sand that had dared to be on her suit. "They say white sets off a tan."

Gordon didn't know who *they* were, but he did know that it wasn't only the tan that Mary's white suit was setting off. "Are you going to get it wet?" he asked. "I mean, it's new."

"You bet I am, and you're coming in with me."

They swam and laughed and listened to rock and roll, ate their lunches savoring the final day of summer. Laura with David, Charlene with Frank, Tony alternating between Susan Welch and Kathleen Boroughs, they reveled in their last hours of blessed freedom. Eventually, Gordon was standing in water that reached to his chest. With her head on his shoulder, Mary was floating on her back, supported by his willing hands, the length of her lovely body stretched out in front of him.

"You okay?" she asked him turning her head slightly. "You're so quiet."

"Just thinking about . . . things."

"About Hawk Point?"

"How could I forget?" Gordon laughed, trying to make it sound casual. That night was burned into his memory, a sexual brand so vivid, it was as though he was wearing glasses with the image of it etched upon their lenses. But although it was there, tormenting him, he had been thinking about something darker, something that held a different sort of promise. A different sort of pleasure. He couldn't tell her the entire truth. (HEY, MARE! I was just thinking about this MURDER I'm planning. Should I shoot him in the heart or in the head? Or maybe in the stomach so he dies really slowly. I've read that a gut shot is agonizing.)

He kissed her cheek and came as close to the truth as he dared. "I was thinking about Stan."

"I think about him too. He was such a nice little kid." She came to her feet and put her arms around his neck. "You can talk to me about it if you want to, if you ever need to."

Gordon pulled her very close to him. He could feel the warm comfort of her belly against his. "It's hard to talk about him." *Because if I start, maybe I won't stop at just Stan. Maybe I'll have to tell you everything.* "It hurts as much as it did the night he . . . the night it happened." *The night he was murdered*.

"I understand. It's okay. I just want you to know that I'm here and I always will be. I love you, Gordon."

He kissed her — not the way he had kissed her when they'd been parked, there had been little, if any, control in *those* kisses — but with a tenderness that should have been beyond the capability of a boy his age, a tenderness born of more than the loss of his brother. He would not have been able to articulate it, but Stan's death, the abrupt and cruel cessation of the numbering of his years, had added to those of Gordon's. A pall that weighed a million pounds lay over his soul. Mary saw a boy she loved; his face at times haunted by what had happened. A stranger would have seen a teenager with the oldest eyes in the world.

"I know that," Gordon said. "I love you too."

"If you love me, we better get out of this water. I'm starting to get pruny." She showed him her fingertips. "See."

Gordon, grateful for the change in emotional temperature, said. "That's you. Mary the Prune."

They swam in until they were in water too shallow for swimming. It was beautifully warm, but the air was beginning to cool.

"We're going to change," said Mary. "You guys'll wait for us, right?"

"No," said David. "We're going to drive miles and miles up the beach and make you walk. Of course we'll wait for you!"

That had been the plan upon which they had all agreed. With so many people on the beach, it would have been impossible to gather enough driftwood, so Tony and Frank, using Frank's dad's truck, had driven over to the sawmill yesterday and scrounged an enormous load of scrap lumber. They would drive the truck, The Chief, and Mr. Molonovitch's Buick, which David had borrowed, a few miles up the beach where they could have a hot dog roast and still be able to see the fireworks.

■■■

It is impossible to ruin a hot dog roast even when the bonfire, one that you have started with gasoline, is shooting flames twenty feet into the sky. The bonfire was roaring away; and even if the hot dogs had tasted a little bit funny, no one could fault Frank's technique. The only problem was, it was a little hard to see the fireworks. Gordon could sort of hear them above the crackling whoosh of the wind-driven flames. That wasn't good enough. These were the last fireworks of the summer and he was going to *see* them (and perhaps some other things), by God.

He finished his beer, stood, and pulled Mary to her feet. "Come on. Let's go up the beach."

David, his arm around Laura, said, "Don't get lost." He was going to kiss Laura tonight if it killed him.

Tony, stretched out on a blanket with Susan, – he had settled on Susan – groaned. "I just ate six hot dogs. I can't even move, much less go up the beach."

Frank, in heaven because he had *finally* got up the nerve to put his arm around Charlene, said, "I noticed you didn't extend an invitation, but we'll pass. Be good, you two."

"Always," said Gordon, glancing at Mary, who was studiously ignoring the teasing. He picked up his blanket and led her off into the darkness. When the bonfire was a small flame in the distance, he stopped and spread the blanket under a poplar. They would still be able to see, and he would have something to lean against.

"I thought you wanted to watch the fireworks," whispered Mary when he put his arms around her.

"I don't want you to get cold," said Gordon. "See. Now you're not cold." He kissed her and she settled against him.

Fireworks and kisses; there is a sameness about the two things. The heat, the explosion – one pyrotechnical, it must be admitted; the other hormonal, but explosions none the less – the anticipation of just *one more*. Soon, though, there was more kissing than observing fireworks. And then? Gordon pulled away from her just long enough so that he could gently push her down onto her back.

There was an explosion and Gordon could see in her eyes the reflected sparkles of light showering down from the sky. *I love her so, so much*, he thought. His hand touched her belly and began to slide downward.

"No." Mary sat up. "Not that. We can't do that again for a while. We're going too fast. No more petting below that waist. You have to promise."

"What!" *Uh-huh*, he thought. *Let's take something that we both really, REALLY enjoyed the other night, and make a pact not to do it again. Right.* If anything would make him entirely insane, that promise would be it. (We have to lock him up in the *special* ward for the SEXUALLY MENTAL, Mr. and Mrs. Westley. Has he made any promises about not petting below the waist recently?) Gordon, as yet unaware of his own body's nearly infinite potential for pleasure, thought in bleak despair, *Everything I have IS below my waist. Maybe I can have my penis surgically attached to my chest.* (Gordon, the surgery has been a *complete* success, but you are going to have to wear a very funny-looking shirt.) "For a *while*? How long? A week? A year? Come on, Mary, listen."

"No. *You* listen." She stood up and when he did as well, she took a step back. Gordon was stung to his very core. "You know Karen Allen?"

"Yes," he said in confusion. "She's going to school at Bishop Strachan in Toronto this fall. What does she have to do with us?"

"Plenty. She is *not* going to school at Bishop Strachan this fall. She is *not* going to school at all. And how do I know this? I know this because my mom's sister, my Auntie Christine, is a nurse. She works for some guy named Doctor Williams, some Toronto doctor. And Auntie Christine told my mom that Karen is staying with her grandparents because she's pregnant. Karen's pregnant, and if it can happen to her, it can happen to me. To us. Do you want to be a father at the age of seventeen? If I got pregnant I couldn't give up my baby. Karen is giving up hers, I guess, but I couldn't do that. There we would be with a baby! Is that what you want for us? Is that how much you *love* me?"

"God!" said Gordon. "You know I love you."

She was fighting tears now. "Then slow down!" she hissed. "Do you think I didn't . . . enjoy what we did at Hawk Point? I loved it, but maybe next time it won't be just our hands. Maybe next time we'll be going all the way." Struggling for control, Mary said, "I love you, but I'm scared."

"Just let me hold you."

"Hold. How do you spell that, Gordon? F–U–C–K?" Mary whirled around and began to run down the beach.

Not bothering with the blanket, he ran after her. "I'm sorry! I won't touch you!" But she wasn't slowing down. *How can I catch her if I can't touch her?* he thought crazily. When he was running alongside her, he said, "Mary, please. I'm sorry." Gordon grabbed her arm and pulled her to a stop, instantly releasing her. His voice shaking with emotion, in between pants he gasped. "You. Should. Try. Out. For. The Olympics. Jeez."

"It's not funny."

"It *isn't* funny. I'm sorry, but I can't help myself when I'm around you."

"Very pathetic, but you have to, because I can't help myself either. I don't know if you've . . . if you've done it; if you've gone all the way with anyone else."

"I haven't. Honest." His voice husky with *more* than emotion, Gordon went on, "It's just you I want to – *What do I say? I can't say screw! And she'll go wild if I say bone! What's romantic? Got it! Thank you, St. Valentine!* – to make love with."

Mary took a step closer. "I'm a virgin and I'm staying one for the time being, no matter how much I want you. I know I would get pregnant. I just know it!"

"Okay! Okay! I'll even wear a virgin pin if you want. You can loan me one of yours; you've got about a thousand of them. Gordon Westley the Lord of the Virgins." (Anything. *Anything* to calm her down, to make her laugh or even smile a little.)

"I just might."

She didn't back away when he reached for her, and so he took her in his arms. "Can I kiss you? I just want to kiss you."

She leaned her head back and looked into his eyes. "Just kissing. Nothing else."

Gordon, who wanted to latch onto her breasts like a remora (they *are* above the waist and therefore clearly within the PETTING LINE OF DEMARCATION) gave her the most chaste kiss of which he was possible.

"That had tongue."

"Our tongues were above our waists, the last time I checked."

"You are bad."

"Yup." He kissed her again and this time she didn't object to his tongue. "Let's go back for the blanket."

"Just to get it, right?"

"Of course!"

But that was when Gordon became aware of the headlights that were sweeping across the beach as three cars positioned themselves around the bonfire.

"What is it? What's happening?" asked Mary. "Is it the police?"

"No. Those are Sultan cars," said Gordon, his attention fixed on one of the coupes.

It was Lancer Caldwell's.

chapter 19

"A timid person is frightened before
a danger, a coward during the time,
and a courageous person afterward."

— Amos Littlebird, Odawa Sachem

By the time Mary and Gordon had reached the bonfire, all
The Sultans were out of their cars. Lancer was leaning
against his coupe, with one hand in the pocket of his jeans.

"Look who took time off from balling Mary to come
and say hello," he shouted to Gordon. "This is our fire
now. Get the hell off my beach, Westley."

"Get lost, you asshole!" said Gordon. "Go crawl back
into whatever septic tank you came out of."

"You just got one warning, Westley. That's it. You
want the shit beat out of you now or later?"

"Hah! Right! Odds are a little more even now, aren't
they? You want to fight? Fine. I'm not scared of you,
Francis. Nice game of pocket pool you got going there, by
the way."

Lancer flushed, but his hand stayed in his pocket where he was fingering his medal, He had come to think of it as his good luck charm. It felt good to handle it, because when he did, he got sort of a rush of heat, sort of a flashback to that night. He hadn't felt as alive as the night he killed the Westley turd. He couldn't wait to kill Gordon. He had it all planned how he was going to do it. Old Gordy-Wordy would know for sure that what had happened to his crummy brother hadn't been an accident. It would feel pretty good telling him that, and telling him what he had planned for Mary – what he had planned for a girl who had been unfaithful to him. The idea felt so excellent, that the beginnings of an erection stirred in the crotch of Lancer's jeans. Once Gordy was dead, he'd kidnap Mary and rape her and *that* Lancer was really looking forward to. Taking his time, teaching her his entire sexual repertoire, punishing her with love, as the perverted might say, keeping her locked up at his place until he'd had enough of her. She'd have to die too, of course, but not until he'd had his fill. And Lancer had a large appetite where the pussy department was concerned. *Later, though*, he thought; it would all happen in good time. Tonight he'd give Gordy-Wordy just a little taste of what was to come. "You piece of crap, Westley!" he shouted. "You're scared shitless."

"I'm not scared. Not of you."

"Prove it!"

"Fine."

"Chicken."

"Fine."

It took Mary a second to understand that Lancer wasn't calling Gordon a chicken. They were going to *play* chicken.

"Half mile down the beach if you're not too nervous to drive that far," said Gordon. "I'll start from here."

"See you soon." Lancer's eyes crawled over Mary. "Come to think of it, he's probably been too chicken to stick you with his little dick, hasn't he Mary?" He cupped his genitals and lifted them. "Got something nice here for you, babe. Stick around. I'll show you how a real man does it to you."

"You sonofabitch!" shouted Gordon, but Lancer only laughed.

The door of his coupe thunked shut, as did the doors of the two other Sultan cars. Engines started and The Sultans drove down the beach; one car after another pulling off to the side until it was only Lancer still driving. His headlights swept around. Gordon could hear the deep rumbling of the coupe's engine.

"Gordon don't do this!" Mary begged, as he took out his car keys.

He ignored her, walked over to The Chief and got in. Mary scrambled in on the passenger side.

"Get out of the car, Mary," said Gordon quietly. "This is serious."

"No. Listen to me. Please don't do this. *Please!*"

"Get out of the car, I said. I don't want you in here until this is over. I do this, and then we're gone."

"This isn't a movie. It's not *Rebel Without a Cause*. You could be hurt. Killed!"

"Get out of my car." He was staring straight ahead, his eyes on Lancer's coupe.

"No! I won't let you do this. Please, Gordon. Please, let's just drive away. *Please!*" Then, her voice desperate and low, "If we just drive away, we can park somewhere and we can do . . . what we did the other night. And more! Only please, not chicken. Please. Not if you love me!"

"GET OUT OF MY CAR!" He leaned over her, pulled the door handle and shoved open the door. "David! Get her out of here!"

Mary, who was weeping, fought David when he pulled her out, but it wasn't much of a fight. She fell onto the sand and knelt there.

David got into The Chief and slammed the door shut.

"Not you too," said Gordon tiredly. "Out of the car, Ace."

"Look, Wesser. We've been together since kindergarten. If you think I am going to let you get all the credit for this — You. Are. Mistaken. We're The Lakers, aren't we?"

The back doors opened and then Frank and Tony were in The Chief's backseat.

"Heard you were going for a ride," said Beery.

"No guts, no glory," said Breezy. "Roll on, my good man!"

The three other girls were close to tears now, Mary's sobs highly contagious.

"I don't want to see this," said Charlene, who grabbed Susan's hand. They ran off into the night.

"I'm sorry, Mary," said Laura, following them. "My parents would kill me if they knew I was involved in anything like this. If you're smart, you'll come with me."

But Mary couldn't take her eyes off The Chief. Gordon floored the gas pedal; an instant later, Lancer's coupe was in motion, its custom split exhaust manifold and straight pipes playing a Harley Davidson concerto. Faster and faster they went, sand spraying, engines screaming, heading straight at each other. Gordon, as he prepared to shift into high gear at sixty-five miles an hour, could hear Lancer's car's exhaust thundering as the gap between them closed. Five hundred yards, one hundred yards and still neither turned away. It wasn't Wesser who was driving The Chief, arm wrapped around the wheel, it was Gordon Westley, hands in the two and eleven o'clock positions, his entire being focused on his driving.

With Gordon's headlights close enough to nearly blind him, Lancer thought, *Fucker ain't gonna turn!* He jerked his wheel to the right as far as it would go. Gordon wrenched his wheel to the left, The Chief's left front fender just clipping the coupe's taillight. The Chief spun out in the sand. When Gordon regained control, he saw that all The Sultans were driving at high speed away from him, heading off in different directions.

"Cops," said Breezy feebly.

It was true. There was the distant whine of a siren. They could see the small and ruinous flashing of lights as the police car pursued one of The Sultans. Gordon flipped off his headlights and sped back to where Mary was standing. Alone.

"Burn rubber, guys," he said. Frank and Tony were gone within seconds. "Get in," Gordon said to Mary. *How am I ever going to get her to listen to me after this?*

"Wait for me, David," Mary called. She walked up to The Chief and leaned her hands on the door. "I don't want to see you anymore, Gordon. Ever. You would have died on this beach rather than listen to me; you would rather have killed yourself rather than . . . than . . . do what I offered to do with you. I don't know what has happened to you this summer. You don't keep your promises to me, and up until tonight, all you've cared about is the sex. You say you love me, but until a few minutes ago all you've really wanted was for me to jack you off."

"That's not true!" He got out of the car. His voice soft, Gordon said, "I could have taken you parking and, okay; we could have gone all the way. That's what you meant, wasn't it? All the way? But I didn't do that, did I? It wouldn't have been what you wanted."

"I don't want it; not anymore. Not with you. And by the way, I know that you didn't pass up the chance because of me. It was because whatever this *thing* is you have going with Lancer is more important to you than I am. I don't know you anymore and you don't listen to anything I say. You were actually willing to die for this . . . this stupidity." She took off the ring Gordon had given her, picked up his hand and slapped it down. "You're going to get yourself killed and I don't want to be a part of that. I know Stan's death has been hard for you, but you are never going to change. The only choices you are ever going to make are bad ones."

"I do *everything* you ask. At least I try to, but it's not enough for you, is it?" Gordon – overloaded by anger, frustration, and the certainty that his life from this night on would be unbearable – felt something crack within himself, as though his soul, fragile and cold from the cruel burden it had carried for so long, had shattered. (No reason to hold back now, Gordon! Just tear into her and you will feel *so-o-o-o* much better.) Out it flooded. "It's YOU who aren't listening. Everything has to be your way. Everything has to be about you. Never what I want. Just what you want! God, Mary! You loved it! All that moaning when I put my hand down your pants and –"

"Cripes! I do not want to hear this stuff! Come on," David begged. "Cut it out!"

"You give me a little taste of something and then you take it away," Gordon went on. "Is that supposed to be love? Is that how you show love? Maybe all I do think of is sex, but what about you? What about that bathing suit today? What about swimming in our underwear? What about always waving it in my face?"

"Why don't you just rent a billboard?" Mary was crying again. "Or maybe David can help you spread the word. Why don't you write it on the wall of a bathroom?"

"Maybe I will. You remember how you said that Lila Box was a pig? Well, you know what you are? You're a cock tease!"

She swung her arm back. Gordon braced himself for the slap, but before she could deliver it, David grabbed her wrist. "You don't want to do that. You two are both out of control. Guys. Come on. Don't do this," he said. "Why don't you just go with him, so you two can work it out?"

"I'd rather go somewhere with *Lancer*." She pulled away from David and hugged herself. "I hate you, Gordon. I hate you!"

"Nice. Really nice. Why *don't* you go with Lancer, Mary? Why don't you go ALL the way with him? I bet you nearly did; all that crap about not kissing him back. Bet you weren't a cock tease with Lancer. And you know what? I hate you, too!" Gordon shouted. "You think you know it all, don't you? You don't know anything about me, or why I do things! You don't know the first thing about my life!"

"I guess that's true, but I do know I never want to see you again." She turned away, tears rolling down her face. "David, please take me home."

"Gord?" David looked dubious. "You okay with that, man?"

"It isn't up to him," sobbed Mary. "I'm not *with* him, anymore. Either drive me, or I'll walk."

"Okay, okay! I'll drive you home," said David, avoiding Gordon's angry face. He grabbed her beach bag. "Get in."

Gordon watched the Buick's taillights disappear. He stared down at the ring, then squeezed his fist closed on it until it cut into his palm. *I'll throw the goddamned thing into the lake*, he thought. "No," he whispered to himself. "I'll keep it and look at it every day to remind myself how stupid I've been." Then he stuffed it in his pocket. The sound of another siren was becoming louder now, but Gordon couldn't have cared less. Which was a good thing, because Constable O'Driscoll was just rolling up.

■■■

O'Driscoll could have pressed charges; at the very least, Gordon had been disturbing the peace – and then there was the beer – but Constable O'Driscoll was no stranger to the savagery with which death could rend a family. The Westleys' tragedy had left their lives in ruins. The last thing they needed was for their remaining son to be hauled down to the station. Instead, he simply escorted Gordon home, following in his squad car, where he placed him in the custody of his father.

"Give me your car keys," said Ben in a flat tone.

He was astounded when Gordon stared him down and said, "I need my car, Dad. I have to have The Chief."

"So you can race? What you *have* to have, is a serious look at what you are doing with your life and your future. O'Driscoll could have arrested you. He didn't. And you've been drinking; I can smell it on your breath."

"It was only one beer."

"You're sixteen! You're under age!" Gordon's father lowered his voice. "Alcohol and cars, son. How can you be so stupid? Do you have any idea what it would do to your mother if something happened to you? She is just starting to pull herself together. You want to kill her, son? Because that's what would result if anything happened to you. It would kill her. And it would kill me. Then there's the fact that you had Mary with you tonight, for the love of God! Her parents — and we — have trusted you. What would they think of this mess?"

"I'm not going with Mary anymore. She broke up with me. You don't need to worry about her, because I won't be seeing her again. It's over."

Suddenly, everything became clear to Ben Westley. Gordon's reckless behavior had been born of Mary's rejection, by the end of the puppy love that they had briefly shared. "I'm sorry to hear that. Mary is a very nice girl, but she isn't the only girl in Erie View, you know. You can date other girls. As a matter of fact, it's probably a good idea to date other girls, since you don't want to get too serious at your age." (You have no idea how serious it was, Dad. You'll never know how serious it was. No one will.) Gordon's father ran a hand through his hair. "Look. I should ground you. Promise me no more drinking and racing. Promise me. I can accept your promise."

"I promise. (Any idea what a liar I am, Dad? Any clue at all? Goes hand in hand with being a potential murderer.) You have my word."

Ben *knew* his son had just lied to him. He started to reach out his hand, to touch Gordon's cheek, but the look in his son's face stopped him, and so he did not. Something, a nictitating membrane of remoteness shuttered over Gordon's eyes and then was gone. *What have we done to you?* his father thought. *We should never have left you here on your own.* With a deep sigh he only said, "Better get to bed, Gordon. First day of school tomorrow."

■■■

Mary, unable to stop crying, rode home with David. When he pulled up in front of her house, she reached into the backseat for her beach bag, her breathing uneven.

David put his hand lightly on her bare arm. "Listen. I'm not going to repeat any of what I heard tonight," he said. "None of it. Not what you said or what Gordon said. I swear. Whatever you've done together is your business."

"I don't want to talk about this with you, David. Let go of my arm, please."

"I will, but just listen to me. Gordon didn't mean what he said back there."

"Oh, sure!"

"And neither did you."

"What makes you such an expert?"

"I've known him since we were both little. I don't know you as well, Mary, but I'm an expert on Gordon, all right. He loves you and I'm pretty sure you love him, no matter what you said. Look. My parents fight all the time; yours probably do, too. That's what people in love do. They fight."

"Let me go."

He let her go. "You're making a big mistake. Gordon's had a rough summer, but he's been able to get through it because of you."

"That's it! That's enough!" Mary shoved open the door, got out, and slammed it behind her.

"You're making a mistake!" called David to her back.
When she went into the house with no indication that she
had heard him, he shook his head. "A big mistake," he
muttered as he drove away.

■■■

Within an hour or so, Mary knew that David had been
wrong. She managed to get past her parents and Nanna
without too much of a fuss. No, she wasn't crying because
Gordon had done something inappropriate. No; he hadn't
gotten fresh. And NO! She absolutely did not want Nanna
to have a talk with Gordon's grandfather! As a matter of
fact, she wasn't going to see Gordon anymore; they had
decided to date other people, which would be much
better. She was just tired and it was the first day of school
tomorrow and she was going to bed.

Mary undressed in her room. Wrapped in a bathrobe,
she went into the bathroom, ran a hot, deep bath, let the
robe drop to the floor, stepped into the tub, sat down, and
sobbed. She didn't bother washing; she just sat there and
added to the water with the tears she was shedding, and as
she cried, she became increasingly certain that David was
wrong. She hadn't made a mistake; she had made the
biggest mistake of her life.

I feel so awful, she thought. *The things I said to him in
front of David! God! Gordon will never forgive me for that.*

Mary got out of the tub, drained it, and toweled herself dry. She tossed the towel into the hamper, put on her robe, and brushed her teeth. Then she went into her bedroom and put on a clean nightgown. She didn't get into bed; she just sat on the edge and stared at the telephone on the nightstand. Then she reached out and picked up the receiver.

On the other side of town, Gordon, freshly showered and wearing only jeans, was standing in the downstairs hallway, the telephone receiver in his hand. He was nearly sick with despair, because it was in the shower that he realized he had made the worst mistake of his life. He had hurt Mary intentionally, and with something close to enjoyment; wounded her, lashing out mindlessly. In doing so, he had lost her. But maybe he could beg, crawl, plead, and promise anything. Maybe she would listen to him if he did it right; if he said the right things.

Then, at almost the same time as Mary hung up the phone, knowing he would never forgive her, Gordon set the receiver gently in its cradle.

She'll never forgive me. Who am I kidding?

Mary cried herself to sleep that night. So did Gordon.

chapter 20

"Education is the best provision
for old age."

          — Amos Littlebird, Odawa Sachem

Gordon suffered through the first four days of school. Mary would not look at him, much less speak to him. She kept a buffer zone of girlfriends between them — not Laura Crane, though; Mary's friendship with Laura had dissolved the night she had left her on the beach — and sat as far away as possible from Gordon in the classes that they shared. The only thing he knew for sure was that he thanked God he hadn't called her. She would have hung up.

"Give her time," David told him. "She likes you too much not to come around."

"You're wrong," said Gordon. "She hates my guts."

"Man, you are so wrong. She loves you."

"If she loved me, she never would have said what she said about . . . you know . . . us. That was private."

"Look. That all stays with me. Period. And you know, you were slinging it as much as she was. You have to be the two most stubborn people on the face of the earth. Why don't you just talk to her?"

"I can't. I just can't. She would just crap all over me again. I couldn't take that. Just let it go, man. I don't want to hear about it anymore."

By Friday, although Gordon had lost Mary, he had gained something. He now had a plan. All those hours sitting in class had paid off. He hadn't absorbed any math or English; science and French had left him untouched educationally, but he had a plan.

He would kill Lancer in Lancer's own house, the way Lancer had killed Stan. Different method; same result. DEAD. Gordon had taken the Luger from his mother's brassiere drawer this morning while she was making breakfast. It was now in the locked glove box of The Chief along with two boxes of the .9 mm cartridges it used. First, he would drive out to Russet Woods to practice, then after dinner, he would drive to the house that Lancer rented from Old Man Richardson. He would wait until Lancer came home from his shitty day or from his shitty night out, and he would kill him.

If Gordon had not been so caught up with murderous intent, if he had not lost Mary, he might actually have enjoyed those first few days of school. The other Lakers certainly had. Not because of the superiority of the academic programs, but because life at Erie View District Collegiate Institute, always shaded with mayhem, had gotten off to a rousing start.

The school had a new wing. Just to christen it, someone had blocked every toilet in the guys' washroom and then flushed them all. The entire wing had been flooded and evacuated. The principal, Mr. Carson, who had about as much influence over the student body as Mr. Ligonier had over the audiences at The Palace, had been livid. Mr. Carson had yelled over the PA system with such vehemence, that Gordon thought he might have seen drops of spittle coming out of the speaker. It hadn't mattered. No one confessed, and in fact, the "Phantom of the Outhouse" struck again the next afternoon, this time vandalizing the girls' washroom.

And Mr. Clark, who taught geometry, was wearing his tweed sportscoat for yet another term. He had worn the same coat every day for seven years. This he did, because as he walked up or down the aisles, he knew that at least one student would whip a fully loaded fountain pen at his back. Mr. Clark had the coat cleaned every few months, but the green, blue, and black stains never truly came out. He bore this abuse with the stoicism of a secondary school samurai. It had occurred to Gordon that Mr. Clark's crown in heaven (Why crowns? Stan had once asked him. Why not cowboy hats or helmets or maybe coonskin caps? *Crowns*? Did that mean you have to carry a scepter? Neat!) would not be studded with stars. His would be encrusted with fountain pens.

By Wednesday, the stall doors of both new washrooms were veritable tomes of lavatory wit as people waxed toiletic. There were drawings of male and female genitalia, some surprisingly correct, others looking like the reproductive organs of an alien species. There were missives. ANYBODY CAN PEE ON THE FLOOR; BE ORIGINAL AND SHIT ON THE CEILING. FART LOUD IF YOU LIKE MR. CARSON. There was poetry. HERE I SIT AND CONTEMPLATE; SHOULD I CRAP OR MASTURBATE? There were tests. WHAT'S LILA BOX'S FAVORITE NURSERY RHYME? HUMPME DUMPME.

By Thursday, Marty Fallbrother had managed to tear off his finger in shop class. This was because he had tried to change the drive belt speed on a wood lathe while it was running. Mr. Bennett, the shop teacher, had come storming over and yelled, "Get out of here, Fallbrother. You're bleedin' on da hardwood!" Just for good measure he had added, "An' take your finger." Marty's response to this had been to roll his eyes so far back in his head, that he must have been looking at the inside of his own skull. Then he had passed out. Mr. Carson had rushed him to the hospital where a doctor had tried to reattach the finger. Rumor was, if it didn't take, Marty was going to dry it out and wear it on a string around his neck. None of this meant anything to Gordon, who somehow made it to the end of the week. Exhausted and heartsore that Friday afternoon, he tossed his books into the locker he was sharing with David this year.

"See you at Kitchie's later?" asked David. "We can play a few games of pool? Mess around with the guys?" *Man, he looks awful*, David thought. *Gord looks like he hasn't slept all week.*

"I don't know. Maybe. I'll see," said Gordon, but he wasn't looking at David. His eyes were riveted on Mary, who was at her own locker. There was such hopeless longing in those eyes, that David felt as though he had just seen something so intimate that it should never have been shared.

He slapped Gordon's shoulder and said, "Good enough," but he was thinking, *Not good at all. This is definitely not the Gord I know.*

David watched Gordon walk down the long hall and out the front door of the school. He waited until Mary was passing by and said, "Are you having fun?" He stepped out and blocked her way. "Are you enjoying yourself? I sure hope what you are doing to my best friend is worth it to you."

Her eyes blazed at him. "I'm not doing anything to him. He's doing it to himself."

"Right. Do you have any idea how much he needed you? No. Let me rephrase; *needs* you. Was it the stupid game of chicken on the beach? Was it that I know you guys were doing more than necking? Big deal. I told you it goes to the grave with me. I meant that. Or is it that you can't control him? That he doesn't jump when you snap your fingers? You're killing him, Mary."

"I should slap your face for that!"

David spread his arms out and laughed. "Hey! Be my guest! I can even call Frank and Tony and make appointments with them for you. You can work your way through all of us."

"Gordon needs something, but it isn't me. And I *can't* control him. That's right. Nothing I said that night meant a thing to him. You call yourself his best friend? A best friend wouldn't have let him play chicken. He would have killed *himself* if he could have killed Lancer; you know that don't you?"

"I am his best friend," said David quietly. "His best male friend. The Lakers stick together. You, though, were supposed to be his best female friend, his girlfriend."

She hit the door of a locker with her fist. "The Lakers! Driving around, acting like toughs. Like hoods! The beer! When are you going to grow up? When are you going to be able to see that it's the stupid Lakers, and your stupid cars, and . . . and, your stupid nicknames that are behind all this? *Wesser. Ace.* You're all so immature it makes me puke. You think you're such big men? You're idiots!" She was crying now; tears had spilled from her eyes and were running down her cheeks. "I'm not killing him, David. He's doing it to himself and you're helping him. And don't even think about bringing Stan's death into this. Don't you *dare* dump that one on me!" she sobbed.

"I thought you guys were in love. You don't stop loving someone just because of an argument."

"That's exactly right, David. You don't." Mary turned and walked away from him, her back straight. "Leave me alone!" she shouted. "Just leave me alone!"

Gordon, sitting in the parking lot in The Chief, its engine idling, stared at her unblinkingly when she came out of the building. The red curtain of her hair hid her face so he didn't see that she was weeping. He watched until she turned the corner and he couldn't see her any-more. Then The Chief screamed out of the parking lot.

It had begun.

■ ■ ■

Gordon used nearly an entire box of ammunition before he gave up, shaken and soaked with sweat. He couldn't hit *anything* with the Luger. NOTHING! Not at twenty feet, not at thirty feet, and certainly not at fifty feet. Point-blank range? Yes. How would he ever be able to get close enough to Lancer to kill him? He kept a shotgun at his place; Mary had told him so. Lancer would be able to kill *him* with a shotgun. What he needed was a high-powered rifle, something accurate to at least a hundred yards. He didn't just want to kill Lancer, he wanted to live to enjoy the fact for the rest of his life. He would wound him badly. Two quick shots to the knees would put him out of commission and unable to reach his shotgun; he would get him to give back Stan's medal, and then he would kill him. This was a mere bump in the road, just a slight delay.

But he had to get a rifle.

■■■

The Luger cleaned and back in his mother's dresser drawer, Gordon played pool at Kitchie's with The Lakers, game after game, until he was sick of it.

"I can't blame Laura and the girls in a way, you know; for running like that," said Frank. "Can't blame them, but got no use for them either."

"Not after they left Mary alone," Tony agreed. Both he and Frank had severed their ties with Susan and Charlene. "Pretty crappy move. What about Laura? She's worse."

"Well, I don't care if I *ever* see her again," said David. He shook his head and mouthed *stop it* to Tony and Frank. Just the mention of Mary's name had caused Gordon to wince. "Want to get a burger before Gertson's closes, Gord?" he asked. "Or we could go over to Denison's?"

"I don't think so. You guys go ahead. I'm going to stay here for a while and then just head home."

David – a small frown of concern creasing his brow – Tony, and Frank paid Mr. Kitchie for their part of the game and left. Gordon had never thought he would be glad to see his friends walk away from him, but he was. Because he couldn't talk to Joely with them, or anyone else around. The poolroom slowly emptied until it was only Gordon playing; Mr. Kitchie went home, leaving Joely to close up.

"Want me to clock you out now?" he asked Gordon as he wiped down the counter with a damp cloth.

"No. I'll just practice a little more. You start your cleanup and I'll check out when you're done."

Joely shrugged. He locked the door and painstakingly brushed and then covered tables, making certain the covers were just so. He got his push broom and swept the center aisle all the way to the door. He locked it and began working his way back to where Gordon was pretending to line up a shot on the black ball to bank it into the three-pocket.

"You burning the campfire pretty late, Kimosabi," said Joely.

"Haven't been getting tired too early, lately, Tonto." said Gordon.

Joely laughed softly. "I haven't been tired early for more years than I can remember."

"Listen, Joely; I was sort of thinking about going

hunting tomorrow afternoon, but I don't have a rifle. Would you lend me yours? *If he can't hear my heart pounding, he's deaf.* I'd be careful with it. *God. I'm sweating like a pig!* I'm a good shot."

Joely stopped sweeping and leaned on his broom. "Hunting what?"

"Whatever is in the woods. Rabbits."

Joely leaned his broom against the wall and stuck his hands in his pockets. "Just about the only words of Indian wisdom my grandfather never told me were 'don't bullshit a bullshitter,' Gordon. I learned that myself. The hard way. Why don't you say what's on your mind?"

"Nothing," said Gordon, his eyes on the floor, knowing he wouldn't be able to outlast Joely's patient silence, feeling himself losing control until, unable to stop himself he said, "I can't."

"Can't or won't?"

"I CAN'T!"

"Are you in some kind of trouble?" asked Joely gently. "I'm no stranger to trouble, and I don't mean trouble with the law. Maybe I can't help, but whatever has been gnawing at you —" Gordon's eyes flew up. *How can he see through me like that?* he thought. Joely smiled a little sadly. "You're pretty easy to read, Gordon. It's all in your face, in your expression, and all someone has to do is look to see that something has been eating you alive for weeks.

Maybe I can't do anything to help out, but I can listen. And getting it off your chest is always a wise thing. I'm a good listener, Gordon."

Gordon tried to fight it, but it was as though Joely's kind words were breaking the seal on his grief.

"That fucking Lancer Caldwell murdered Stan, and I'm going to kill him for it." There it was, a capering nightmare of a story, gushing out of Gordon unchecked as he told Joely about the medal, the scooter, his plan for revenge, the Luger. He talked and talked until he had to stop because he was crying. Joely didn't ask him how he could be so sure. He didn't say a word. He just stood there, thoughtfully nodding his head.

"Do you believe me?" Gordon asked, wiping his eyes with the backs of his arms. "If you won't lend me your gun, I'll just get another one somehow, even if it takes years. I'm going to kill the prick, no matter what."

Joely was quiet for a long while, nodding his head, watching Gordon, but not really *seeing* Gordon. His eyes were so far away that maybe he was gazing into another world or listening to something poignant and terrible. He didn't *seem* like Joely really, at this moment; this wasn't Injun Joely, sweeper of the poolroom, emptier of the spittoons. Gordon felt a small, cold prickle run up his spine. I don't care if he is creeping me out, he thought furiously; I *have* to get that gun! "Joely? You believe me don't you?"

"Why wouldn't I believe you?" Joely blinked rapidly several times. He crossed his arms over his chest and leaned against a pool table. "You're a level-headed guy. Smart. Loyal to your family. It sounds perfectly logical to me. Hey! Bastard killed my brother, I wouldn't hesitate to kill him.

"Did I ever tell you what the hell I did during the First World War, Gordon?" He laughed a little. "That's silly; of course I haven't. Well, I was in the Canadian Expeditionary Force." Joely pulled a pack of cigarettes out from under the counter and lit up; Gordon had never seen him smoke, or for that matter, heard him swear before. Joely examined the glowing tip and shook his head. "Man's gotta have at least one bad habit. Anyway, we were recruited in Canada, trained in England, and killed in France. Your grandfather was in my division, if I'm not mistaken."

"Yes. He was." (THE RIFLE! I WANT THE RIFLE!)

"He and I were some of the guys who made it back to Canada." Squinting through the cigarette smoke, he laughed again. It wasn't a very nice laugh. "We were supposed to be the lucky ones. You know, my friend, I think the lucky ones are buried at Flanders. No bad memories, no nightmares. Just poppies.

"I joined up in the spring of 1915 with a bunch of buddies from the reservation. They melted us down, poured us into the same mold and when we were ready, sent us off to fight the dirty Hun. Our cause was on God's and England's side, we were told.

"At first, it was our own army that made short work of us. It was easier to hate the generals than the Germans for chrissake, because it was the ineptitude of the generals that made certain we were cold, wet, unshod, and pretty much always confused. Hey! Want a beer?" He went to the refrigerator in Mr. Kitchie's office, got two bottles and an opener and cracked them open. Handing one to Gordon, he clinked his against it. "Death to the dirty Hun!" Then he swallowed down most of the bottle and hoisted it in a second toast. "Here's to fallen comrades.

"That all changed at the front. The shelling killed some of my friends; you never forget that sound when someone you know is screaming because their arm or leg has been blown off. By then we were all pals, you see; life in the trenches did that to us. Sometimes one or two guys would disappear at night. We would get replacements and *those* guys would become our buddies.

"Then there were the snipers. They picked away at us." He winked and smiled. "Damned good shots, some of those Germans. Our commander asked for volunteers to be trained as snipers. Tit for tat, Gordon! I was a pretty good shot, so what the hell; I volunteered. They gave me a rifle with telescopic sights, one that had been regulated to an extremely high degree of accuracy." He crossed the room and took the rifle out of the umbrella stand and showed it to Gordon. "Like this Ross. See? The wooden fore-end is cut away so the barrel floats freely, and that helps conceal it from the enemy. Very accurate in the right hands. They also gave you a really fine pair of binoculars for reconnaissance. We would not only be killing the bloody Hun, we would be finding targets for our artillery to shell. Efficient, eh?

"I was a natural. I killed Germans under every circumstance you can imagine. Relaxing behind the lines, on watch, taking a shit, sleeping, talking to their friends."

Joely dropped the butt of his cigarette to the floor and crushed it with his shoe. "One day I was moving forward with my platoon, and I came across some Germans I had sniped only a few minutes before. One of them had been reading a letter. I tell you, Gordon, the bullet hit him so hard and fast that he didn't even have time to drop that letter or the photograph of a girl he was holding. He looked absolutely astounded. I will never forget the look on that kid's face.

"Shit! I was even awarded a medal for gallantry. Imagine Sergeant Joely Waters getting a medal; knew they'd never believe that back on the reservation. After a while, I was given a battlefield commission and promoted to lieutenant. My new job was to organize and run a brigade-wide school to train and lead snipers, which I did with great gusto. Loved every minute of it. I was doing my duty, I was avenging my comrades." Joely set the Ross on a pool table and lit another cigarette. "After the Armistice was signed, we were shipped back to Canada and demobilized. Kind of hard to return to civilian life when part of your everyday activity has been killing the dirty Hun. No dirty Huns on the reservation, Kimosabi, no siree! I went home and learned that my girlfriend had run off to Winnipeg with another guy. I didn't give a damn; the bitch was no good anyway.

"I started to have trouble sleeping; started to drink. I ended up in a veterans hospital where I was told by the psychiatrist that all I was doing was looking for a handout. 'Stop being a burden to society and start acting like a man.' Needless to say, I beat the living shit out of him. First chance I got, I ran away and I've been on the move since." Joely spat in the general direction of a spittoon and missed.

"Now don't get me wrong. I do not regret killing a single man; I don't even regret killing prisoners in cold blood. I did that, you know. Yup. Couldn't understand what they were saying, but it was pretty clear they were begging for their lives, as though that mattered! I was doing my duty to my country. But the thing about killing even one person, is that you get to live with it. Some guys do that without a problem. Others? There isn't a night they don't see those faces, those letters, that surprised look. I did my job as a soldier, but I couldn't kill anyone now to save my own life. Just the thought . . ." He shuddered, actually shuddered.

"Which sort would you be if you killed Lancer? My grandfather used to say that to regret deeply was to begin afresh. Couldn't say I agreed with him on that. You'd better know, because if you are wrong, you'll be spending the rest of your life paying the price. Sleep on it. Give it some time. You decide. If you want to kill him, come back and I'll give you the Ross. If you decide against it, fine, I won't think you a coward. You make the choice. You. And either way, no one ever knows about this conversation. I'm very good at keeping secrets, Gordon."

"He killed Stan," was all Gordon could manage.

"I believe you; all I ask is that you think it over."

Gordon swallowed and nodded, setting his untouched beer on the pool table. "Okay." Joely didn't say anything more, and so he walked to the door, unlocked and opened it, and stood in the doorway, his back to the pool hall. "Joely?"

"Yes?"

"Have you ever found it? The Third Song for Courage?"

"No. I have not."

■■■

Gordon, feeling like he had been beaten, walked into the house. The front porch light had been left on for him, but otherwise, the windows were dark. Everyone would be asleep. When he entered the front hall, though, there was his grandfather sitting on the bottom step of the staircase. John Stanford looked up.

"Are you all right, Grandpa?" asked Gordon.

"I'm all right. Just couldn't sleep is all. Sometimes when I can't sleep I come down here and sit and think about Stan. Helps a little. Somehow, being here, where he . . . died . . . makes me feel as though I'm close to him again. Foolishness, right?"

"I don't know. I don't know about anything anymore, Grandpa."

"I vaguely recall thinking the same thing myself at your age. Life is a confusing business at times."

"You never talk about the war."

"I do not," his grandfather said harshly. Then, with a great weariness, "Someday, maybe. Maybe someday when you're old enough to hear about it, but Gordon, I'm not sure you'll ever be old enough to hear that story."

chapter 21

"To regret deeply is to live afresh."

— Amos Littlebird, Odawa Sachem

Gordon's day of delivering groceries was unspeakable. He had slept poorly the night before, his sleep punctuated by a recurring dream in which a sobbing Mary was on her knees in the mud. Joely, rain streaming down his face, his uniform soaked, was holding the Ross in his arms, stroking it like a lover and regarding her with infinite pity and sadness. It didn't make sense, but Gordon couldn't get the dream out of his mind, anymore than he could forget what Joely had said in the pool hall last night. By the time he was done work and driving home, he was bushed. But, not so bushed that he wasn't planning to go to Kitchie's tonight and talk to Joely. He'd need to ask his dad for money, though. School meant he was only working Saturdays and he was a little short.

He found his father alone in his den, reading the evening newspaper. "Dad, could I please borrow five bucks?" Gordon asked.

Ben Westley looked up. "When you don't pay something back, it can hardly be called a loan," He set down his paper and took out his wallet.

"Okay. Can I please have five bucks?" His father handed him the money and Gordon shoved it in his pocket. "Thanks, Dad."

"I know where you might be able to pick up a few hours of work on Friday nights; if I can convince your mother, that is," said his father.

"Would it be as much fun as ripping guts out of chickens? Would it be as much fun as watching the Fournuts kids dress up a pig? It has to be at least as much fun for me to consider it."

"I think you might like it. Right up your alley, actually," said his father mysteriously. Ben savored the moment and his son's raised eyebrows. *He looks better today*, he thought. *Tired, but better.*

"Come on, Dad! What is it?"

"Kitchie's."

"Kitchie's?"

"I do believe you are familiar with the establishment." He gave Gordon a wry look. "Apparently Joely Waters has quit his job, and John Kitchie is looking for someone to clean up. I don't think he would expect you to keep your bed under a pool table and he's offering —"

"Wait! What do you mean *quit?*"

His father shrugged. "Just quit with no warning, took his stuff and didn't even ask to be paid."

"He didn't say goodbye!" Gordon felt dizzy. How would he be able to tell Joely *anything* if he had left town? How would Joely ever know that he had decided he wasn't the sort to be able to live with killing someone? Not yet, anyway. Not if *that* was what it could do to you; Joely and his grandfather were living proof of it. That he needed to think, and how grateful he had been that Joely had even listened to him —

"Gordon, I said why would he want to say goodbye to you?" When Gordon hesitated his father added dryly, "Son, one of these days, when you have teenagers of your own, God help you, please remember that your mother and I were not as thick as you thought we were. We *know* you play pool there." *Please God, let it be the worse thing he ever does with his life*, thought Ben Westley.

"I . . . sort of knew him. I mean, he was always there and he became kind of a friend in a way. He used to tell me stuff that his grandfather had told him." Seeing his father's questioning expression, Gordon racked his brain. "Like last night he said his grandfather once told him that to regret deeply was to live afresh. Stuff like that."

His father rubbed his chin and said thoughtfully, "Well, if Joely's grandfather said it, he wasn't the only one to say so." He got out of his chair, stepped over to the bookcase and scanned it. With a grunt he pulled out a book and began to flip through it. "This is *Bartlett's Familiar Quotations*. Look. Henry David Thoreau: 'To regret deeply is to live afresh.' And the only reason I happen to recall that particular quote, is that there was a fellow in our unit . . . Sam Kinders was his name . . . never made it home . . . anyway, he had a copy of *Thoreau's Journal*. Used to read aloud from it; drove us all crazy."

Gordon took the book to his room and poured over it. It was true. He couldn't remember all the Indian wisdom Joely had shared, but had his grandfather been Aristotle, Benjamin Franklin, or Thoreau? Gordon didn't know. He ate his dinner and then went back to Bartlett's, reading quote after quote; he didn't go to Kitchie's. Joely had said he could keep a secret. He had kept the biggest secret of all: that he was a liar.

Finally, his eyes ready to drop out of his head, Gordon had taken the book back to his dad's den. His father was still up, even though it was well past midnight, an unopened book on his lap, a glass of sherry on the table next to the leather wingback chair in which he was seated.

"You're up late," said his father. "Something on your mind?"

Gordon put the book on the coffee table and sat down on the couch. "Why would he make all that stuff up, Dad? I mean, what was the point in stringing me along all this time with the Indian wisdom bullshit."

Ignoring the *bullshit*, his father said, "Well, maybe his grandfather did say some of those things. Have you considered the idea that his grandfather could have been a well-read man? Not all education is formal. He could have been self-taught." There was nothing but doubt on Gordon's face. "Son, Joely spent time in a veterans hospital and I don't suppose it did him much good. Your grandfather? I'm not certain it helped him much more than it did Joely, but Grandpa has us. Joely had no one here. Except maybe you. Don't judge him too harshly, son. I don't think he was a well man – I mean well in his mind. That first war did terrible things to people, just like the second one did."

"I know that, Dad. Joely said that even though he wasn't sorry he had killed all those guys, he'd never be able to kill again."

"That hardly surprises me. And if he *was* lying, remember that if you live a lie long enough, you can become the lie. Always be honest with yourself, Gordon."

Gordon leaned forward, his elbow on his knees. "Sounds like a song."

"What do you mean?" His father picked up his sherry and sipped it.

"Oh, Joely told me that his grandfather said there were three songs — sort of like important lessons, I guess — that everyone had to learn about life."

"Well, three is a good place to start."

"Dad?"

"Yes, son?"

"You don't talk much about the war, either." Gordon cleared his throat carefully. "Did you kill anyone?"

Ben Westley sighed and put down his glass. "I did. Nothing I like to think about too much; I just pray to God that you never have to do the same thing. There are nights I wish I had never enlisted. Nights I wish that I had been here when you were born and learned to walk and said your first words. I can't make that happen; can't turn back the clock. I just hope to God that what I did — what *we* did — means that you'll be here when your son or daughter is born, Gordon, not on a battlefield somewhere." Ben Westley slapped the arms of his chair and stood. "Now that's enough. This is getting very maudlin. Get to bed."

Gordon stood up and going to his father, put his arms around him. "Thanks, Dad."

Ben Westley, caught off guard, returned the unexpected hug, his heart aching with love. He watched his son leave the den and climb the stairs. *He is so young*, he thought. *There are so many things that can happen to make it all go wrong for him. One stupid thing and that's it; his life could be ruined. Dear God, let him be safe. Let me give him the right advice when he asks.*

Caught in the powerful grip of his love for Gordon, an emotion so strong that he felt as though he were choking, it would not occur to Ben Westley for quite a while that Gordon had just thanked him for far more than his advice.

■ ■ ■

"You are never going to believe this, man!" whispered Tony to Gordon. It was four days later and they were in history, the first mind-numbing, brain-wilting, soul-searing, meaningless, and BORING period of the day with which The Lakers and thirty other unfortunates had been cursed. Mrs. Dare had a voice that could peel the label from a can of beans. But it was THE DARE GLARE, an expression so venomous that pit vipers would have curled up and whimpered "Uncle!"

"What am I never going to believe? That this period is ever going to end?" said Gordon out of the side of his mouth. You had to talk out of the side of your mouth in Mrs. Dare's classes, because not only did she have the long-distance vision of a harpy, she had the personality to match. Everyone who whispered in Mrs. Dare's classes looked like they had permanent cases of Bell's palsy.

"Lancer Caldwell is dead."

"*What?*"

"Would you like to share that with the class, Mr. Westley? STAND UP AND SHARE THAT WITH THE CLASS, MR. WESTLEY."

Gordon stood up and shared. "Lancer Caldwell is dead."

■■■

He *was* dead. Old Man Richardson, having gone out to collect his rent, had discovered the body and thrown up all over his own overalls. There were all sorts of rumors: a single shot had done the deed, the corpse was riddled with bullets, Lancer had been partially eaten by feral dogs, he had committed suicide, there was a mass murderer loose in Erie View. Nothing was accomplished in a single class at school that day. It was as though a new course of study had been added. LANCER CALDWELL D.O.A. 101.

Gordon wasn't certain what he felt at first. Relief that he might never be able to change his mind and act on his plan? Anger, that although he had chosen not to kill Lancer, the option was no longer there? He didn't know. Maybe it was the uncertainty of his feelings that kept him from thinking too much about Lancer's death and Joely's sudden departure. (No. Joely had been telling the truth there. That much I know; I could see it in his eyes. They looked dead when he said it. Dead eyes. Empty eyes. Tonto had been telling the truth.) Tonto. The dumb nickname made his throat tighten a little. (Put it out of your head, Gordo. Joely was a pretty good guy, but he's gone. Let's get some HAPPY THOUGHTS into the old Westley cranium, because there is no reason to have anything but HAPPY THOUGHTS. Caldwell is dead, gone, zorched, done with.) But in spite of the happy thoughts with which Gordon tried to fill his brain, the veritable mob of happy thoughts, like so many Munchkins tippy-toeing through the Land of Oz, he still didn't know how he felt.

Gordon read about it in the paper the next day. Lancer, it seemed, had been shot in the middle of the forehead while sitting in his car. His keys were in the ignition, so he was likely just leaving or had just arrived. The windshield and rear window had been shattered. No bullet had been found.

"Old Man Richardson crapped his pants as well, throwing up on himself," said David. "I mean actually crapped his pants. I guess it must have been a pretty high caliber bullet, because most of the back of Lancer's head was gone. I'm not making that up either. Constable O'Driscoll told my dad that there were brains everywhere."

"You wouldn't have thought Lancer's brains would make much of a mess," said Tony. "He had the smarts of a squirrel."

Nobody laughed at that, though.

"He was smart enough," Gordon said harshly. "I won't miss the asshole."

None of The Lakers or anyone they knew went to Lancer's funeral. Nor did they go anywhere near the horrendous party the two remaining Sultans threw afterwards, one that they held in the men's beverage room of the Bayside Hotel. Fights broke out, the cops were called, and Dutch and Eddie were arrested.

"And you know what I heard?" said Frank. "The Sultans had whores in there. They were arrested too. There have been whores, ladies of the night, *prostitutes* working at the Bayside all along, and now we'll never get a chance to see them!"

"How will we go on?" moaned David.

It was discussed ad nauseam in the school showers over the next few days, in the halls while they were eating lunch outside, and when they were walking between classes. Gordon still didn't know how he really felt.

On a moonlit Sunday night, he drove out to the cemetery, not the cemetery where Stan was buried, but the small Catholic cemetery. It didn't take long to find the bare rectangle of soil, the raw wound in the earth that was Lancer's grave. FRANCIS MARTIN CALDWELL 1937–1956. That's all it said on the stone.

Gordon stood there for a while, the last of the summer's crickets chirping in the darkness, the wind rattling through the nearly bare branches of the trees, the unwanted question, *Who killed you?* rising up in his mind like a terrible ghost. (Who also hated you enough to kill you, you damned asshole? Whoever it is I hope he's sleeping well at night because he did us all a favor. Whoever it is deserves a medal. *A parade!* Whoever it is deserves to have a statue cast of him.) Those were the thoughts he *wanted* to be thinking; those were the vitriolic things he had planned to say aloud, a bitter, angry prayer of pure hatred incanted over Lancer Caldwell's earthly remains.

But he didn't.

Suddenly, in this dark and lonely place it was Stan, and only Stan who now counted. It was his memory, like cream rising in a bottle of fresh milk that was with Gordon. He turned his back on Lancer. To hell with everything else. Almost everything, that is.

■■■

Gordon would always recall the events of the next few weeks of that fall as a series of snapshots. Cruising Main Street, working at Floyd's Market – he did *not* apply for Injun Joely's job; he didn't even like going into Kitchie's that much after Joely's departure – school, all these things would in time blur together into a period he thought of as AFTER STAN, the way such memories do.

There were a few incidents that happened to Gordon though, the *snapshot* things, that would forever remain fresh and clear, as though they had just happened.

SNAPSHOT NUMBER ONE: GORDON TAKES A BIG CHANCE

She was babysitting Robbie Colons. This he knew
because, the Colons', Gordon's parents, and the Davidsons
were having dinner at Mary's house. Gordon had
rehearsed his speech. He could have delivered it in
Parliament and brought hardened politicians to their
knees. (Forgive me, give me another chance, I love you. I
will always love you.) He looked as good as possible (not
that looking good has done anything to make her
acknowledge the fact that you were dying for her these
last weeks, Gord; even if you were James Dean, she
wouldn't have cared). He was just going to do it no
matter what. He hoped.

Now he stood at the Colons' door, his heart thumping, his hands damp. Gordon knocked. He waited. He had
lifted his hand to knock again when the door opened.

In shreds and snippets, his carefully rehearsed words
blew away in the glacial blast of derision that came from
her, something cold enough to instantly freeze the planet
Mercury. Mary said nothing to him, though; she simply
stood there.

Gordon's torso was suddenly drenched in sweat, but
his mouth was so dry he could barely part his lips. "Mary,"
he croaked. He coughed and then licked his lips. "Mary, I
just wanted to say that I'm sorry. Everything . . . everything I said . . . I should never have talked to you that way.

Never. The only thing I ask — and I don't have the right to ask you for anything — is for you to believe that I *have* made good choices. One anyway." Gordon looked down at the porch and back up at her. Could he have had less of an effect? "That's it, then." With a brief nod, he turned and walked away.

Mary's rigid posture and blank face were the only way she had been able to keep from crying when she saw him. *I love him no matter what*, she thought. *If I let him go now, this is it. If I let him go, then it's for good, and I don't think I can do that*, and then she was running down the steps and across the grass. "Gordon!" she called sharply.

Gordon didn't know whether to stop or make a run for it. He didn't know whether he could stand the rotten things she would say to him. He faltered, then stopped, and in doing so, set the course for the rest of their lives. Mary came up to him and put her hands on his shoulder blades, on his damp T-shirt, and when he didn't pull away, put her arms around him, feeling his ribs, and resting her cheek against his back.

He's lost weight, she thought. *It's because of what I did*. "I am so, so sorry for the things I said to you. I'm sorry for the way I acted. You're so much braver than I am; I was afraid you would never forgive me."

He turned around then to the sight of her red and miserable face.

"I'm not brave. It's just that I love you." Gordon took
her in his arms and said into her hair, "I really love you.
Can we start over again?"

"Oh, Gordon. I have missed you so much."

"Me too, Mary. Me too." He took the ring out of his
pocket and slipped it onto her finger. Then he kissed her.
It was a long, long kiss that left them both dazed and out
of breath. He kissed her lips, then her cheeks, then her
neck. "I've missed –"

"HEY! YOU GUYS!"

It was Robbie Colons. He was standing at a window
on the second floor of the house. Mary and Gordon separated as though they were on springs.

"Robbie!" yelled Mary. "You get back to bed!"

"How long do you think he's been standing there?"
whispered Gordon. "HOW LONG HAVE YOU BEEN STAND-
ING THERE?"

"The whole time. It was better than a movie,"
quacked Robbie cheerily. "He won the bet."

"Who?" asked Gordon. "What bet?"

"Stan! We had a bet that you guys were doing *oogy*
stuff. Kissing. *Oogy!* Wait a minute!" He disappeared from
the window.

Robbie came tearing out the front door in his pajamas
and bare feet. He handed Gordon a comic book.

"*Blitzkrieg, Searing Battle Sagas of WWII As Seen
Through Enemy Eyes*?" read Gordon. "What is this?"

"It was his favorite," quacked Robbie. "That was the prize if he won, and he did, but I have to give it to you, since you're his brother. Since I can't give it to Stan. He was my best friend; he was the only one who never made fun of me and if I live to be a hundred, Gordo – no, a thousand – there will never be anybody as good as Stan."

Gordon could say nothing. He just nodded, his eyes brimming with tears.

It was Mary who said, "Thanks for that, Robbie."

SNAPSHOT NUMBER TWO: THE LAKERS FOREVER

David's mother finally broke down and permitted her husband to buy David a car. Gordon's dad gave him a good deal on a '53 Buick Skylark Convertible – one that David christened The Lark – that was absolutely gorgeous. Rain was the only thing that kept that car's top up; David drove with it down even on cold nights, the heater blasting away, and the radio turned up so loud that you could hear him coming five minutes before you saw him. Frank and Tony, pooling their money, bought a 1938 Woody Wagon from Gordon's dad. They were also given a good deal, but mostly because the Woody had seen better days. Its wooden paneling was dried out and chipped, but Frank and Tony had plans.

"We have plans," Tony explained. They were sitting on a big log that had washed ashore on the beach, drinking beer, only one each, since Marc Ducharme and the other migrant tobacco workers would soon be gone. "We're gonna keep it in Tony's uncle's barn over the winter and work on it. Gonna drive it this way for a while though."

"To get a feel for her," said Frank. "I know. I know what it looks like, but when we're in it we can't see it."

"Got a name for it yet?" Gordon asked.

"Not yet," Frank admitted.

They sipped and relaxed and considered the possibilities. The Motivator? The Woodster? That was a good one. The Sex Mobile?

David laughed. "Mobile? Sex Mobile makes me think of those mobile things you hang over a baby's bassinet. Only, instead of bunnies you'd have people screwing. Think of the complex a baby would have."

"Is sex all you ever think of?" asked Tony. "I mean, have we made absolutely no progress here since we were twelve and trading information on the best way to jerk off so's your mother or father wouldn't know?"

"Not really," said David. "I do remember that you, Tony, thought the best place to jack off was in your sock."

They laughed and drank their beers and talked about the girls they wanted to bone. (Gordon reserved commentary on that one. He *knew* who he wanted.) Debated whose tits had grown during the summer. Discussed the various techniques of removing a brassiere from a girl. Farted and laughed their guts out about it, smoked a few fags, told stupid jokes.

"Do you think we'll all be friends in twenty years?" asked David during a brief lull.

"Man, if I have to keep hanging out with you for twenty more years, I will go mental, insane, berserk, crazy, *and* retarded," said Tony.

"Ditto," said Frank. "Add ape shit to that, by the way."

"How will we be able to tell?" asked David. "Ape shit? Man, I am definitely changing your nickname to Cheetah!"

The Lakers, thought Gordon. *The best bunch of guys in Erie View.*

SNAPSHOT NUMBER THREE: THE AFTERNOON GORDON GETS MAIL

It was on a strangely mild day in November, one of those fall day gifts rich with smoldering colors and musky scents of autumnal perfection, that Gordon received the package. He had picked up the mail, something he did now, because Stan wasn't there to do it. Stan who had *adored* mail but had never got a single letter in his life (birthday cards didn't count) until Gordon, who couldn't stand it any more, had written him one. (Dear Stan, you idiot. You had better frame this letter. You had better get it bronzed like our stupid baby shoes. THIS IS YOUR FIRST LETTER!!!!! Your very smart and good-looking brother, Gordo.)

There was a hydro bill and the telephone bill. And a flat package; one that was addressed to him, one whose return address entirely baffled Gordon.

Mrs. Geraldine Ryan,

1253 Sutton Road,

Ottawa, Ontario.

Who the hell was *that*?

He tossed the bills on the telephone table along with his books, dropped a loud smooch on his mother's cheek as he passed through the kitchen, and headed out the back door to the beach.

"Just bills, Mom," he said. "On the telephone table."

"Nice to see you too, Gordon. Clean up, please; Edith is coming over for dinner."

"I'll be back in a few minutes," he shouted.

Gordon's grandfather and Mary's nanna were still a hot item. John Stanford had proposed to her and was limp with relief when she turned him down saying, "Been married, John. Never been a loose woman before. This is too much fun to spoil with wedding bells."

Gordon sat down on the still warm sand and tore the brown paper from what turned out to be another, but smaller brown paper-wrapped package and an envelope. A newspaper clipping fluttered to the sand; Gordon picked it up, smoothed it out, and began to read it:

LIEUTENANT JOSEPH WATERS, 60,
TAKEN BY DEATH.

Waters? thought Gordon. *That's Joely's last name!*

Funeral services for Joseph Waters, 60, who died on Monday, October 22, will be held Wednesday, October 24. The funeral will be at 10:00 a.m. from the Harvard Brothers Funeral Home, Ottawa, to St. Peter's Church, Ottawa, for services at 10:30 a.m. Father George McNabb will officiate. Burial will follow in Mount Olive Cemetery. There will be no visitation beforehand.

The son of the late Colonel Robert Waters and Mrs. Lillian Waters, Joseph Waters died by accidental drowning while swimming in the Ottawa River.

Born in London, England, June 17, 1896, a graduate of Laurier University with a B.A. in Classical Studies, Joseph Waters served in the Canadian Expeditionary Force from 1915 until 1918 (If blood could actually run cold, Gordon's was on the verge of freezing; *this CAN'T be real*, he thought.) and was awarded The Distinguished Conduct Medal, the citation having read in part: He showed complete devotion to his duty and an utter disregard for all and any danger. Joseph Waters received a battlefield commission, and returned to Canada as a lieutenant.

He is survived by his sister, Mrs. Geraldine Ryan.

Gordon put down the clipping and tore open the envelope; at least he tried to tear it open. His hands were shaking so badly he could barely do it.

Dear Mr. Westley,

My brother spoke often and fondly of you in the few brief weeks that remained to him, once he returned to Ottawa. He was never given much to relating his experiences regarding The Great War, preferring to forget that period of his life. Perhaps you shared his predilection, having been, as he referred to you, a fine comrade in arms.

My brother's life was not an easy one, as you must know. Perhaps things might have been different for Joseph, had his fiancé not died of influenza while he was in France. I hope, Mr. Westley, that you, a fellow veteran, have not suffered as he did. To fight for your country for three long years and survive, is a miracle. To be doomed to fight that war every day for the rest of your life is a horror beyond comprehension.

As the executor of my brother's will, I have enclosed this package, unopened, as per Joseph's wishes.

Sincerely,

Mrs. Geraldine Ryan

Gordon let the letter fall to the sand. He picked up the small, flat package and just held it. He smoothed his fingertips over the paper. Gordon did *not* want to open the package, because as long as he didn't open it, then maybe Lieutenant Joseph Waters of Ottawa was someone he had never met. Maybe Lieutenant Joseph Waters, who had accidentally drowned in the Ottawa River was a complete stranger. He *had* to be a stranger, because Joely *couldn't swim*. Joely would *never* have gone into the river to swim. Joely might have gone into a river for some other reason, but NOT to swim. Uh-uh, *non*, *nyet*, negative; not to swim.

Dreading what he would find, he picked off the tape and slowly opened the package. Inside were three things: a Distinguished Conduct Medal, one that had Sergeant Joseph Waters' service number, rank, initials, surname, and service impressed on the edge, a World War I service medal (Stan's medal, this is STAN'S MEDAL, I would know this thing anywhere!), and a folded square of paper. The two medals resting on his bent knees, Gordon unfolded the sheet of paper.

Dear Gordon,
I was almost 100 percent sure you would make the right decision regarding a certain matter. Almost. But as you well know, I am not a gambling man. The last time we were together, you asked me if I

had ever found my Third Song for Courage. I think it will please you to know that I did. My Third Song is, and always will be you, Gordon. My Third Song was to do what I had to do, so that you would have a chance to find your final song. May you sing it with great joy, Gordon.

Your friend,

Injun Joely.

For a long while, Gordon sat with his cheek on his knees, sometimes on Joely's medal, sometimes on Stan's. Sat unhearing, when his mother called him in for dinner, and when his father said that Gordon perhaps needed to be alone for a while. He sat while the sun went down in a sky filled with violet wisps of clouds.

Perhaps God, in His infinite and enigmatic wisdom, *had* chosen to ignore Gordon's deranged implorings these last months. Now though, God did one of the things that He does best: He answered a prayer unspoken. For all his life, Gordon would remain untouched by the double-edged rapier that had been Joely's gift. There would be no guilt, no uncertainty. He would find, with the slow, revealing passage of time, only the singular and comforting knowledge that he had been saved from himself.

But not yet, not tonight; on this night, it was only what the package had contained. He pocketed everything except Stan's medal; that he clutched in his right hand.

Gordon stretched out on his back on the sand; eyes closed, he moved his arms and legs until a perfect sand angel was there beneath him.

"Stan," he whispered. He climbed to his feet, and looking down at the sand angel, he cried. Up to this moment, even when mourning his brother, Gordon's tears had been in part for himself. Now though, he wept only for Joely; for a man who had prayed on a lonely beach at sunrise. And it was the second entirely adult and selfless act of his young life.

Then, with the inevitability of the moon's path across the night sky, with the simplicity of the closing of a perfect circle, came the next one.

Gordon Westley left the darkness behind him and headed for the house calling, "Mom! You'll never guess what I found!"

■■■

"He who is brave is free."

      — Seneca

"They never fail, who die in a good cause."

      — Lord Byron

"My name is Duty."

      — Unknown

Quotation Sources

1. "Live well. It is the greatest revenge." – *The Talmud*.
2. "Friendship makes prosperity more shining and lessens adversity by dividing and sharing it." – *Cicero*
3. "All the world's a stage and all the men and women merely players." – *William Shakespeare*
4. "A bully is always a coward." – *Proverb, early 19th century*
5. "The pleasure of loving is in loving." – *François de la Rochefoucauld*
6. "No one ever suddenly became depraved." – *Juvenal*
7. "The heart has its reasons which reason knows nothing of." – *Blaise Pascal*
8. "Work saves us from three great evils: boredom, vice and need." – *Voltaire*
9. "Of all noises, I think music is the least disagreeable." – *Samuel Johnson*

10. "A handful of patience is worth more than a bushel of brains." – *Dutch Proverb*

11. "Fear not death, for the sooner we die, the longer we shall be immortal." – *Benjamin Franklin*

12. "When one man dies, one chapter is not torn out of the book, but translated into a better language." – *John Donne*

13. "There are some defeats more triumphant than victories." – *Michel de Montaign*

14. "Abandon all hope, ye who enter here." – *Dante*

15. "Love is composed of a single soul inhabiting two bodies." – *Aristotle*

16. "Practice, the master of all things." – *Augustus Octavius*

17. "If you wish success in life, make perseverance your bosom friend, experience your wise counselor, caution your elder brother, and hope your guardian genius." – *Joseph Addison*

18. "All good things must come to an end." – *English proverb*

19. "A timid person is frightened before a danger, a coward during the time, and a courageous person afterward." – *Jean Paul Richter*

20. "Education is the best provision for old age." – *Aristotle*

21. "To regret deeply is to live afresh." – *Thoreau*
"He who is brave is free." – *Seneca*

"They never fail who die in a good cause." – *Lord Byron*

"My name is Duty." – *Unknown*